RENA ROCFORD

ACNE, ASTHMA
AND OTHER SIGNS
HALF YOU MIGHT BE DRAGON

CURIOSITY
QUILLS PRESS

A Division of **Whampa, LLC**
P.O. Box 2160
Reston, VA 20195
Tel/Fax: 800-998-2509
http://curiosityquills.com

ISBN 978-1-62007-039-0 (ebook)
ISBN 978-1-62007-043-7 (paperback)

For my family

CHAPTER ONE

Seven Days Before

Before I was close enough to be slathered in anti-acne cream, the kiosk lady had her bottle at the ready. Her eyes locked on me, the easy target. The stink of acid and rubbing alcohol told me the cream was fake. There was no magic bullet for acne; I'd already tried it all.

The woman held out her hand in the hopes I might mimic her and extend my arm–this wasn't my first rodeo.

"The salts from the Dead Sea have natural healing properties. I guarantee you'll see a difference immediately."

Her smile was as fake as the gold around her neck, and I would know. I could smell gold.

My mother said I was crazy, but I could smell metals. Gold had a scent like butter. Silver smelled of rain in a forest. Fake gold smelled like burning bread, and this woman was covered in it.

"No thanks." I kept my hands firmly to my side.

My friend, Beth stretched her lower lip in serious consideration. "Oh, but how do you know if you don't try?"

I punched her in the arm, but Beth was six-foot-three with a tendency to make refrigerators seem dainty; nothing I did was likely to make a dent in her. With the punch, I threw her a withering look, and Beth smiled, wagging her eyebrows.

I gave the saleswoman my most pleasant smile. "Thank you, but no thank you."

Desperate for a sale, she reached for my arm. I grabbed her wrist before she could catch me and twisted her arm across her body. The motion smeared the fake Dead Seas salt across her sleeve.

"I have sensitive skin."

Beth sputtered a laugh, but she walked to the nearest store window, making a show of examining the mannequin on the other side. I slipped away from the kiosk and joined her.

"I like this jacket." Beth squinted, sighing.

"Then you should try it on."

"Ha! The clothes in this store never fit"–she pointed at her chest–"they're always a little too optimistic." Her golden ponytail bounced as she shook her shoulders suggestively. Beth was many things, but curvy in the right places wasn't one of them. On the other hand, she could go pro-roller derby at the drop of a hat. Beth was like a force of nature, and she didn't mind tussling with anyone dumb enough to get in her way.

I was like a reject from a geisha convention. My hair was too straight and black for the Irish heritage of my mother, and my eyes were too green for my father's Japanese heritage. I was caught in the middle. Half. Mutt.

"How do you know if you don't try it on?"

"Honestly, Allyson, you sound like a school counselor. 'How do you know you won't enjoy fixing farming equipment unless you try?'"

"I was mimicking *you*."

Beth arched her eyebrow at me. "Are you saying I sound like the school counselor?"

Before I could respond, a guy our age came into earshot, watching Beth as he walked, even as he passed. His wide eyes tracked Beth like search beams in the fog. He craned his neck, but his legs kept moving forward, as if the two halves of his body weren't on speaking terms. He smashed into a cardboard ad of a man giving a woman flowers. He fell, his legs tangling in the chain holding the two halves of the ad together.

Beth ran to his side, pulling the cardboard off. "You okay?"

He stared up at her, blinking, like he saw a miracle, not Beth. His lopsided face fit his crooked expression, as if he'd been beaten about the head but more solidly on one side. What he lacked in symmetry, he made up for in size, easily topping Beth's six-foot-three by another head. He clearly outweighed her by nearly a hundred pounds of lean muscle.

His mouth moved, but no words came out. A half smile of disbelief bloomed on his face as he grabbed the cardboard ad and broke off the flowers still tangling his feet. He took a deep breath as if steeling himself or taking in the fresh scent of a new day. With a mumble, he thrust the cardboard flowers at Beth. The rest of the ad ended up in a pile of broken commercialism.

"Uh, thank you." Beth's words sounded like a question, and we all stood there, waiting for the next minute to save us from the most awkward conversation on the planet.

Scratch that. To be a conversation, he'd have to say something. Anything.

"John, I told you to stay away from the—" another man said, stopping midstride when he saw his friend attempting to give Beth fake flowers. The new guy was nearly as tall as the first.

Where John looked like he was lopsided through an unfortunate accident, the second man's face was actually skewed. One brow was higher than the other, and his rock-breaking hands could have come from two different people. His patchwork appearance made him look like he spent more time working out one half of his body. He even stood with an off-kilter slump to his shoulders.

He glared at Beth, then returned his gaze to his friend. "We don't have time for anything fancy. Just bag the unicorns and get a move on," he said, looking Beth up and down. A shiver of danger danced down my spine. I checked over my shoulder for something that looked like a unicorn, but saw nothing.

Maybe unicorn was code for something.

Oh crap, maybe it was code for kidnapping girls. Wasn't that a problem in some places? People would kidnap girls and sell them as prostitutes. I hadn't been in Albuquerque for that long, but I hadn't heard of that being an issue here. Though, really, who advertised their neighborhood was a haven for sex traffickers?

And these guys were big. My self-preservation alarms blared.

In my mind, my gym teacher's words came back to me in a way her name never would. When being attacked, we were supposed to yell fire because no one would come to the rescue if we yelled rape.

I wasn't much of a runner, so I prepped to yell fire. The sharp scent of gunmetal and copper reached my nose, kicking my heart into high gear.

My breath rasped in my lungs.

Not good.

I had no reason to suspect them of anything, but big guy number two had the stance of someone used to resorting to physicality to get what he wanted. I cracked the scales at a whopping one hundred pounds, soaking wet. I wasn't going to take anyone in a straight fight anytime soon. I scanned the mall; aside from a couple of shoppers beating a hasty retreat from the kiosk lady, there was no one. No cops. Not even rent-a-cops. And there was no one big enough to come to the rescue if these giants decided to drag us off.

I grabbed Beth's arm. "I sure hope we aren't late meeting your overprotective boyfriend who just went to states in taekwondo." I pulled her back a step, but she moved like a puppet, wooden and only half as believable.

"What's the hurry?" A third voice said from behind me. I froze. My stomach cramped and my chest tightened into the beginnings of a full-blown asthma attack. So much for running or yelling.

"It looks like this pretty one is well on her way to getting a bonus," the second lumpy man said. He turned to Beth. "What you got there, sweetie? A bit of gryphon? Some unicorn? I hear unicorn's real common 'round these parts."

Unicorn? Gryphon? How many code words could a bunch of kidnappers need?

Beth's face turned to ash. "I don't know what you're talking about."

"You're pretty young to be on the payroll," the third man said.

Beth's panicked eyes darted between the men, but her weight shifted to the balls of her feet.

Their faces froze in a confused mask, like they were trying to solve a math problem—something really complicated like two plus two.

John stepped between Beth and the second guy. "I saw her first. I get the bonus."

"Yeah, well this one's mine." He grabbed my arm in his boulder-sized hand, twisting me around to face him. The grip crushed muscles, grinding them into the bone. He could break my arm without even trying. There was no way to break that hold, and I was no match for a three hundred pound bruiser. I took a breath to scream, but my lungs cramped shut as my heart continued to race. My chest burned. I needed to scream. I wasn't going to be one of those kids on a milk carton.

Air squeaked into my lungs, rasping through my shrinking trachea. It wasn't enough, but I wasn't going to magically stop having an asthma attack without my inhaler. He dragged me closer. This was it. I wasn't going to get any more air than the feeble breath in my lungs now.

Clenching every scrap of muscle in my body, I forced the air out.

The debilitating tightness around my throat released, and the scream unfurled in all its blood-curdling glory. My throat burned with the force of my yell, and the noise raged between my teeth, vibrating like a chainsaw of sound.

Orange flames streamed from my mouth like a fountain. The fire splashed into the huge man, engulfing him in an inferno. The whole world ground to a halt as a raging blaze poured out of my mouth. I gasped, and the fire stopped as quickly as it had come. Smoke stung my eyes, and my chest ached. The scent of burning hair filled the air.

What was that?

What the hell was that?

I blinked, but this new freakish reality kept marching forward like a roller coaster.

My hands jumped to my mouth, but there was nothing there but skin—shaky, clammy skin. It had to be a hoax, but no cameras looked down on us, just people blinking like owls.

I breathed fire like a freaking dragon.

Like a dragon!

Fire!

The soft crackle of flames brought me back to reality. I'd just spit flames at the man who could star in a McBeefcake commercial. Flames licked up through the remains of Mr. McBeefcake's buzz cut. He scowled and let go of my arm, patting out the burning hairs on his head as if he extinguished fire from his scalp regularly.

I just shot flaming death from my mouth.

And my throat burned to prove it!

But he wasn't even fazed.

The strong taste of ammonia filled my lungs. Was there some scary chemical in me now? How did this work? I touched my lips, but they weren't burned.

I ran my tongue across my teeth, but nothing seemed out of place, no burned out gaps where teeth used to be.

Holy crap, I just breathed fire! Actual flames. Out of my mouth!

McBeefcake patted his head in slow deliberate strikes to smother the oxygen from his burning skin. "I thought we'd taken care of all the dragons."

Flames caught lazily on a cardboard ad behind McBeefcake. He wasn't burned. His hair burned, but he was undamaged. The blaze crept up the wall behind him, consuming the cardboard. Real flames—from my *mouth*! —so why wasn't he screaming in pain? He was more worried about his hairdo than his face burning off.

The alarms blared to life, startling everyone out of the tableau. Like the world had been on pause, the siren jumpstarted the crowd into motion.

I spun, grabbed Beth's arm, and bolted between the other two. "Run!"

Other shoppers screamed. The crowd pushed for the doors, and the crush prevented anyone from getting there. I dragged Beth toward the fleeing shoppers. Smoke curled up through the second floor, and the chaos of flashing lights and screaming shoppers added to my disorientation.

"Get her!" The words carried over the cacophony of the mob.

Did they get their lines from Rent-a-Thug? *Stop thinking, keep running, Allyson.*

We charged down the center of the mall avenue, avoiding the traffic at the obvious stores with exits. My feet pounded on the tile floors, but my lungs wouldn't recover. I just couldn't manage to draw a breath. The hallway spun, and I bounced off a pillar, only keeping my feet because I clung to Beth for dear life.

I can't have an asthma attack now! I'm running for my life! Sweet god of asthma relief, could we reschedule this for another day?

Mechanically, I kept throwing my feet forward, one in front of the other, but the vertigo would drag me down soon. The constriction got worse, running up from my diaphragm right to my jaw. My gorge rose in the back of my throat, but I kept pounding past stores. The world spun, and I crashed into a trashcan. The decorative ironwork caught me in the stomach, threatening to spill my lunch into the trashcan right then.

Beth kept running, dragging me along. After three more steps, my stomach had voted lunch off the island, but I pushed on. My breath squeaked into my lungs, and smoke filled my nose. If I could just get it over with, maybe I could run. A rock solid hand hit my shoulder, spinning me around. The whiplash sent me reeling, and I couldn't hold it in any longer. I puked.

Right on his shoes.

He froze. Slowly, he tilted his head to look at his feet. The pile of puke smelled like ammonia, and lazy flames licked up from the stinking mass like the dying embers of a large campfire.

He looked from his shoes to me and snarled.

I smiled back. The world had already stopped spinning, and I felt one hundred percent better.

His face turned red as his hands shook and he roared.

Beth grabbed an autographed baseball bat off a nearby vendor's table and smashed it into the guy's teeth. The bat rang with a deep *thunk-click*. McBeefcake stumbled backwards, tripping into a kiosk of glass animals and chili peppers. He tilted over like a tree, landing butt first in the display case. Glass sprayed the walls, chunks skittering across the floor.

He moaned from the ground, but stayed down. I scanned for his two cohorts, but they'd vanished into the mall. Where were the cops?

"Come on!" Beth yelled over the blaring alarm. She dropped the bat on the table.

We ducked into the nearest store with an outside exit and ran for the doors among the herds of people. When we burst outside, the cold air stole past my jacket. Wind swirled at my hair, and cable-thick locks flew in my face. Some people milled around the exit, but others fled to their cars. We cut through the crowd, keeping our eyes out for the big guys.

Beth muttered and shook her head. We'd come out of the mall on the opposite side from where we lived. Without talking about it, we walked around the mall toward our apartments, clinging to the shadows as much as possible.

When we were nearly to the road dividing the mall parking lot from the apartment complex, I stopped. "What the hell was that?"

Beth shook her head, pointing at a nearby entrance to the mall, now swarming with escaping shoppers. She kept walking toward the pizza joint, the last establishment before the road.

When we reached the drive-up window, Beth slipped behind the shrubs. They didn't block any wind, but they seemed safer somehow. At least we couldn't be seen easily. Between the bushes and the cinder block wall, stumps of dead trees waited, making our own private haven.

Beth paced silently. I bent over at the waist and panted to catch my breath. Beth stopped but wouldn't look at me.

"You okay?" I asked.

"It smelled me."

"It? I was pretty sure they were male."

Beth turned around. Escaped strands of hair from her ponytail floated on the dry wind. "They weren't human. Not even part. Those were trolls."

My heart flip-flopped in my chest. *Just bag the unicorns*, he'd said. This couldn't be real.

I'd breathed fire. *Real* had a whole new meaning today. "What do you mean by trolls?"

"Trolls, you know, live under a bridge, eat goats; trolls." Beth raked her hands through her hair, but only managed to pull some strands free. "And what about you? Hasn't your mom had 'The Talk' with you?"

I snorted. "My mom has more secrets than the CIA. She did have the 'please use a condom' talk."

Beth shook her head. "Not condoms! You're half freaking' dragon, and you didn't even know?"

"Dragon? But how?" My questions boiled out of me. "How is that even possible? How could anyone be half fantasy creature, let alone fire breathing lizard?"

She bent a branch, releasing it before it snapped. "You're one of the Kin. You're half or part creature of legend. I don't know how that happened, but that's what you are."

My questions rolled around inside my brain, never quite taking form. All I heard was not human, and my brain short-circuited. It was impossible. "How?"

Beth shrugged. "Magic, for all I know. And your mom never told you?"

"Nope." I leaned against the trunk of one of the trunks.

"That's rude."

"What about other creatures? Are there phoenixes?—wait, would that phoenii?—but you know what I mean."

"I don't really know what all is out there, only what I've run across. Unicorn, here and there, and, of course, trolls and dragon."

Unicorns.

This was too much. I shook my head. "This is impossible."

"What's impossible is that you didn't know. How come you didn't guess?"

"I have asthma. In what doctor's office is there a poster saying, 'Have asthma? Talk to your doctor about a possible dragon heritage.' I thought what everyone else thought. Dragons are in books and movies."

Beth grinned. "Rare, but real."

Then it hit me. "You knew?"

"Are you kidding? Strength, smarts, lightning reflexes, you're hard to miss. I just didn't realize you were dragon. This could change everything."

"What everything? You haven't told me anything. What the hell is going on? Who were those guys? How did you know they were trolls?" I stopped when I realized I was yelling.

Rimmed in white, Beth's green eyes glowed through the night. I'd never yelled at her. Sure, we'd only been friends for three months, but she was by far the best friend I'd ever had. And I'd collected more "best" friends than birthdays.

Beth resumed pacing.

"How did you know they were trolls?" I asked again.

Her head twisted to the side like she was in pain. "I'm half."

"Half what?"

"Half troll."

Her quiet words haunted her face. She stopped pacing and stood as far from me as the shrubs would allow. We said nothing for a small slice of forever. She fidgeted as I waited for whatever came next.

"Well, aren't you going to run or scream or something?" Beth asked.

The idea of being half dragon had completely washed out the enormity of my best friend confessing she was half troll. It just didn't seem possible. Beth wasn't anything like the trolls from fairy tales. She was smart and pretty. And I'd seen her house, it was absolutely spotless. Beth was nothing like what trolls were supposed to be.

But then again, those other trolls had smelled like aftershave and gunmetal, so clearly they bathed more regularly than Grimm would have me believe.

I shook my head as a half-smile crept onto my face. "Seriously, you just attacked a troll to save me from who knows what fate, and you're worried I'll take off like some perfect little princess? I thought you knew me better than that, Beth Whitlocke."

The smile broke over Beth's face. Relief flooded from her, and her whole body relaxed. "I just can't believe you're draconic."

"Draconian, more like."

Her bark of laughter filled our hiding place. "That's funny, Drake."

Wind stole through the tree, and we both shivered. "Will they be back?"

"I think we lost them." Beth scanned the branches as if she could see through the dark, but when I looked, I saw nothing but police cruisers and fire trucks at the mall. "Maybe we should go into hiding or something."

I ran the conversation through my head again. They'd said she was young to be on the payroll. That meant they didn't recognize her. Or me. "They didn't know who you were. It was just really unlucky on our part. Right?"

"I sure hope so."

CHAPTER TWO

Six Days Before

After a bout of terrible dreams involving Beth eating a live chicken before telling me not to worry about it, I woke up. My mouth tasted like the marching band had practiced on my tongue last night.

But what did I expect after spitting fire, minty fresh breath?

When I moved, everything creaked. Every muscle and joint hurt, especially my abs. Best ab work out ever? Well, there had to be an upside. The stench of my own breath would kill a skunk, so I wanted some perks.

Well, perks besides the whole blasting flames in the face of troll kidnappers.

And could I do it again?

I stuffed that thought in a jar and went to the bathroom. The lights were on in the apartment, so I knew my mom was already up. To alleviate the pain of having only one bathroom and both of us getting ready at the same time, my mother did her hair at a mirror in her room. The shower was mine, but before I made it to the water, I brushed my teeth and gargled as much mouthwash as I could handle.

The shower had miraculous healing properties, but rendered the bathroom mirror worthless. Though I didn't need it to put on my makeup—no need for that horror show before breakfast.

My pitch black hair was darker than midnight and, to my great disgrace, my face had more craters than the moon. Regular makeup was too frail for my needs. A face like mine needed more pancake than a waffle house. I ordered foundation from a theatrical company online. It came in a giant tub and disappeared faster than fresh baked cookies. But pancake needed perfectly dry air to keep from caking, so I popped open the door to let the steam out.

"Leave us alone," my mother said at the front door.

Her voice drew all of my attention, and I peeked around the edge of the door. The bathroom was a short hallway away from the front room–and front door–of our apartment. She stood directly in front of the door, hands on her hips, and ready to repel any invaders.

"It's her *birthday*," someone said on the other side of the door. I recognized the voice: My Aunt Aggy. "She'll know something is up if you don't let me talk to her."

Mom straightened. "She'll just think you forgot. You're not known for being around when we need you."

"You think she's that dumb? She is related to me, you know. By blood."

"No, you can't take her away. I've seen what happens to people in your family."

Ice formed around those words. They were fighting words. I had never met my father, and his sister made a special point to give me something on each birthday. Almost always, it was music and a statue of a dragon. I'd always had the feeling that she had a real thing for dragons.

Turns out, nope, she was trying to tell me something. Which side of the family did I get the dragonish tendency to spit fireballs and identify metals by scent?

"And you think you're doing a better job running from everything?"

Mom stood on the balls of her feet, leaning into the front door. Tension poured off her, and her whole body was poised to start a fight. "Go. Now. I will not tolerate this sort of behavior from you."

"Let me in or I'll break down the door."

My mother leaned back and gave a haughty head shake. "Oh, now who's the superior race? Resorting to violence at every turn?"

An image of fire bursting from Aggy's lips filled my mind. If I got my dragon blood from her, then she could toast my mother.

I pushed the door all the way open and interrupted. "Mom, have you seen my—Aunt Aggy? What are you doing here?" I schooled my face into a look of surprise.

"Your mother was just letting me in. Weren't you, Cathy?"

Instead of acknowledging the question, Mom grumbled something that sounded vaguely like "This isn't over, Aggy."

My mother may have been four inches taller than Aggy, but my aunt cowered before no one.

She hopped over the threshold with flare. "Well, how does it feel to be fifteen?"

I twisted my waist-length black hair to squeeze more water out, dripping onto the linoleum. "Wet. How about you?"

Her gaze softened to some faraway memory. "When I was fifteen, I learned to—"

"What are you doing half naked?" Mom interrupted. "Go get dressed. Just because it's your birthday doesn't mean you can be late to school."

My eyes locked onto Aggy, and she gave me the you'd-better-do-what-your-mother-asks look. I nodded and practically ran back to my room. Maybe if I was quiet, they'd start fighting again.

No luck. Even after my liberal application of makeup, by the time I got back to the front room in jeans, T-shirt, and boots, they were sitting at the kitchen table. Waiting there, they were the epitome of yin and yang. My mother's climbing-the-corporate-ladder scarf was artfully pinned to her blouse, and her cup of coffee matched her pants. Her pale skin was powdered to within an inch of her life, and her bright red lipstick drew the perfect attention to the fact that she had red hair and blazing green eyes. She looked like a Gaelic goddess.

Aggy straddled the chair, resting her hands on the back. Tied into a ponytail and braided, her black hair resembled jumper cables, and there was no makeup on her already tanned face. She wore a jacket that buttoned up the side, thick pants, and boots three sizes too big for her short stature–even shorter than me now! She could have been the star in a hard-hitting kung fu film. Wait, was kung fu Chinese or Japanese? Holes in my knowledge like that made me feel like a complete fraud when it came to my Japanese heritage.

Aggy took the last sip of coffee, and dumped the cup back into its non-matching saucer. "Can I take you to school, then?"

"I usually walk."

"Oh, well, in that case, here." She dropped a notebook into my hands.

She wrote music for fun, and sometimes, she gave me her songs. I flipped open the notebook to see. And there it was, a song scribbled out across the page. The notes plucked echoes through my mind, hinting at what it would sound like on my guitar, and my fingers itched to have the string beneath them.

"No, you may not stay home and practice," Mom said just as I started to hum.

"But it's my birthday! How often do I get to turn fifteen?"

My mother drew a line through the air, cutting off all argument. "Absolutely not. You have an education to obtain."

I didn't mutter about how moving in another six weeks would kill any attempts I had at sticking to an education. And since I'd had more schools than birthdays, one could argue that my education with the guitar was my most steady subject. I held up the music, but Aunt Aggy caught my eye and shook her head.

I sighed. "Fine. I'll just put it away." I dashed back into my room and dropped the stack of music next to the four surviving dragon statues my aunt had gotten me on previous birthdays. Their blue, purple, green, and white scales winked back at me, and I hoped she'd gotten me another.

I grabbed my backpack–untouched from yesterday–and headed for the door. I kissed the brass dragon hanging beside the doorway. Mom called it the Guardian. Its swirling tail gave it an expectant look, like the dragon wasn't satisfied without a proper acknowledgement.

The Guardian was the only thing my mother put a nail in the wall for. She'd risk losing the deposit for it.

Maybe I got my dragon from Mom.

More importantly, did they both know, or was one of them hiding a really big secret? Maybe that's why Mom didn't want Aggy around.

Outside, I stood on the concrete landing and shrugged into my jacket. My aunt shut the door behind us. "It's a bit chilly, isn't it?"

"It's March in Albuquerque."

"March is warmer in California," she said.

"I wouldn't know; Mom doesn't like California. Too expensive."

"Too bad. I could keep a better eye on you there."

"I bet," I said.

Aggy arched an eyebrow, and I opened my mouth to ask her about my father. My throat caught. Two giant Harleys roared by on the street, and I chickened out as the buff, bearded men rode by in their leather vests.

There were things no one talked about, and absent family members topped the list. Until last night, I'd thought we didn't talk about my father because he was in the CIA, or something even more secretive, like Disney. Today, I wasn't sure. And how stupid would I sound if I asked someone if my father was actually a dragon? And how awkward would that be if he wasn't the dragon and it was my mom? More importantly, how did I get to that topic gracefully? Uh, hey, Aunt Aggy, accidentally fry any trolls lately?

From the apartment complex, we ducked through big bus stop to the street. Four lanes of heavy traffic stood between the high school and me. We could jay walk, but the traffic was fast and thick, and my asthma kept me from being much of a sprinter. I always opted for the crosswalks.

At the corner, Aunt Aggy grabbed my arm. "Hold on a sec, squirt." She searched my face again.

Heat rose in my cheeks.

I tried to look away, but she caught my chin in her hands. Her eyes met mine, and I opened my mouth to ask her about last night. Then she nodded, and I snapped my mouth shut.

"I've got a present for you—well, it's sort of a present. I mean, it's more like a birthright."

"Is it something from Dad?"

She winced like I'd stabbed her but tried to recover, putting on a brave face. I felt a lot better not asking about the whole fire-breathing thing.

She dumped a package into my hands, a lump heavy as a brick and wrapped in leather. "Not exactly."

"Should I open it here? You are coming to dinner aren't you?"

"Of course, kidlet. I wouldn't miss it." She looked over her shoulder at the bus stop. I followed her gaze to some big guys sitting on a bench waiting for the downtown bus.

Were they trolls?

I took a breath to ask her about the mall, but she pointed at the light. "Better hurry up." Already the light had turned to the flashing red hand of doom, and I took off across the intersection. I made it to the boulevard before the light changed, stranding me on the island of cement. She'd tricked me into coming out in the street, and now I was stuck. And she hadn't followed me out here.

When I looked back to find her, she'd already disappeared. There weren't that many people on the corner, but she could hide in a brightly lit room with nothing inside but her. I sighed in defeat. What good would it do to finish chasing her down if she was already gone?

Still, she'd given me a lumpy package, and I turned it over in my hands as I finished crossing the street on the next light. Leather straps held the rumpled funnies section of a Sunday paper around the present. I untied the first one, but kept my back to the school, just in case someone saw and teased me about getting a gift from my aunt.

Beth walked up next to me. "What's that?"

"A birthday present."

"You gonna open it?"

I tore open the paper and freed the cheap knick-knack, a clear plastic lump encasing a fake sword. It looked like something I would have bought from Six Flags when I was ten. It was smaller than a lunch box.

"What is that supposed to be?" Beth asked.

"My birthday present." I turned the sword-in-the-plastic-stone over in my hand. This had to be a joke. Aunt Aggy gave me awesome dragons, not tawdry, midway keepsakes.

"Is that from your mother?"

"My aunt."

"And she likes funny swords that look like soft serve?" Beth asked.

I held the hunk of chunk up to the light. Sure enough, the sword blade curved back and forth in a ridiculous spiral, like someone had chopped the horn off a narwhal and stuck it on a Lord of the Rings prop. "It's not her usual style."

"Well are you just gonna stare at it? We'll be late."

I dumped the crummy sculpture into my backpack and followed Beth. At least today could only get better.

The bell rang for lunch, and I prolonged packing my books into my backpack. I didn't want to leave math class. Lunch was just a nice way of saying *social gladiatorial event*.

Jed Peterson bumped into me, and my books spilled out onto the industrial classroom carpet. My homework fell out of my math book.

I glared at him.

"Sorry," he said, but when he caught up to his friends at the front of the classroom, he snickered.

"Try not to let her rub off on you. I hear pancake face is contagious," his friend whispered.

Either it was a mock whisper or I suddenly had super acute hearing. Great, I could add eavesdropping to my super powers.

And I used fixative. My makeup wasn't going anywhere.

I mumbled something impolite and pushed through the door. Was I really half dragon? Was that what was going on? Was Beth trying to set me up for something? Could this be an elaborate hoax? A joke would explain why I'd never heard of anything like half-trolls.

Some joke.

But how did any potential pranksters make the fire? Either I hallucinated, or I spit actual fire onto an actual guy who didn't mind having his hair burned off.

Had my aunt really been hiding something this big for my entire life? And what about my mom? Did she know? How could she miss sleeping with a dragon? Or would you? Maybe he looked as human as I do?

Wait. Would this mean Aunt Aggy was a dragon too? She looked totally human, but I guessed it wasn't impossible.

I couldn't think without food in my stomach.

I made my way to the lunchroom with the rest of the stragglers. The constant flow of people in and out kept the doors open, and I slipped inside between a girl balancing her nachos on top of a giant Snapple and a jock. I scanned the room, but already the line stretched to the back wall.

Vending machine lunch for me.

Slipping through the crowd, I made my way to the two machines stacked against the side wall: one for snacks, the other for soda. I got in line for candy and studied the selection. As the week wore on, the choices dwindled away. Today was Thursday; the selection was pathetic. No chips, no pop tarts, no donuts. But my birthday luck finally kicked in: one package of Skittles left. I could manage English if I could have a taste of the rainbow first.

Sticking my dollar into the machine, I waited. It spit out my dollar. I fed it into the slot again. The machine protested and sent the dollar out. I rubbed the bill on the metal edge of the machine and tried not to listen to the fidgeting behind me. The world is completely unfair–I could spit fire, but the freaking vending machine wouldn't take my dollar.

"Here, I have an extra." Steve June held a dollar out to me. His wavy black hair smelled like hickory and moss, reminding me of the forests in the northeast. My heart almost hit my ribcage.

I nodded, too afraid I'd squeak if I said something.

He handed me the dollar bill, and I handed him mine. I practically touched him! I fed the money into the slot and dialed the number for Skittles.

"What's taking so long?" Jed's whiny tone rose above the dull roar of the cafeteria.

"She eats so many Skittles, she has rainbows for brains." Ed Harris laughed, and some of the other guys in line laughed with him.

My face burned. I didn't know what it was about Ed, but he hated me. My mom said it was a sign he liked me. Sometimes my mom was thick in the head.

Steve hit Ed with a lazy back handed slap. "Shut up."

Come on, machine, go faster.

Jed laughed louder than the rest. "She eats so many Skittles, if you pop her zits, they're blue inside." The boys all laughed.

Forget the Skittles. I turned to leave.

"Hey, Allyson, I think you've got Skittles under your face. No wonder you wear so much makeup. If my face were breaking out in a case of–"

"Whoops." Beth slammed her shoulder into Ed, who fell into Jed, dropping his soda to the ground.

"Hey, watch where you're going, ogre." Jed brushed at his shirt.

"I'm so sorry." Beth's voice was falsely sweet, ruining any actual attempt at an apology. "But sometimes I'm just *so* clumsy."

"You'd better watch it," he said.

"Or you'll what? Tell Mrs. Alister?" Beth raised an eyebrow at him. "Yeah, I'm sure that'll go well."

"You're a hippo, I swear."

Beth grabbed the front of his shirt and twisted her fist. "Surely you meant to say something else, perhaps an ox, or a gorilla, or anything that can run a touchdown, or twist your sorry little neck into a pretzel." As she spoke, she pulled him closer to her face, which meant she lifted him off the ground, one handed.

Yeah, Beth could scare a werewolf out of his hide.

"What's going on here?" Vice Principal Blanders rushed over.

Beth set Jed down. "I was just straightening his shirt, Mr. Blanders."

"I'm sure, Miss Whitlocke. Move along, then."

Beth hurried to me. "Don't listen to those rats."

"Hey, Skittles!" Ed yelled.

I heard a rustling and spun on the spot. Before I'd come to a stop, I sensed something hurtling toward me and snatched it out of the air. Opening my hand, I revealed the projectile. He'd thrown my Skittles at my head. I looked up from my hand to the three boys still standing in the line. They all stared at me, their eyes rimmed in white.

"Shit," Jed whispered.

"Mr. Harris!" Mr. Blander's lips pinched into a tight circle at the indignity of such words.

Ed's eyes looked like golf balls. "Freak."

Steve kept staring at me, barely blinking. Then he nodded in agreement with the others.

My blood turned cold. How could I have thought he was cute? Jerks. The world was full of jerks.

"Ignore them." Beth forcibly pushed me toward the exit. As we hit the doors, she grinned. "Why don't you try out for the football team? What a receiver!"

Dry wind pelted into me as we stepped outside. We cut across the courtyard to Mrs. Gunderson's classroom, and slipped inside. Today's journal topic was written on the chalkboard.

Actual chalk; I swear, this place was in the Stone Age.

Beth snorted at the board. "'What mythical creature would you most like to be?' Great, now I have to reminisce about that in English, too."

"It doesn't sound so bad. What would you pick?"

Beth stared at the chalkboard without seeing it. "A Pegasus."

"Why?"

"Are you kidding? They've got everything, strength, speed…" She paused. "Grace. And they fly. It's the triple threat of mythical creatures. You?"

"I don't know, maybe the dragon thing isn't that bad. But what are the rest of them like? I wouldn't want to live with a bunch of twits, even if they are superior warriors, fire breathing, wise beyond all measure…" I stopped when Beth raised an eyebrow. "What?"

She checked the room to make sure we were still alone. "The point is to fantasize about something you're not." It was the first mention of last night between us all day. I held my breath, but Beth kept smiling at me.

I rolled my eyes. "Well, what? Am I supposed to say kraken, or Minotaur or something? How about a unicorn, would that be corny enough for you? I could pick a My Little Pony while I'm at it."

Beth's laughter rumbled across the room. Mrs. Gunderson came in through the door to the teacher's rooms.

"Oh, don't mention the unicorns, they're such jerks," Beth said. "They sparkle like vampires, and think they're saving the rest of the world from evil. Who do they think they are? Repressing ingrates incapable of–"

"Ladies, is something wrong with your lunches?" Mrs. Gunderson asked.

"I just wanted to get a head start on the assignment," I lied. I still needed to do my homework from last night.

Mrs. Gunderson pursed her lips, and all thought of magical creatures and kidnapping trolls fled my mind.

CHAPTER THREE

The afternoon passed in a blur, and I tried to keep my head down. My hair drooped across my face, but it failed to create a field of invisibility around me. It was like a black curtain of doom, no light in, no light out. Damn zits. Why did I have to have so many?

The gong of the last bell reverberated through my American Institutions class, cutting off Mr. Andrews. At least the bell meant he had to stop talking about our civic duty to pay taxes. I was only in the class because nothing else fit into my schedule. That was the joy of transferring every few months. I'd never completed a class, but I had lots of snippets. Last semester, I took most of Driver's Ed., even though I wasn't old enough. Sometimes school was more like glorified babysitting. At least in math they let me go on in the book like I'd been there the whole semester. Math was the same everywhere. Add two and two and it equaled four. It didn't matter what school, what state, and no one ever questioned me after I passed the exam.

I lagged behind, gathering my stuff and waiting for the other students. I tucked each and every pencil into its little slot in my backpack. I wasn't OCD, I just wanted to give everyone else enough time to clear out so I wouldn't have to deal with Jed the jerk or Ed the ass.

"Miss Takata, is something the matter?" Mr. Andrews asked.

I hated when they called me Miss.

"Just waiting for the rabble to clear."

"Ah, well, if you'd like, I think we should talk about your grades."

I drew in a deep breath. *Here it comes.* He was going to ask why I didn't do a good job on my homework. And I needed to try not to hurt his feelings when I told him his class wouldn't even matter because I'd transfer out of here by April. My next school might have me taking woodshop for my sixth period.

"I'm sorry, Mr. Andrews. I'll try harder on the next exam."

"Actually, I thought you did fine on the exam. I want you to start turning in your homework. It's obvious you know the material."

"But you have a no late work policy."

"I'll waive it if you give a presentation next Monday on what it's like to live in a city other than Albuquerque," he said.

I stood there like a deer caught in the headlights.

"That shouldn't be too hard. I just want you to give a fifteen minute presentation and answer the other student's questions. Most have never travelled out of the metro area, let alone the state. It might be nice for them to know that McDonald's doesn't serve green chili on cheeseburgers in Vermont."

I laughed, and it rang off the walls. Vermont had its graces, but spicy food wasn't one of them. My mother couldn't handle small towns. Burlington wasn't big enough, and if your neighbor knew your name, that was too much information as far as she was concerned. Worse, Vermonters thought ketchup was one of the Three Spices made by God. The other two were salt and pepper. All other spices were just crazy, and quite frankly, ketchup was a little wild.

"So, you'll do it, then?"

I hesitated. Hell, knowing Mom, we might pack up and leave by Sunday.

"Sure, I'd love to."

"Great, then I'll see you tomorrow, with tonight's homework in hand."

I grabbed my bag and fled before Mr. Andrews could come up with something else I could do to earn back the right to turn in my homework. I hit the door with my shoulder, and it swung away in the breeze, banging into the doorstop. The wind pinned it to the wall, and I had to manhandle it closed. One nice thing about having a school in the desert, people didn't hang around the outside lockers once the winds kicked up. And Albuquerque had winds. I wrapped my jacket around my chest and leaned into the gritty air. The lockers ran along three buildings connected with walkways and windbreaks.

When I got to my locker, I turned the knob and yanked open the flimsy metal. As I dumped all the books inside, I considered the American Institutions tome. A little homework wouldn't kill me. I dropped the book into my bag, and slung it over my shoulder.

"There you are." Steve appeared like magic, blocking the entrance to the locker alcove. "I was starting to think you were avoiding me."

Imagine that. "What do you want?"

Tumbleweeds blew by, rolling into the side of the building before following the wind around the corner. It was practically a scene from an old western. Now, if we could say our lines and be done–

"I just wanted to apologize."

"For what? Demeaning me in public or throwing candy at my head?" Okay, compared to being chased through the mall by trolls, the candy thing was nothing, but I didn't have to tell him that.

"I tried to stop them," he said.

"Yeah? Well, who threw the Skittles?"

He looked away, his amber eyes almost golden.

"That's what I thought." I pushed past him.

"Hey, wait, I'm trying to apologize here."

I kept walking. All I had to do was make it across the giant street, through the bus station, and then I'd be free of him. He wouldn't dare follow me into the apartment complex, would he? Head down, I swam through the wind.

"Look, I'm sorry, okay? I just needed to know."

I glared at him. "Needed to know what? How much it might hurt if you hit me?"

"Is that what you think?"

He sounded genuine, but I'd seen these tricks before. People played each other up with ridiculous things. Then, once someone admitted something embarrassing like believing in aliens, or whatever the game was that day, the others would mock the confessor. If they caught it on film, it'd be on the Internet before the sucker finished blushing.

That was all this was. He probably just wanted to get me to say something damning, and then his friends would jump out from around the corner with a camera going. My humiliation would be plastered all over YouTube by dinner.

"Wait, can I just explain? Please!"

It was the please that got me. I stopped mere feet from the stoplight with its fist-sized pedestrian button. I turned back to watch Steve stumble up the curb. I couldn't believe I used to have a thing for him. Then the wind caught his hair and ruffled it in that I'm-too-good-for-you model way. Well, he was nice to look at.

"Fine, explain, but don't think I'm waiting for you." I took the last two steps and hit the button for the light. I pounded it three times just in case the number of hits made any difference in how fast the light changed.

"It was a test," he said.

"Did I pass?"

He nodded. "Oh, yeah, you passed." He watched as motorcycles drove by. They looked like the same guys from this morning, but then again, all grizzled old bikers looked alike. For a second the smell of fog wafted over me, but this was the desert. There wasn't fog here. Their bikes rumbled like a thunderstorm, cutting off all attempts at conversation.

Steve squinted into the sun, following the bikes. "You don't belong, do you? No one ever fits in with you. That's why you hang out with Beth, right?"

"I like Beth." My words were calm, but my heart pounded in my chest. I'd known her secret for less than twenty-four hours. I didn't want him asking about it.

Steely ice pounded through my veins. What would happen if he knew? I'd never heard of dragons and trolls except in fairy tales. Would it cause social anarchy to know that there were trolls living among us? I tried to shake the feeling.

He puffed out his laugh. "Of course you do. She's the only one in school who gave you the time of day. That's why she's your friend."

I turned my back on him, pretending to watch the street. "I don't have to listen to this." And maybe he was right. Beth was scary big, really strong, and the football coach wanted her on the team just to intimidate the opponents. She wouldn't even have to touch the ball to scare the other guys out of their pants.

Oh, and she was a troll.

But she was the only person who talked to me when I got here in December. I'd wondered if I'd be more popular if she hadn't been the first to extend the hand of friendship. There's one thing all high schools have in common: the new girl might as well be bait. They would fight over my love and affection for the first month or so before I started to 'fit in.' But not here. Albuquerque had a way of scouring right down to my desiccated soul. My grades didn't matter, because I'd never finished a semester in one school. I'd never been around to take the state boards for my grade level, but I'd studied for them in nine states.

And no matter how much they fought to be my friend in the beginning, they never texted me after I left. I got unfriended faster than mud dries in this desert. I was a pawn. A prize. An outsider only worthwhile for their popularity games.

Then there was Beth.

She was worth thirty popular friends.

"It's just that you two are sort of–you know–similar." His voice carried over the traffic.

How could he know? I only found out last night.

The wind buffeted into my face, and if I wanted to avoid eating sand, I'd have to turn back to him. At least he had to look into the wind to look me in the face.

And he did. He looked right into my eyes. "You feel like you don't belong because you're different."

"Newsflash: duh."

He shook his head. "No, you're really different, and so is Beth."

"Really? So, other than scaring the football team, how is Beth different?"

"Haven't you ever wondered why she doesn't go out for sports?" Steve asked. "It's because someone with her heritage would blow away the competition."

The light turned and traffic stopped. *Finally!* I jumped into the crosswalk.

"You're crazy," I called over my shoulder before he started walking.

"Wait! Why won't you listen to me?"

"Because you're about to say something like 'Beth is a Cyclops with a good plastic surgeon.' I'm not listening. It's not like I'll be here long enough for you to humiliate me. Go find someone else to play with."

He followed me across the street. I took the sidewalk instead of cutting through the bus stop. I wanted plenty of time to lose him.

"I can't believe you don't know what I'm talking about." He ran his hands through his hair. "Okay, what if I can prove that you're different? Will you hear me out then?"

"Fat chance." I plowed forward, giving him no opportunity to sway me from my path.

He stopped for a second. A gust of wind drove a tumbleweed bush the size of a compact car onto the sidewalk. I had to step into the street to dodge around. Steve ran to catch up. "What if I prove I'm different? Will you listen then?"

I spun on him and jabbed him in the chest. "You? Different? Do you think I was born yesterday? My god, what kind of idiot girls do they keep here in the desert if you think I'll fall for such a stupid line?" I scanned the road before I turned the full force of my contempt on him. "You're just like every other pretty boy on the planet. You're so used to being worshiped that you can't fathom a girl not falling for your charms. Well, guess what, model boy? I'm a freak, remember? So go back to whatever game you play with the normal girls, and leave me alone."

I turned to leave, but he grabbed my arm and pulled me back. His steel grip clamped down on my forearm. "I'll show you." His face froze, jaw set. Still holding my arm in one hand, he pulled a knife from his pocket. It was a tiny thing, little better than a pencil sharpener, or a keychain. Illegal at school, but the metal detectors wouldn't go in until next year–according to the vice principal. Steve flipped the blade open with his teeth.

My heart thumped in my chest, and the wind blew harder, as if sensing the change. I pulled to get my arm away from him as the knife moved closer. He brought it down on his arm.

I drew my arm away, pulling it tight against my chest. "What are you doing?"

He pointed at his arm with the knife. "There, see, I'm different too."

Blood welled up, and the scent of metal and moss filled the air, only to be whipped away by the wind. Along the line of the knife cut, a silvery material like liquid mirrors collected along the knife blade. As it dripped down his arm, it turned to the rusty red of regular blood.

"Well?" he asked, shaking his hair back away from his face. He raised an eyebrow at me, daring me to disagree with him.

This can't be real.

"Let me see the knife." I held out my hand. I couldn't tell if I wanted there to be a trick or not.

He gave me the knife, handle first, but I didn't need to see it. That was blood. I could smell it. And he always had an earthy smell of forests and things that grow. Loam, that's what they called it. He smelled like loam.

The blade was silver. I searched for a hidden compartment that would let out the silvery stuff, but I already knew the blood was real. He had silver blood. When I looked back at Steve, he held up his arm and pinched it. More silver liquid flowed from the wound and turned red as it fell to the sidewalk.

"What are you?" I leaned away from him.

"I'm Kin, like you."

I narrowed my eyes at him. "You don't know what I am."

"I know you're different. You're Kin if I ever saw one."

"What is that, Kin?"

"It's just a name for the non-normal people."

"And you're not human?"

His eyebrows came together. "I bleed silver. Did you ever come across that in Biology?"

"How come the text books don't know about you?"

He sighed. "We hide. And what about you? Are you running from something?"

I shook my head. "Not that I know of." But he had a point. We moved all over the country, never back to the same place. We never stayed longer than a few months, and we always just picked up and moved. But why would we be running?

Why would they hide?

"So what? You're Kin, but what does that mean?"

"I am descended from a long line of unicorns who—"

A horn blared as a BMW drove up and stopped right in the road.

My heart leapt. *Unicorn.* He was part unicorn.

This was too much.

The horn kept blaring, and Steve rolled his head in the sign of the long-suffering teenager. "My father."

The tinted window rolled down, and I got a glimpse of a man in designer sunglasses. He had the same wavy hair as Steve, only peppered with silver. His baby-butt smooth face had to be shaven by some sort of servant to look that clean at four o'clock in the afternoon.

"What the hell do you think you're doing?" he yelled.

"Dad, I just wanted to—"

"I was worried sick when you didn't show on time."

Wow, he must run a tight ship; Steve couldn't have been more than fifteen minutes late for anything.

"Just give me a minute, okay?" Steve asked. "Look, can I call you or something?"

I dumped the pocketknife back into his hand. "I think I have enough crazy on my plate right now."

"Can I come over or something? I haven't met anyone outside our–"

His father leaned on the horn, cutting off all attempts at conversation.

Steve's shoulders slumped, and he shot a glare at his father but took a step toward the BMW. The horn stopped, and Steve turned back.

"I'll see you tomorrow then."

"Sure." I stepped away from the road, but his father's words carried over the wind.

"What were you thinking, being seen with that girl?" The door slammed as Steve got in the car, and I kept my head down, watching but pretending not to hear.

"She's one of us, Dad. I saw it."

"No, she's not, and you'll stay away from her kind. She's dangerous."

Steve looked up, and across the distance, his amber eyes caught mine. *Sorry,* he mouthed.

CHAPTER FOUR

I walked away from the scene of crazy, rich, overprotective father being a complete twit and ducked through the wrought iron fence into my apartment complex. It was a giant gated community with multiple buildings all painted the same brownish-beige color. Conveniently, it matched the local dirt, so they never had to wash the buildings. Cars parked in the spaces ranged from brand new Mustangs to dilapidated Hondas from the eighties. My Aunt's MGB sat there next to the other cars, a collector's car lurking among the others. Good, she was still here somewhere. I wanted to talk to her.

I tore across the strip of lawn–a luxury in this desert–and caught the smell of earth and water. The grass was brown, but maybe that's what grass looked like in Albuquerque.

As I stepped off the patch of lawn, I caught a hint of gunmetal and copper. I froze, searching the parking lot. Three big guys wrestled a lumpy bag into the back of a moving van. They had their backs to me, so I couldn't see if it was the same guys from the mall. I ducked behind a wall, my heart racing.

I stood frozen in panic for a moment before I peeked around the corner. The three guys came out of the truck and went to a storage unit nearby. They grabbed a large box and carried it into the truck.

Just movers then.

Damn, why am I so jumpy?

Oh, right, trolls in the mall and a crazy guy who bleeds silver. And, of course, the whole me puking fire thing, 'cause that's not strange in the least.

The movers closed the door of their truck, piled into the cab and drove away. I didn't move from my hiding place until they'd left the apartment complex. When they were gone, I rushed over the last patches of pavement to the stairs.

When I opened the door, the smell of flowers rolled over me. The spicy, almost cinnamon scent of the carnations mingled with the perfume of the stargazer lilies. The green smell reminded me of a garden, or what a garden should smell like. I'd never lived in one place long enough to grow anything. I chased that thought from my mind and kicked my boots into the corner by the door. The flowers sat in a vase next to a card on the kitchen counter.

My mother gave me the same present every year: cash, so I could buy clothes or jewelry or whatever. But there was one rule regarding all belongings, if it didn't fit in the two trunks when we left, it didn't come with us. I usually blew my birthday bucks on ice cream and pizza at the mall. And books. I loved books; I just wish they didn't take up so much space. Maybe there'd be enough cash in the envelope for an e-reader.

I picked up the bulging envelope. Maybe she got me gift cards this year. It wasn't her handwriting on the envelope, but my aunt's messy scrawl. Mom's handwriting could win contests. She claimed it had 'gotten out of shape,' but apparently going to school with nuns for teachers instilled great handwriting.

Maybe they should send doctors to those schools.

I tore at the edge, and the flap popped open. A key fell out and clattered to the counter, followed by a card and a folded piece of paper. The card was blank, just a picture of a kitten on the front with nothing inside. I picked up the key and turned it over in my hand. The piece of paper was written in the same bold hand as my name on the envelope. An address for somewhere in Nevada was written on the paper, and that was it. Flowers and a strange key from my aunt qualified as the weirdest birthday present ever.

'Cause, seriously, I was totally going to get in a car and drive eight hundred miles to figure out what she just gave me…

I slipped the key into my pocket and went straight to my room. I pulled out my guitar and tried not to purr as I tuned it. I loved music. Songs were the only thing I got to do everywhere. I played through the chords of the song, adding in the lyrics as I went. I wasn't a great player, but my aunt wrote incredible music. Even I sounded good when I played her stuff.

I practiced until I memorized the piece in the off chance I might get to play it for her tonight. If I did, she might play, too.

But what was the deal with the key?

I stopped playing and pulled out my phone, flipped it open and dialed Beth.

"Hey, what's eating you?" Beth asked.

"You could wait for me to at least say hello."

"Okay, say hello."

"Hi," I said, dragging it out.

"What's eating you? Birthday blues? Did your mom cancel dinner, 'cause if she did, you can come over here, and I'll order a pizza or something. It's your birthday. It'd be a crime not to celebrate."

"Your dad still out of town?"

"He'll be back on Monday."

"Doesn't he worry about you partying or something?"

"Yeah, no. I'm about the most boring teenager on the planet. Besides, he racked up a bunch of Xbox points before he left. Someone has to spend them." She paused. "You're avoiding the question."

"Yeah, well, I ran into Steve on the way home," I said. What to tell Beth? His dad is an ass, and he bleeds silver, so don't cut him.

Does he get silver road rash?

"Tell me you didn't listen to him and his pack of nags. They are completely worthless." Something on the other end of the line broke and Beth swore.

"Pack of nags?"

"Unicorns. He's some sort of protégé monohorn. Anyhow, he had tapes of me healing crazy fast and they were going to post it on YouTube. He and Jed were trying to get attention from some

Hollywood big wigs in town. They tried to use the school computer lab, and that's when they got caught."

"Seriously?"

"Yup."

"Are you okay? I mean, you didn't crush any skulls or anything, did you?"

"Nope, I found their parents and told them what their children were doing."

Her smug smile rang through the phone in her voice.

"Wait, you ratted them out to their parents and you weren't branded nark of the century?" I asked.

"Honestly, Ally, does it look like I have a gang of devoted admirers?"

"Did you tell your dad?"

"He was on a business trip to Africa and didn't get back for weeks. By then, well, I'd done everything I could. It was enough humiliation all around, no need to involve the parental unit."

Silence fell, but I didn't know what to say.

A key scraped in the lock of the front door. "I should go, that's probably my mom."

"Is that your super hearing coming into effect? Shall I add it to your wicked vomit aiming skills?"

"Oh, shut up."

"Fine. Just remember, if she cancels on you, I've got pizza."

"Bye." I flipped the phone closed.

"Honey, are you home?" my mother asked from the front door.

"I'm here, Mom."

I went back out into the front room as my mom pushed into the apartment with a bouquet of flowers in one hand and an envelope in the other.

"I've got some big news," she said.

"Oh?" I cocked an eyebrow for effect.

"I got transferred. We'll be moving in a month."

Not again. I sagged into the couch.

"Isn't that great? It's a big raise, too; I'm actually getting promoted." She laid the flowers on the counter and dropped an envelope next to them, then opened the refrigerator and pulled out an uncorked bottle of wine. "Happy birthday!"

She poured the golden wine into a plastic cup, then poured some sparkling grape juice for me. She handed me my glass.

"Congratulations." I dutifully lifted the cup to my mother. She glowed in the moment. I put the cup to my lips and took a swallow, trying not to taste the week old refrigerator smell.

She took a long sip of wine and sighed. "So, how was your birthday?"

Great, Mom, my best–only–friend is a troll, and the only guy I've had a crush on in years is an asshole who bleeds silver. Oh, and I'm half freakin' dragon and you couldn't have mentioned that during the honey-we-should-talk-about-sex-and-drugs lecture?

I held back my sigh. "Fine."

She seemed to see me for the first time since getting home. "Here's the deal, kiddo. When we move, I'll be able to afford something special."

I narrowed my eyes at her. "What sort of special."

"I was going to make it a surprise, but it is your birthday. I was thinking I could let you pick out a new guitar."

"An electric one?"

My mother sighed. "If that's what you want, then sure."

Visions of a purple Fender danced through my head. Who doesn't want a new guitar? Yeah, so it was bribery. When it came to music, I had no integrity. I was all about the bribes.

She pinched me, and I tried not to giggle, but her happiness was infectious, drawing a laugh out of me. "So, is there anyone you'd like to invite to your birthday dinner?"

"Beth," I said automatically. "Her dad's out of town."

"He sure travels a lot." She looked at me frowning. Her brow furrowed as she took a gulp of wine. She passed over the envelope, and I opened it. Six twenties flapped at me as I read the card.

"Thanks, Mom."

She held up her drink. "To a new home."

I tapped my cup to hers, but kept my mouth shut. In my pocket, a mysterious key burned in mind, begging for attention. To a *home*.

CHAPTER FIVE

Five Days Before

After a birthday dinner that mysteriously did not involve crazy Aunt Agnes–I fully suspected my mother had something to do with that–I woke and dressed for class as usual. I still got goose bumps thinking about those trolls, but now it seemed more like a bad dream than real life. Besides, Fridays always held a certain appeal: the hope of the weekend. There was something magical about two days off. Two days of not needing to try to fit in and pretending the whispered insults didn't hurt my feelings. Why did I even go to school? I didn't have the grades to get into college.

"Mom, can I just stay home today?"

"Absolutely not," she called from the bathroom.

She curled her hair to perfection–someone should have told her you don't have to impress the boss after you get the career-altering promotion. It was her new boss she'd need to kiss up to. Still, she put on her climbing-the-corporate-ladder dress, and her makeup looked great. Nothing could make her hair prettier, but she'd been giving it a go for the last twenty minutes.

"But yesterday was my birthday." That sounded whiny even to me.

"And today is not. Chin up; I want you to take some good grades to your next school. Is that understood?" My mother smacked her lips as she reapplied her lipstick. "Oh, and your aunt called; she said she was sorry about last night."

"When did she call?"

"She said it was lunch, but the message didn't show up until last night."

41

Damn it. I really wanted to pin her down. If I was half dragon, then she must be too. Or maybe she was full. I was hoping to get some real answers from her, but now she'd probably disappeared for another year. Would I have the guts to ask her over the phone?

"You'd better hurry up, young lady. I know when the first bell is."

I rolled my eyes, but grabbed my backpack, utterly untouched since I'd gotten home yesterday. So much for a new leaf and all that. I slipped it over my shoulder and hopped out into the cool morning. Fruitless plum trees lined the streets, blossoms filling the air. I loved how they looked like little clouds of magic, and just in time for my birthday. The wind tore through the apartment complex, and the pink petals rained down like snow, blanketing the walkway at my feet. Late March wasn't a terrible time to have a birthday; I just wished I'd gotten some answers.

And what was at that address in Ely, Nevada? I'd spent half my night wondering about the key and the other half dreaming about turning into a leathery, scaled monster. Just on the cusp of morning, I'd dreamt I'd been given a castle in the desert.

I'd never be lucky enough to inherit a castle—or the fortune I'd need just to have it—but I enjoyed rolling the thought around in my head. A castle perched on some red sandstone cliff, overlooking a deep valley like the Grand Canyon. The wind would sweep up the cliffs, and I could fly. I could watch the seasons change in one place, dusted by snow in the winter, dotted with flowers in the spring. Would it have thunderstorms through the summer? I painted them on my imaginary castle. *That would do.*

I hit the crosswalk button and waited for the light to change. Across the street, Beth leaned against the light post, waiting for me. She smiled when she met my gaze, and my whole body relaxed. We would go about our normal business, and pretend the whole troll-dragon-guy-bleeding-silver thing hadn't happened. When the light changed, I practically skipped across the road as I mentally imagined Beth in my castle with me. It would get lonely all by myself, after all.

She could have the east wing. I'd take the west wing.

"Was it a satisfactory birthday?" Beth asked.

"Well, my aunt called to say sorry, but I didn't get to talk to her." I spoke with my usual light-hearted tone, but Beth gave me the penetrating eyeball.

"Maybe you can come over this afternoon and watch some movies. I've got an ancient copy of *Legend*. They cut off some unicorn horns," she said, and flashed a malicious smile.

"Any word from your padre?"

"Pwha! As if. Look, if you can talk your mom into it, you can come over and we could get into loads of trouble. I don't even have any volunteer work this weekend."

When I raised an eyebrow in question, she rolled her eyes. "I'll tell you some other time. So, what do you say, explore your inner-self, watch movies with me?"

I sighed. "Right, well, we could watch *The Last Unicorn* or *Dragon Heart*, or something."

"Hey, you okay?" Beth elbowed me in the ribs, searching my gaze with bright green eyes. Sure, they were a touch larger than they should be, and her right eye was a little higher than her left, but even if she was half troll, she cared. Which was more than I could say for all my former classmates.

"I'm just disappointed. I wanted to grill my aunt."

"You could always ask your mother."

"Ha! There are two forbidden topics in my house: absent family members, and the past." I held my hand over the side of my mouth. "Besides, what would I say? Mom, I accidentally lit the *mall* on fire? I'm probably wanted for arson. These are not the ways to open conversations with the parental unit."

"I'm just saying." Beth rounded the yellow bars that marked the edge of the parking lot. Tires screeched across the asphalt, and everyone turned. The rumble of anti-lock brakes warred with the squealing tires as a silver BMW slid to a halt next to the sidewalk.

Startled expletives broke out through the crowd heading onto campus.

Steve's dad jumped out of the car. "You!" He jabbed an accusing finger toward Beth and me as he stalked forward. "You blubbering, festering pile of puss. What have you done with him? Where is my son?" He pushed me aside and grabbed the lapels of Beth's jacket.

She towered over him in size, but shrank before his fury. "What? I don't know! What's going on?" Beth looked to me then back at Steve's dad.

"I knew you'd turn on us." He shook her jacket, and Beth rattled in the canvas. "I'll kill you. We never should have taken in one of your kind!" His red face threatened to pop, but his hands moved from Beth's jacket to her throat. He had to reach up to get a grip around her neck. If he hadn't been screaming mad, it would have been a classic example of a Chihuahua taking on a Bull Mastiff. Except the Bull Mastiff had frozen.

Beth's face paled to paper white. She stared wide-eyed at Steve's dad, unable to muster any defense.

His hands tightened, and a squelch escaped Beth's mouth.

The rapid beating of his heart rose over the din of the crowd. It drummed impossibly fast, and my senses sharpened. His clothes smelled of cologne and cigarette smoke. His breath was tinged with sugar and jelly–a donut, maybe? His tear-streaked face held a full day's worth of beard growth.

Beneath it all, he smelled like his son–of moss and forests.

And he was *choking* my best friend.

A knot in my stomach unraveled, and I bent my knees to gather my strength. In one step, I threw my elbow into his armpit and he cried out. He released Beth with one arm, and I brought my doubled-handed fist down into the soft spot of his shoulder. He crumpled under my blow.

Beth fell backwards, gasping.

Feet pounded the pavement, running toward us, but I didn't care. Let them see me fight. What did it matter if I got expelled? I'd be moving in a month.

I took two steps, rounding between Steve's dad and Beth. If he wanted to attack her, he'd have to get through me.

"You!" He pointed at me, and his eyes widened. Crazy eyes. The eyes of a man who had lost everything. "You did this. What have you done with my son?"

"I haven't touched Steve." I spoke calmly, but my mind raced.

"Liar!" He launched himself at me, and I blocked his attack. He grabbed my backpack, pulling me to the ground. A foot caught me in the back of my knee, and I fell forward. He threw all his weight into the blow and my head whipped to the pavement. I turned my face to spare my nose, but my cheek slammed into the rocks next to the sidewalk. From the ground, my hand found his arm, and I twisted, hard. He screamed, and I levered myself off the ground. His bones ground and popped in my grasp. If I pressed harder, I could break them.

He swung with his free hand, and I ducked. I swept out my leg, catching both of his, and spun him in the air. As he fell, I caught his free arm behind his back, keeping him from hitting the cement. He writhed in my hands, but he couldn't break my grip. I squeezed my hands around his wrists.

Teachers erupted from the crowd, surrounding us. Someone took his hands from mine, and someone else pulled me off him.

"Miss Takata!" Principal Hawthorne yelled.

Mrs. Gunderson shook her head, standing between the Principal and me. "Mr. June attacked her."

The other teachers pulled Mr. June off the ground, holding his hands behind his back. He struggled, wildly tearing away from the other adults. He searched the area, and his eyes locked onto me once more. "You!"

I stepped forward, fists clenched. Mrs. Gunderson grabbed my shoulder, pulling me back.

He struggled against the others, but when he couldn't break free, he spit at me. It nailed my jeans.

Actual spit.

I pulled against the hands holding me back. "What the hell is wrong with you? I haven't done anything!"

As I tried to step forward, more people moved to hold me back. My whole body shuddered with the need to wring his neck.

"There will be nothing left of you!" Mr. June screamed. "When I'm finished, they will only talk about how your hide made good *tack*!"

I surged forward, but Beth's hand crushed my shoulder. Adults filled all the spaces between us, blocking my view of Steve's dad.

"Come with me, ladies." Principal Hawthorne beckoned with a wave of her hand.

I picked my backpack out of the dust. Beth shook, but with rage or fear, I couldn't tell. I followed along, demurely, Beth beside me, until I reached up to wipe at an itch on my face. My hand came away bloodied.

"Shit."

"Miss Takata, please!" Mrs. Hawthorne widened her eyes at me.

"I'm sorry, Mrs. Hawthorne, but I'm bleeding."

Her eyebrows pinched together in concern, my previous transgression forgotten. "Is it bad?"

Beth took a peek at my face. "Just a scratch."

"Still, I'll call the nurse when we reach my office. I want to keep an eye on you two until the police arrive."

By some unspoken agreement, Beth and I lagged behind.

"Can he do anything to you?" I whispered.

"He sort of runs my trust fund." Her voice shook when she answered.

Well, wasn't that just swell? He had control over her life, and he was a raving lunatic. Make that a raving monohorn lunatic. Today was off to a great start.

When we reached the front office, Mrs. Hawthorne pulled the first aid kit off the wall on her way to her office.

Beth took the kit from her. It looked like an artifact, something from the 70s, but Mrs. Hawthorne pulled out some sterile wipes and passed them across the table. Without saying anything, Beth took them and turned me toward her.

"Please put some gloves on, Miss Whitlocke."

Beth rolled her eyes but put on the latex gloves that came with the kit. Her face set in a business mask, she daubed at the mess, and a few blood-soaked wipes fell into the trash. Beth reached up to daub again, and paused. The muscle in her jaw jumped. She looked into my eyes as if willing me to read her mind.

"That ought to do it, do you have some medical tape in there?" she asked. She held my gaze, but her stony face gave no hint of what was the matter.

My stomach did that awful flip-flop thing.

What's wrong with my face?

Before I could panic, Beth taped a big wad of bandages to my left cheek. "You'll probably want to keep that covered until you can have a good look at it." Beth pitched one eyebrow up. "You know, like in a bathroom or somewhere with good lighting, and privacy."

Oh, crap.

Mrs. Hawthorne scowled. "You should have that looked at by a professional."

Beth gave a sharp shake of her head when Mrs. Hawthorne wasn't looking.

"What's going on? What happened to Steve?" I asked.

"He is missing." She handed me a tissue. "If either of you ladies have any information, we'd greatly appreciate it if you would tell the police."

I shifted from foot to foot, the tape on my face burning.

Those trolls were still out there somewhere. They hadn't managed to catch Beth and me, but what if they got Steve?

But how to tell the police? *Uhm, excuse me, but I think some trolls kidnapped my classmate.*

It sounded nuts just thinking it.

"Well," Mrs. Hawthorne said at last, "in light of the current situation, I can understand if you ladies wish to be excused from classes today. Shall I call your mother, Miss Takata?"

"Can't I just walk home? I live right across the street."

Mrs. Hawthorne favored me with a sympathetic look. "I'm sorry, but given the severity of this morning's events, I cannot release you to anyone but your guardian."

Translation: Here at Ellison High, we like to cover our asses when our students are attacked by raving, rich pains in our butts.

She picked up her phone and talked briefly with someone else. I guess the calling of parents didn't actually fall under the cranky Principal job title. "Miss Whitlocke," she said, "I presume things have not changed with your father?"

"That's right," Beth replied, a picture of perfect stoicism.

"If you ladies could, please wait at the front desk for things to settle out." Mrs. Hawthorne held the door open and flashed a wan smile at us.

"I'll wait with you," Beth said.

"What, someone doesn't have to show up for you?"

A half smile cracked her stony expression. "I'm an emancipated minor in certain regards. Rides home fall under the legal definition. I get to check myself out if I'm ill, etc. I can always call on–ahem– *family* friends, if I'm too sick to get home, but that has yet to happen. I'm pretty sturdy."

I paused. "The whole bridge domicile issue?"

"You're funny, Drake."

The secretary picked up the phone. "Mrs. Takata?–Oh, I'm sorry, I just assumed."

I could just see Mom's blood pressure rising. She hated when people called her that.

"Yes, well, if you could come and pick her up… No ma'am, given the severity of the situation, we have to release her to a guardian."

My mother's voice blared through, none of it understandable from this distance.

The secretary hung up the phone and smiled at me. "Poor dear, do you need an ice pack or something?" she asked.

"Oh, I'm fine except for the pain and the bleeding."

She blinked.

Beth elbowed me in the gut, and for the record, getting elbowed by a half troll was not pleasant.

"Well, if there's anything I can do to make you more comfortable, just let me know. Your mother will be here soon." She smiled, and I wondered if somewhere, they bred happy people to work front desks like a puppy mill.

CHAPTER SIX

My mother burst through the orange office door, and scanned the room for her only brood. Her gaze scoured me from top to bottom, but when she looked back up to my face, she focused on the bandage. "What happened?"

I bristled. *I came to the rescue. I should be some sort of hero, and everyone is just shy of throwing me in jail.* "I don't want to talk about it," I said, grabbing my backpack off the floor. I pushed past her and headed for the door.

She peeled her gaze from me and turned to Beth. "Do you need a ride home, Beth?" my mother asked.

"No thanks, Ms. Brown." Her voice was bright and cheery, but there was a tremor in it.

I turned back, and Beth put her thumb to her ear and pinky to her mouth. I nodded, and continued my headlong escape of the office.

We didn't speak as we walked to the ancient Ford Ranger. Green paint had chipped off the hood, but it still ran. I climbed in the passenger side and slammed the door behind me.

"What happened?" Mom asked, once she was settled behind the wheel.

"It's not a big deal." She turned the key, and the engine fired up. She ruthlessly backed the pickup out of the parking spot and sped across the pavement to the light. As she drove, she narrowed her eyes at the road. "They said a man attacked you."

"Yeah, Steve's dad went nuts at Beth. I pulled him off. Do we have to talk about it?" I played with the door lock, pulling up the little plastic nub and stuffing it back into the door.

She blew through the red light, and the tires squealed as she took a left turn onto the road next to our apartment complex. "Yes, we have to talk about it when you get into fights at school."

"It wasn't a fight, okay? It was little more than self defense."

"You listen to me, young lady. I will not have that sort of behavior from you."

I snorted. "And what behavior is that? The kind that gets me in trouble at school, or the kind that inconveniences you from taking the dream job you really want? Scared I'll screw up your promotion?"

She slammed the brakes as she turned into the apartment complex. "This has nothing to do with me. I'm only trying to look out for your best interests."

"And you think moving every five months has been in my best interest? How the hell am I ever going to get into college like this? How am I supposed to get a job? All you ever do is run. Was Dad some sort of criminal? Did he scare you so much that you can't live in one place longer than it takes the neighbors to learn your name and start asking questions?"

A muscle in her jaw jumped as she ground her teeth together. She parked the truck in front of the staircase to the apartment. I looked anywhere but at her, focusing on the faded MGB still parked in the same spot from yesterday. If Aunt Aggy's car was here, where was Aunt Aggy, and why hadn't she shown up last night?

My mom took a breath. Her hands were shaking, and she gripped the steering wheel. "Everything I have ever done has been for your protection," she said.

"So, you're trying to keep people from calling me bastard or something? Well, I don't care. I don't care what happened before you had me. I just want a normal life!"

She took a deep breath. "I have been the best mom I could be. I'm sorry it hasn't been easy, but you'll understand, someday. Maybe when you have children of your own."

I pursed my lips, but only because rolling my eyes would pull the tape on my cheek. "No, I don't understand, and I'll never understand why a life with you–running!–could possibly be better than having a real father." The words spilled out of my mouth. I held my breath, waiting for her to say something.

She took a long, slow breath. "I'm sorry you feel that way."

I'd mentioned Dad and there were no fireworks. I might live through this.

She pursed her lips. "Now, I have to get back to work." Her face set, jaw clenched and no hint of her real feelings. "You're grounded until we can talk about this. Do you understand?"

"That's completely unfair! I haven't done anything."

"I'm trying to talk to you but you're making this impossible. I know what it's like to be your age. I remember how hard the first–well, I just know, okay?"

"No, it's not okay. You know nothing about me. You don't know what it's like growing up on the run, having a new school every four months."

She sighed. "Is that what this is about?"

I said nothing. My mother was relieved my issues might be something so mundane. I nodded to confirm her reality. She focused on the dashboard, where the clock blinked, then cussed. "I've gotta go, but this isn't over, young lady."

"Fine." I pushed the door open and slung my backpack over my shoulder. I slammed the door for good effect, but Mom had already hit the gas. I wanted to scream at her. I wanted to break things, but a deep burning swept through me, and I remembered the gout of fire in the mall. For the fiftieth time, I wondered if someone had a security video of that.

I stormed up the stairs, stomping, but who would notice? Who would notice if I just disappeared? My mom and my aunt? Oh, and Beth. So, yeah, three people in the whole freakin' world. I'd called thousands of people my friend, and no one cared. I'd already blown out of every life I'd come into contact with, and in a month, I'd lose Beth too.

And what the hell was wrong with Steve's dad?

I locked the door behind me and kicked off my shoes on the strip of linoleum. Dumping my bag with the shoes, I headed for the bathroom. Since I didn't know what was actually wrong with my face, I fished out the first aid kit to have the supplies I'd need to rewrap whatever was wrong. At least the bandage had been over my worst zits.

The tape stuck to my skin, pulling out hair. I ripped it free and had to blink to hold back the tears. When I was sure I'd saved the world from a flood of worthless saline, I checked the mirror for the damage. My cheek had burst open over two of the three zits on my left cheek. Peeking out of the ruined flesh were two unmistakable scales.

"Oh crap! No, no, no, no!"

My phone buzzed in my pocket.

I punched the dial. "What?"

"How's it going over there?"

"Beth, I thought you were my mom."

"Are you having that much fun?" Despite the sarcasm, her voice cracked.

"I'm sorry, I've just, you know." I pulled the phone to my other ear and whispered. "I have *scales*. What the hell?"

Beth chuckled. "What did you expect, hatchling?"

"This isn't funny," I hissed.

"Well, what did you think would happen? You spit fire, now you have scales. You're half dragon, or at least part dragon. Enough for physical manifestation at least."

I looked back in the mirror and touched the vibrant blue scale. Down the center of the scale, red pulsed to a darker purple. Was that my blood below the surface? "That's great, but what the hell do I do now?"

"Come on, Allyson, you wear enough makeup to hide Lady Gaga under there. Just use more than usual."

"Beth," I said, trying not to sound like I was explaining to a small child, "the texture isn't the same as my skin. It doesn't matter how much makeup I use, it will just look like a flesh colored scale on my face."

"Relax, we can go buy some Halloween makeup from Duke City Party Supply," she said.

I nodded as if she could see me. "The one that's in the mall where trolls chased us last night?"

"It's only in the parking lot across the street; I doubt they're canvassing the place like cops."

"No, just like kidnappers." Beth didn't respond, so I went on. "Why do they call Albuquerque Duke City anyway?"

"The first Spaniard granted land here was a duke: the Duke of Albuquerque. It's Spanish. They even spell it differently. We took a fieldtrip to the museum in fourth grade."

"You remember stuff like that?"

"It's not like I have friends, and the teachers are nicer to you if you get good grades. You're changing the subject. Are we going to buy you some Halloween makeup, or what?"

"I can't walk around with scales on my face."

"Just put a Band-Aid on it and say you got in a fight—which you did—then make some joke about the other guy." Beth at least sounded kind of normal.

"Fine. Meet you there in thirty minutes."

"Wouldn't dream of missing it."

I pawed through the first aid kit and pulled out a Band-Aid the size of my palm, then stuck it over the scales. Why couldn't I just slowly deteriorate into normal teenage angst and trauma? Wasn't that enough for one person? Why did I have to be the overachiever at Freak High?

The Band-Aid packaging crumpled in my hand, and I tried to calm my breathing. I pulled the inhaler out of my pocket and considered taking a puff, but would it work on a building fire attack?

Forget it. If I spit fire, then maybe I needed to. What if my asthma has just been me holding back my fire all this time? Could I run track if I just spit fire before I jogged?

At the entryway, I paused to stuff my feet into my shoes. I mentally flipped off my mom as I flew out the door. Grounded? Yeah, how was she gonna check?

When I got to the store, the lights were off but the door was open. Rows of floor to ceiling party gags filled the store. No one stood at the register, but a camera watched from the black dome stuck to the ceiling. I waved before heading into the stacks of party merchandise.

They had every theme I'd ever dreamed of and a number I hadn't. Weddings and baby showers took up the first three rows, and after that it was two rows of princesses, a row of pirates and finally, Halloween costumes.

Beth stood in the middle of the aisle with the only store clerk. "Is this all the makeup you have?"

"Yeah." He shook his head and shrugged his shoulders. "It is March. We won't get our first shipments for Halloween until August or September."

"Bummer." Her eyes scanned the merchandise before tilting her head at me. "See anything?"

I searched the products for a moment and found a couple pots of liquid latex paired with red and black paint. The picture on the package showed someone with a grotesque hole in the side of his face. Shock and awe makeup.

"This'll do." I picked up three. Who knew how long I'd have to cover it up. A day? A month? How many of my birthday bucks was I about to flush just to have a normal face?

Maybe I could make a prosthetic piece I glued on every day.

My life unfolded before me, gluing a piece of fake skin over my scales, trying to be normal. I'd be buying this crap online 'til I died. I could get a job working at a costumer's shop and claim that I was really into strange makeup. Could I ever do anything normal again? And how long would the glue last? Could I put it on and go to a slumber party? Or was another normal venue of teenagerhood just yanked from me?

Would it last through a date? I'd never been on a date, and now I never would without having some prosthetic pasted onto my face.

My *face* was defective.

Would it get worse? Would I break out in a rash of scales? Would I look like a dragon, or a cross between a human and lizard?

"Is that all for you?" the clerk asked.

"Uh, yeah. Um, do you take cash?" *Oh, hell, do you take cash?* Could I sound more like an idiot?

He chuckled. "Yes, we still take cash."

Yup, I definitely wanted to spend birthday bucks hiding my defective face.

CHAPTER SEVEN

"You okay?" Beth asked as we left Party Center.**

"Sorry, I'm just," I paused, grasping at the air, "this whole thing is insane. Dragons? Trolls? Everything I've been told is a lie. That's just crazy, you know?"

A derisive huff left her lungs. "Boy, do I ever."

"I mean, what's out there? So, I'm—" I dropped my voice in case some invisible hermit caught us talking, "—I'm half dragon, but what about centaurs and pegasuses—would that be pegasii? —or ghosts and wraiths? Zombies?" I widened my eyes.

Beth closed her eyes and gave a short shake of her head. Her lips moved slowly in an exaggerated *no*.

We got to the edge of the busy road that separated the high school from the mall. Our homes flanked the school: Beth's condo on the left and my apartment on the right. I kept my silence, but I wanted to know more. The world was suddenly filled with all kinds of possibilities. What else had every history book lied about?

She tipped her head toward her place. "You wanna come over? We can watch the Tom Cruise horn chopping."

I hesitated. I wanted to. I burned to know more. There was just one little problem. "I'm grounded."

"Oh, please, what are they teaching kids these days? Violence is bad, but if you save your friend from the raving lunatic, you're grounded?"

I smiled. "I think it was for something else."

"So then why did you go to Party Center?"

"You gonna interrogate me, or are we going to watch some unicorn horn chopping?"

She smiled and punched me in the shoulder. I rubbed my arm. She play hit like a Mac Truck. We dodged the little traffic in the time-honored jaywalking tradition. A couple of college kids at the skate park watched us cross the street. I checked to make sure they weren't trolls, but they seemed human enough.

But were they unicorns?

Were they gryphons? Harpies? Ooh, I bet my English teacher in Vermont was part harpy. She was definitely the flesh eating, soul-crushing type.

I wrenched my mind back to the present as we crossed the street to Beth's place. Where my apartment building matched the dirt, hers matched cactus flowers and insects, bright reds, oranges, and yellows. Mine looked like a blob of dirt artfully crafted into a rectangle.

We climbed the stairs two at a time, and my chest tightened. Asthma or fireball?

"You're thinking too hard, Drake," Beth said.

"Do you have to call me that?"

"I'm sorry, does it bug you?"

"Would it bug you if I called you 'troll,' or 'trollop,' or whatever the girl version of troll is?"

Beth smiled, enjoying some private joke. "As far as schoolyard teasing, there's nothing you can do to troll to really make it sound more awful than it is." She looked away, her eyes dark with some distant memory. Behind her hardened rind, Beth knew all about schoolyard taunts. Then she closed up again, hiding any truth behind her cavalier smile. Her stocky frame didn't fit with beauty magazines, but her smile was indestructible, a shield against a world obsessed with beauty.

And in my little plastic bag I had three pots of gunk designed to hide my face. I'm such a hypocrite.

She pushed open the door, revealing a well-appointed apartment. I'd been here before, but the place was nice. Really nice. Designer furniture and custom paint nice. White couch, white carpet… I found it nearly impossible to believe a place like this was in a condominium complex.

Beth went to the fridge and pulled out two bottles of cream soda. She sat in the corner of the couch opposite me, undid both bottle tops, then handed me one. We clinked the bottles together.

"Cheers," I said.

"Cheers."

The *Legend* DVD case sat opened on the coffee table. She had everything from *Hairspray* to *Singing in the Rain*, all filed in orderly shelves. Beth picked up the remote and started the movie.

After a good half hour of Beth's fidgeting, I pulled my attention from the movie. "So, what's going on?"

She pretended to watch the heroine rescuing a unicorn. "It's complicated."

"More complicated than finding out I'm part dragon and have scales on my face, making me the school freak?"

"I'm just glad you took the title from me. Maybe I can get a date to prom now." She snorted. "Well, at least my chances are now greater than zero."

"How many unicorn halves or Kin, or whatever, are at the school?"

"Any descendant are called Kin, not just unicorns. As for the monohorns, they have something like twelve at the school." Beth stared at the screen, but I knew she wasn't watching. She was trying not to think about the things Steve's dad had said.

"Are there others at the school?"

Beth flashed me a quick smile with shake of her head. "Nope. Unicorns don't really play well with others."

"So, what's the deal with them?"

"I'm half troll. They would usually kill my kind, but I'm some sort of humanitarian effort. I'm a philanthropy project. That and it's useful for training to have a real, live, half-troll." Her face contorted like she'd just bitten a lemon.

"I don't understand."

"I have most of the natural abilities of a troll. Great strength, exceptional healing, you know," she snorted, "a solid desire to eat roasted goat under a bridge."

I gawked at her, eyes wide.

"The goat thing is a joke, jeez. I can't even eat lamb without getting queasy." She took a drink of her cream soda, staring at the TV but not seeing it. The dark thoughts slipping through her mind practically played across her eyes.

"You're not exactly vegetarian though."

"That doesn't mean I like to eat cute, fuzzy things for breakfast."

"What about your dad?" I asked.

She crushed the soda bottle in her hand. Blood trickled down onto the white carpet. It had a slight green tint as it fell, but the color staining the carpet was just as red as any other blood. Beth opened her hand and pulled shards of glass out of her palm. She collected the glass in one hand, blood still dripping from the wound. The ragged edges of the cut closed like drops of water slipping together. The skin sealed together, erasing the cut.

She held up her hand and waved at me. "See, exceptional healing."

"I've never met my father," I blurted.

We locked eyes, and a half-smile pulled at her face, part empathy, part envy. "You're lucky then. Mine's an ass."

Beth took a moment to pick the glass out of the carpet before going to the kitchen. She came back with a bottle of cleaner and sprayed it on the carpet, then fell onto the couch in a *whompf* of leather and cushions.

"My dad sends me a stipend to cover my living costs. He sends it through the unicorns so they can keep me in line. If I don't get good grades and help with training, they don't go grocery shopping."

"That sucks," I said. It was the understatement of the century.

"Huh. I've taken some precautions." She stretched out and put her hands behind her head. "What about you? You're dragon; that's awesome."

Except for the scales on my face. And how exactly did I breathe the fire? How did that work? Could I just decide I wanted to spit fire and have fire come spraying out of my mouth?

Was breathing fire bad for me? In general, I wasn't a fan of things that make me feel sick to my stomach. I scowled.

She held her hands out, palm up. "What, you don't like breathing fire? That was pretty awesome."

"And then I puked," I said.

Beth tried to hide her laughter, but it rolled out like thunder. "Right on his shoes. That was brilliant. Remind me to puke on the next guy who tries to attack me."

I punched her in the shoulder, but it only made her laugh harder.

"Your secret power is vomit. Does that make you the Power Puker? Or the Villainous Vomiter?"

"Shut up," I said. "Or I might be tempted into a repeat performance."

"Try not to vomit fire on the couch, I almost like this one." Beth rubbed the leather gently. She broke bottles in her hands when she was upset. What happened to the furniture when she was mad? Did she crush chairs for fun?

The doorbell rang, and I jumped.

Beth stared at the door. "Shit, you'd better hide. That's probably the monohorns."

"I hope the monohorns are here to apologize," I said.

"Hah, I doubt it." She waved me toward the door to a room off to the side.

I grabbed my soda and disappeared into the small bedroom.

As I slipped into a space next to Beth's dresser, the doorbell rang again.

"Yeah, give me a minute," Beth yelled. She stopped the movie before she opened the door.

"Miss Whitlocke?" The voice was masculine, and I trained my ear to the conversation.

"Hi, Dr. Targyne."

"Do you have a moment to go over the charges?"

I froze. I didn't want to hear this, but part of me was dying for answers. Were they going to talk about unicorns and trolls and, most importantly, dragons? I took careful, slow breaths, holding everything perfectly still, and focused my attention on the conversation at the door.

Something crunched in the other room. For a second, I thought I could hear Beth's heart beating.

"Charges? But I didn't do anything."

"Of course not, Bethany. But you have been formally charged by Mr. June. He thinks you had something to do with Steve's abduction. You were also seen associating with another of the Kin. An unregistered." Metal clanked, like someone rattling a watch in a nervous twitch.

A delicious, buttery metal smell wafted into Beth's bedroom. It smelled like my childhood: forest fires of summer; salt spray from the time my mother and I went whale watching; the first strawberries after winter. The memories flooded through me, and I needed them. I was intoxicated by the sudden idea of home. The metal rattled again, and the smell intensified.

"What have I been charged with?" Beth asked.

I inhaled, letting the memories of my life drown me in the feeling of home, a place that, in a hundred years, would hold all my past teddy bears, my books, my treasures. I saw guitars lining the walls, and in my mind, that house was in a painted desert where the sun beat down to bake the rocks. The images came faster, drowning me in memories.

"You've been consorting with dragons and trolls. You are aware of our laws. If you are found guilty, it will mean censure." The man paused. "The permanent kind."

Spaghetti, chocolate cake, my mother's shampoo, mint along the riverbank, blackberries in summer, snow in pine trees. I took a step forward, and I bumped into a dresser. The bottle fell from my hand, and time slowed. The cream soda dropped toward the white carpet. Without realizing I moved, I reached for it. Faster than lightning, I caught the bottle. Cream soda splashed over the side, hitting the dresser.

"What was that?" the man asked.

The world cleared, coming back to focus. I blinked at my surroundings, surprised to be in Beth's apartment.

He put a spell on me! That son of a cactus put a spell on me! How?

A sound of a foot on the custom tile in the entryway sent a shock through my heart. He could spellbind me, and he was on his way. I searched the room for a place to hide, but there was only the closet. Everyone hid in the closet, but it beat standing in the open.

"What was what?" Beth asked.

I jumped into the closet and pulled the door shut, stuffing myself between winter jackets and summer dresses I doubted Beth would ever wear. I stilled, willing my breathing to slow, and caught the earthy scents of silver and forest–all moss, decomposing leaves, and ferns.

"Oh my God!" Beth yelled.

The footsteps clomped onto the hard floors, like heavy boots.

Or hooves.

Beth cried out, and something smashed into the wall with a *thump*. The sound of hooves on the floor thundered into the bedroom. In a torrent of shattering wood, a curling, white horn crushed through the closet door, spearing the flower dress beside me.

"What are you doing?" Beth roared.

Adrenaline surged like fire through my veins, and with the unicorn horn just inches from my face, I slammed my whole body into the door of the closet. It parted from the wall and smashed into the unicorn. A real, live, white unicorn.

Debris fell around, me, and the scent of buttery metal grew. Waves of memories washed over me, and I shook my head to hold onto the 'now' as thoughts of home flooded through me again. The unicorn stood in front of me, shaking its head to get the rest of the door off its horn.

Without thinking, I smashed down on the remains of the door. The unicorn squealed, trying to shake me free. Thoughts of hunting down prey and digging my claws through hide and hair raced through my limbs.

But I didn't have claws.

In my brief confusion, the unicorn scrambled out from under me. He shook his head, jumping back. The ruined remains of the closet door flew off his horn, smashing into the wall. The splintered wood broke apart, and I stared at my hands half expecting claws to extend from my fingertips.

The unicorn leveled his horn at me, then charged.

"Allyson!"

Time slowed as the unicorn loped toward me. I heard its heart beat almost in time with its hoof beats. As the tip of the horn came into reach, I pushed it down and away from me. The horn caught in the rug, and the forward momentum of the unicorn in full charge flipped the beast into the air. It somersaulted into the wall before sagging to the ground, limp. The smell of that buttery gold arced over me, and I caught a glimpse of the gold bracelet around its leg.

"Shit, is he dead?" Beth pushed past me.

"I don't–" I clamped my hand over my mouth, but my whole body quivered with the need to spit fire at something. My eyes watered, and my throat burned.

Beth turned back from the unicorn, her eyes wide as she focused her gaze on me. She pointed down the hall. "Bathroom!"

I lurched across the hallway to the bathroom and fell inside as the door swung open, flames erupting from my mouth. I aimed for the bathtub, but missed, sending fire splashing off the side of the tub. The inferno spread across the pink bathroom rug, consuming the fabric quickly. I grabbed a corner and threw it into the tub, fumbling with the faucet. Smoke and steam filled the room as the water sprayed onto the burning rug. The fire alarm blared to life, and putrid water rained down from the fire suppression system.

The cold water sprayed down in a nauseating downpour of filth. My abdomen went into spasms, and I was sick into the bathtub again. I clutched the side of the tub, willing myself to feel better or at least to regain control of my stomach. The heat of my fire burned at my face, baking the nasty water onto my cheeks.

And to think I almost stayed home today.

As the blaze died down, my stomach calmed. With the need to puke fire subsiding, I left the charred bathroom. Beth scrambled around her room, throwing clothes into a bag while foul water sprayed down around her. Blonde hair clung to the sides of her face, and her normally bouncy ponytail clung to her neck, a soggy survivor of our escapades.

The unicorn had turned back into a man wearing a designer suit. Even without the fur and horns, he looked the same.

Beth glared at him. "Grab the stupid unicorn. We can't leave him in here. This water is disgusting."

I shifted an arm under his shoulder and hauled. I expected him to weigh a ton, but he was no harder to lift than a trunk of clothes. Maybe I got superhuman strength with my fire puking. Great, I could probably drive nails through boards with my bare hands, but if I needed to start a campfire, someone would have to attack me. Oh, and I'd need a place to puke afterwards.

On the landing, I laid Dr. Jump-the-Gun down and caught sight of the gold bracelet. It hung loosely from his arm, and a part of me seethed with the need to own that buttery gold. Beth smacked my shoulder.

"Hey, snap out of it; that stupid charm bracelet nearly got you killed."

"What is it?"

"Bait." Without another word, she ducked back into the bog of eternal stench.

I slipped the gold from his wrist and dropped it into my pocket. No need to leave him with something that screwed people up– especially people like me. Diving back into the filthy water, I rescued my makeup kit. I'd be damned if I would lose sixteen bucks of makeup for that twit.

I mean, seriously, whose first response is to gore the person hiding in the closet? With a unicorn horn? What was wrong with these people?

The intensity of the sprinklers seemed to have increased. That, or time sped back up from super human, unicorn slayer to normal person. I found the soggy bag of makeup and checked in on Beth. She leaned into her ruined closet and pulled out a shoebox from the upper shelf. She covered it in a towel and headed toward me.

"Come on," she said. "This stuff is dangerous."

"How dangerous?"

"Like anaerobic bacteria breeding since the building was installed, bad for you," she said. She grabbed a duffel bag of sopping clothes, and we headed out. "Grab those papers." Beth pointed, and I picked up the thickly folded parchment.

Outside, we stepped over Dr. Targyne, and I turned for the stairs.

"I ought to kick you," Beth said to the unconscious unicorn.

I grabbed her arm. "Come on, let's get out of here."

She looked at me, her green eyes welling with tears.

"We'll make this right."

"How?" Her plea cut through the air.

"We need to take showers and get out of these nasty clothes, first of all. Let's go back to my place. You can shower there, and we'll put a load in the wash. Then we'll read these papers." I waved the parchment. "Even unicorns have to have procedures."

"But they want to censure me," she said.

"What, like, pull your school work or something?"

"No, they'll kill me. Censure is a euphemism for execute."

CHAPTER EIGHT

I f there was a god of wind, he lived in Albuquerque in March. Soaked in stinking clothes and swimming through a nearly forty mile per hour wind, we shivered our way across the football fields. The chill cut right through my wet jacket. My legs shook, but I kept putting one foot in front of the other. The adrenaline coursed through me, but it was all uncontrolled power. I could jump ten feet straight up, if I could get my feet to agree on a direction to jump.

We crossed the last street to the apartment complex, cut through the bus station, and climbed the stairs in seconds. When we got inside, Beth leaned back against the door.

She sobbed, sucking in gulps of air in ragged hiccups. "They're gonna kill me."

"You don't know that." A conciliatory lie I would hate to hear if I were in her shoes. "Can we fight them?"

Beth dragged a soggy sleeve across her puffy eyes. "Allyson, you've got the strength and the reflexes, but you're new to this. Those horns they have? They're sharp."

"Big deal; you're, like, super healing girl, and I have acne scales. We can take them."

Beth pursed her lips, then nodded her head. "Right, I can see you don't get it." Beth walked around the little half partition into the kitchen area. She pulled out a giant carving knife. I knew what she was about to do, but I couldn't make myself move. I was paralyzed by horror and curiosity.

Beth plunged the tip of the knife into her forearm. She pushed it through until the knife poked out through her arm on the opposite side. Over the stench of our clothes, the fresh scent of blood and something deep and earthy, like cabbage or copper, drifted through the room. Beth yanked the knife out with a hiss, and blood fell to the linoleum in a stream and pooled at her feet. She held her arm out so I could see. The bleeding stopped, and the holes where a knife had torn through her flesh knitted back together in a matter of seconds.

My hand flew to my mouth. There was no wound. Thin pink lines marked the entrance and exit point of the knife wound, but even that faded before my eyes until only Beth's pale, smooth skin remained

"Holy–"

Beth held up one finger, and I stopped mid word. She pulled up her shirt, and across her stomach, grotesque scars stretched from one side to the other. The wavy lines crisscrossed her midsection, a spider's web, except these were scars. They traced out a history of terrible pain. The ragged edges of tears and rips could have only come from violence. No surgeon's cut would leave marks like that. Not even a regular knife would leave marks like that.

I held my breath.

She met my eyes. "That's what a unicorn horn will do to a troll. I don't think we'd last long."

"They did that on purpose?"

"They don't have many, ah, domesticated trolls. So they use me to train their children. Those who can manifest get to use me as a practice dummy." She put a finger to her forehead and mimed a unicorn horn.

"What's manifest?"

"They can change shape, like Dr. Targyne."

I narrowed my eyes, hunting for the reference. "Crazy monohorn who attacked me?"

Beth nodded.

"But how can they do that? How come that isn't illegal?"

"Before two days ago, you didn't even know, and you're one of us. It's not like we advertise." She chewed on her lips.

My stomach rolled, and it had nothing to do with dragon fire. "Are you telling me there's no police? There's no one you can go to?"

"What would I tell the cops?"

"But what about the others? You said there are other Kin, not just unicorns, right?"

Beth crossed her arms. "I've never talked to anyone but the unicorns. And outside of the conclave, everything is hunted." She slid down the cupboard and sat on the floor. "They make weapons out of special materials–mostly parts of their horns, or stuff wrapped with hair from their tails–and they use it to hunt down the other Kin. All for the protection of mankind, but it's pretty simple. I'm with them, or they'll kill me."

"And your dad lets them do this to you?" I asked.

"My dad was just happy to be rid of me. He set up a trust fund and got Dr. Targyne to take care of any big issues. Hence, the emancipation. I can sign myself out of school, but I can't blow my nose without a note from the good doctor." She pounded her fist on the cupboard door.

I knew Beth had never told anyone about this. It was a gift of trust, but a terrible gift; hideous even. What could I do but nod and try to accept? I had my mother. I even had crazy Aunt Agnes. Beth had a flock of horn happy unicorns and a trust fund. She'd trade me for moving across the country every six months in a heartbeat.

And now the crazy monohorns thought she'd done something to their star pupil.

Beth wiped her face clean of any pain and put that indestructible smile back on. "You stink."

I rolled my eyes. "Fine, I'll shower. Just clean up the blood. I'm supposed to be grounded."

When I got out of the shower, I stuffed my nasty clothes into a garbage bag, and Beth followed suit. "I should wash these." I counted quarters out of the laundry money jar.

"What's the point? They're going to come and pick me up. And you, they might decide you're too dangerous."

"First, the not smelling part–"

"Not everything got covered in stink juice."

"And secondly, you've got to fight this." I grabbed the crumpled parchment from the unicorns and waved it at Beth. "What does it even say?"

Beth pointed at me. "You read." She pointed at her chest. "I shower."

If I was going to help, then I needed to know the rules. It's not like they covered unicorn tribunals in American institutions. Seriously, who put a fifteen year old on trial for the death penalty? Even normal people would need a brutal and heinous crime, not just chatting with some trolls and dragons. And what's so bad about trolls and dragons?

I sat on the couch and read the papers.

The letters were done in gold ink, but it being done in pretty–if almost impossible to read script–didn't change the facts. If Beth did anything that revealed the location of the conclave, she could be censured. If she directly contributed to the abduction of one of the members of the conclave, they would kill her.

Basically, they claimed to have the power to kill her for no good reason, but especially if something went belly up.

Like Steve going missing.

Beth came out of the shower in a cloud of steam. She'd wrapped her hair in a towel like a turban. "Solve it all?"

"They kill you for staying. They kill you for going. Why didn't you tell anyone?"

"They'd kill me for talking."

I dropped the papers on the couch next to me. "Seriously, I could have lived my entire life without the personalized lesson in how the US justice system really is much better than many options."

"You're funny, Drake." Beth, still wrapped in a towel, dropped to the couch. The papers bounced on their cushion. "Any recommendations?"

I had nothing. They were charging her for helping outsiders kidnap someone. Without Steve, there was no way to prove her innocence.

Without Steve.

Steve.

"All we have to do is find Steve!"

Beth blinked at me. "What are you talking about?"

"There's only one way to prove you didn't do it. We find Steve, bring him back and you get off."

"You're nuts. How are we going to find him?"

I hadn't thought of that, but with the question before me, my brain raced through to find answers. "Those trolls from the mall, they said unicorns were common in these parts. Maybe they know what happened to Steve."

"You are crazy; we can't just wander around the mall. As soon as Dr. Targyne comes to, they're going to start looking for me. They'll try everything nearby, including the mall."

"If the trolls are canvassing the area, maybe they're at the other mall, too. We go find the trolls at the Coronado Mall, interrogate them, use the information to find Steve, and you're off scot free." I handed over the bag of clothes with a flourish.

"Just like that?" Beth asked.

I nodded in triumph.

"And how are we going to get to that mall? It's on the other side of town. The monohorns know I take the bus–they'll watch the station."

An image of the faded MGB flashed in my mind. "We'll drive, then."

"Did your mother leave you with her truck?"

"No."

"And where are you planning to get a car?" Beth asked, as if asking a child.

I smiled. "There's a car in the parking lot. It hasn't been moved in a while."

Beth held her hands out. "Oh no, no, no, no. I am not stealing a car."

"Just get dressed, okay?"

Beth gave me a wary eye then retreated to the bathroom with her duffel bag, reemerging a few minutes later in fresh jeans, a t-shirt, and a jacket. "You're absolutely insane, Drake."

I picked up my backpack, just in case I needed the tiny toolkit I kept with my pencils. It could be just the ticket to get into the convertible. It's not like I knew how to hotwire a car or anything, but I was willing to try if we could clear Beth of all charges.

"Look, it's been there for days, and I'm pretty sure it's actually my aunt's car."

"If it's her car, then can't you just call her up and ask to use it?"

"It's easier to beg forgiveness than ask permission. Let's just take a look, okay? Maybe it's dead. Who knows?"

"You know car theft is a felony in pretty much every state?" Beth followed me out of the apartment and down to the parking lot.

"I'm ninety-nine percent certain it's my aunt's. And, as a bonus, if it is Aunt Aggy's, she'll have to talk to me." I raised my eyebrows at Beth.

Beth sighed, but she never got farther than a half step behind me.

The car sat, innocently waiting, top down and tonneau cover snapped into place. It had lines similar to a 60s Porsche with the two headlights perched at the ends of two ridges and the hood in the middle. The steering wheel was on the wrong side. Even if the paint was faded, this was an expensive car, a hobby project. As we got closer, I knew beyond a shadow of doubt it was my aunt's. I'd sat in those seats.

I snapped back the tonneau cover and the scent of Aunt Aggy radiated out of the leather seats. Like the unicorn's bracelet, it wasn't just the smell of leather, it was the smell of family–no, home–but I'd never had a home. How could I know what one smelled like? But the gold, *that* was real. So was the smell of Armor All and piñon, the scent of my aunt.

With the cover removed, sunlight winked off the keys on the floor. No need to hotwire. The keys might as well have been an invitation, really. I mean, car, keys, and unsupervised time… my aunt even showed me how to drive it. Yeah, it was a few years ago, but driving was like riding a bike, right? How much could I have forgotten? I'd even taken driver's ed–well, three quarters of driver's ed. In another state. Of course, the laws were similar. I bet I would have passed that final if my mom had just stayed around for another month.

"This is the car you want to steal?" Beth asked.

"Borrow. It's my aunt's car."

Beth looked the car over and twisted her lips to one side of her mouth. "Are you sure it can make it to the mall?"

Running my hand along the dash, I scowled at Beth. "I'm certain it's in great condition."

"Right, great condition for a dinosaur."

"Hey," I said, feigning pain, "it's a classic."

"Especially if you take the standard definition of classic being anything older than fifty years, I'm sure it qualifies." Despite her ribbing, Beth unsnapped the rest of the fasteners and helped me fold the cover. We stuffed it behind the seats, and I dumped my backpack on top of it to keep the cover from flying away. I sank into the seat and breathed in the smell of refined automobile.

The second my butt hit the bottom of the seat, I broke out in a sweat. *Dear patron saint of stupid people, don't let my aunt find out and, if you're listening, don't let me bunny hop the classic car. Please, please, please.*

I turned the key, eased off the clutch, and the car slid out of the parking spot. Beth flashed a rare smile of pure joy. If you're going to be an idiot, do it in a convertible. It feels better.

As we made it to the road, students funneled off campus for lunch. We got caught by the red light and a couple students I didn't know whistled. Beth blushed. I tried to stay focused, but I felt the power of looking hot in an awesome car.

"Hey, Takata, nice car." Jed's unmistakable nasal voice pitched over the idle of the MGB.

Ha! That jerk gets to see me drive this *car.* Today was finally taking a turn for the better.

The light changed, and I threw the clutch too fast. The car lurched forward, throwing Beth and me into our seatbelts. Then, much to my horror, it leapt again, and again. My cheeks burned, and the MGB bunny hopped for a solid twenty yards.

The car made so much noise, I couldn't hear if Jed was laughing or not.

Either way, I'd have to kill him later.

CHAPTER NINE

I didn't know how much hairspray they used in car commercials where there's a woman with long hair riding in a convertible, but my guess was somewhere between two and three bottles, because the second the car got up to thirty-five, a wicked back draft blasted our hair forward. I chewed on strands of jet-black hair all the way to the mall. I'd have to arrange my locks with something more than a prayer next time.

The other great myth concerning convertibles was comfort. No sweet, skin-caressing breeze. By the time we arrived at our destination, the cold air had blasted my skin into chapped hide. Decidedly unpleasant.

And yet, despite having my own hair in my face, freezing ears–I reached up to make sure they were still attached–and skin sandblasted clean, I loved it. This wasn't driving, it was flying. But I wanted earmuffs and hair ties before I tried this again.

We pulled into the Coronado mall parking lot windswept, but otherwise unharmed. I dumped my backpack into the foot well and snapped the tonneau cover over the passenger compartment. Hopefully, no one wanted to steal the car, but I took the keys just in case.

Beth wasn't taking any chances. She kept her duffel slung over her shoulder.

I raised one eyebrow.

"I have cash in the bag."

"What, like, your life savings?" I asked, half joking.

"Something like that."

I gave her a sidelong glance as we walked up the concrete

sidewalk. Above the mall doors, a sign spelled Coronado in jaunty, offset letters and symbols similar to the petroglyphs. Just like a major consumer to cash in on the only perceived natural resource: Native Americans. Even the mall here was a tourist trap. Inside, the first shop to the left was a Native American Emporium, where they sold crap made in China and advertised as authentic Native American.

Past the cheesy shop, the rest of the mall was exactly like every other mall in the US, complete with a food court, a Macy's on one end and a Sears at the other. We walked the length of the mall, scanning the crowd, but no trolls.

"No esta aqui," I said.

Beth wagged her eyebrows. "They mostly come out at night."

"Mostly," I said, quoting another ancient movie.

She sighed, leaning against a wall. "Well, any other great plans?"

"I saw that jacket from the other mall in a store we passed."

Beth turned on her heel and started back. "Yes, I like this plan. Your aunt's car is freaking cold. Did you see any place with some earmuffs and scarves?"

"We could check Sears, I'm sure they'll be on clearance. I hope you like orange plaid." I jogged to catch up and, in no time, Beth bought the thick blue jacket, despite the roominess in the chest, and the shortness in the sleeves. She took a wad of cash from the duffel bag to pay, and when she was done, the roll of twenties still rivaled her fist in size.

I guess Beth didn't spend all of her allowance on clothes.

She caught me watching her and handed me a wad of money. "You should buy something, too."

"I can't take your money." I said it automatically, but deep down, I knew exactly what I wanted.

"Bull pucky. Take the money. It's nothing but paper to me anyway." She extended her hand, fingers wrapped loosely around a roll of cash. "My father gave it to me," she added.

That clinched it. She probably hated the money just because it came from her father. Well, I wouldn't want to distress her with unnecessary exposure to unwanted money.

I took the wad and unraveled it, discovering a hundred dollar bill wrapped in three twenties. More than my mother gave me for my birthday. I ducked into a store selling bomber jackets. I'd always wanted one, and I finally needed one. I also grabbed some gloves.

Even if we hadn't found any trolls to interrogate, at least we had some awesome clothes to go with the awesome–cold–car.

"Now what?" Beth shrugged into her new jacket and tossed the bag into the trunk. The blue fabric set off her green eyes. She twisted her hair into a bun and slapped on a new hair tie, courtesy of The Accessories Store. Three inches of bright blonde hair stuck out at wild angles, but the wind-blasted car look would probably go well with the poky end-of-the-ponytail look.

"Honestly, I have no idea. We need to find Steve. Either that, or we find his body. Do you think we could risk the other mall?"

"No, the unicorns will have dropped any hope for a tribunal. They'll be out for blood after what happened to Dr. Targyne."

I shivered, and it had nothing to do with the cold. Pulling my hair into a ponytail at the nape of my neck, I divided the thick coils into three parts and braided. My hair draped down to my butt, so braiding took a while; a long while. When I'd finished, I opened the driver's door and slid into the seat.

"Where to, boss?" Beth asked, folding the cover and stuffing it behind the seats.

"I–"

The dashboard buzzed, then stopped. I raised an eyebrow at Beth before watching the dashboard again. It buzzed, rattling the hinges of the glove box.

Beth grabbed the knob, and the compartment fell open. Inside, a cell phone lay next to a lug nut wrench. Beth handed me the phone.

The screen said 'Dave.'

My heart jumped in my chest. My father's name was David. David

Takata. The shock of the idea shot through my chest. My heart beat too hard for my lungs to work, hammering against my chest. This could be–

No, there were millions of Daves in the world. How could this one be him?

The phone buzzed in my hand again.

This was my father. It had to be.

My whole body went numb as I tried to hit the talk button. I got it on the third try, but my mouth turned to cotton. My arm was stiff, moving like a slab of wood instead of my own body, as I moved the phone to my ear.

What would I say? What could I say?

My father was on the other end of the line. I opened my mouth, but all my questions crammed into my mind at the same time. *Why did you leave? How come you never talked to us? Was there something wrong with me? Why?*

I cleared my throat to speak.

"Agnes! Thank god!" His voice rang through the phone in a deep bass and a thick English accent, relief lifting his tone. "Don't talk, I don't have much time. I need you to destroy the key. They're looking for you. I think they know what we've been doing. Get Cathy and Allyson out of the US. Tell her it's an emergency. Tell her it's time to go to Ireland. They're coming."

He paused as a door on his end opened with an ominous creak.

"Ah, Mr. Takata, there you are," another voice said. The new voice was higher in pitch, younger sounding. "How is the new market?"

Something moved over the phone, like someone had covered the voice pick up, but I could still hear the muffled conversation. "The new Kirin supply is coming along, Mr. Stein. I believe they'll have a full shipment, sooner than I thought. I'm arranging it now." Then, as if he'd been interrupted, he spoke back into the phone. "And don't forget to have the shipment by the twenty-sixth. Pier 22 1/2, at a quarter to midnight. Do you understand?"

"Dad?" The word escaped my mouth as if pulled by some magnetic force.

He gasped. "What?" The stunned response pretty much summed up our whole conversation.

"Mr. Takata, if you are done, I believe we have something to talk about," the other man said.

"Takata out," my father said

The line went dead.

"Wait! Dad? Dad? Are you there, Dad? What's going on?" I fumbled with the phone, and hit the call back button. It went straight to voicemail. "Shit." I pounded the steering wheel, and my hands shook.

"Talk to me," Beth said.

"It was my dad. He thought he was talking to my aunt."

Beth grabbed the official Tribunal Notification and handed it to me. "Write everything down, before you forget."

I flipped over the heavy paper and wrote everything I remembered, but I finished writing all too soon. It seemed like the first conversation I ever had with my dad should last longer than a few seconds. And he hadn't even known it was me. What would he have said differently?

I should have let him know sooner. I had my father on the phone, and I didn't say anything.

My entire life, I'd dreamed of the day I would meet him and what we would talk about if he ever called, and our first conversation was meant for my aunt?

Why did he want Mom and me to leave? What was so important about not being in the US? Kidnappers? If those were the kidnappers who took Steve, then we needed to find them.

Beth took the paper from me. "Not good," she said when she finished reading.

Beth had a way with understatements.

"And?" I was only half paying attention.

"Kirin, it's an Asian unicorn."

I shook my head to clear my disappointment. "Unicorns? How do you know this stuff?"

"I was pretty much raised by monohorns, and they really wanted to impress upon me the awesomeness of their history and diversity." Beth spit over the side of the car. "In short, something's going on with your dad and some unicorns. And if I don't miss my guess, your dad is a dragon."

"That would explain the scales and the fire breathing."

Beth rolled her eyes. "You don't have to be half to manifest the gifts. Quarter, eighth–they had someone who was a thirty second manifest–but the stronger the gifts, the closer the tie."

The image of purebred dogs flashed into my mind. "Do they try to breed for it, like with sheep? Arranged marriages, that sort of thing?"

"The unicorns are as inbred as a pack of poodles." Beth fiddled with the official papers. "So, I guess we try the other mall?" She folded the papers and held them up. "According to the decree, I only have two weeks to prove I didn't kidnap Steve and feed him to a dragon."

"No," I said. "No matter what else happens, we need to actually find Steve. If my father knows about who is 'supplying unicorns,' we need to talk to him."

"You are insane." She narrowed her eyes at me. "How are we going to do that?"

"We'll meet him at Pier 22 1/2 at midnight." The wind blew again, pulling strands of my hair into my face.

"Running won't help my case any." Beth picked at the trim around the window as her jaw muscles clenched and released. "And how do you know that last part was the truth? Is he really meeting people at that pier?"

"His boss was there; would he have lied with his boss in the room? That would be awkward, right?"

"That's pretty flimsy." Beth finished plucking at the trim and looked at me.

Tapping the steering wheel, I shook my head. "Do you have *any* material evidence to indicate you don't associate with dragons or trolls?"

"Well, no, but–"

I held up my hand to cut her off. "What will they do if they find you guilty at this tribunal?"

She wilted. "Kill me."

"Right, so we're going to the source. We'll find my father and get some answers out of him. Besides, you said unicorns hate dragons. Maybe my dad can help you." It sounded so simple like that. Just walk over, and say, "Hey, could I have a word with you?"

"I think this is a really bad idea. You don't even know where Pier 22 is. What if–?"

"San Francisco," I said.

"San Francisco is not the only port city with pier numbers."

A tumbleweed rolled by and popped up over the decorative fence around the parking lot. The aloe plants swayed in the wind, and leaves swarmed in the breeze like it was fall, not late March.

"Look, there's somewhere else I need to go, in Nevada," I added.

"Where? What's there?"

"I don't really know, but it could be important." Yeah, like my inheritance, or a secret decoder ring or something. Unlocked by a key my father wanted my aunt to destroy.

"I'm supposed to follow you on a gut feeling?"

I pursed my lips. "No, but here are the facts: my father was talking about a new supply of unicorns; the trolls we met asked if you were bringing me in, and they asked if I was unicorn because 'they're common round these parts.'" I paused to sum up my thoughts. "What if those trolls are working for the guy my dad was talking to, and they stole Steve? If that's the case, then we can ask my dad about it."

"That's really far-fetched." Beth fussed with her hair.

"Aren't dragons supposed to be really smart?" I asked.

"Wise. You're supposed to inherit wisdom. Smarts are earned." She looked around at the corporate buildings across the street, as if she could see the future in the gleaming glass. "This is the wrong choice; you know that."

"Is a wrong choice worse than no choice?"

CHAPTER TEN

Beth gave a long-suffering sigh. **"Fine, let's go with your plan."**

"Yes." I pumped my arm in the air. "So, where do we start?"

Beth snorted. "A map."

"We could just use Google or something," I said.

Beth shook her head. "Nah, do you really want to be driving through the desert in the middle of the night and find out there's no reception? And, should we take 40 or go up to Shiprock? We need a map. And some gear for camping."

"Camping? This isn't a field trip."

Beth blinked as she rolled her eyes. "And who do you think will rent a hotel room to a couple of teenagers without a credit card? Besides, it's still five days until the twenty-sixth. How long does it take to drive that far?"

I'd driven that far a number of times, but never in a straight shot. Whenever we took off from a place, my mom and I only drove a few hundred miles a day. Then, one day, she'd make up her mind, and we'd be off to some specific city in no time. "A day or two. Three, tops. So that would be four days. We could sleep in the car for four days."

"Do you know how to put the top up? I haven't even seen a top, and it's still snowing in Taos. Do you want to sleep in that?"

"Point. We have some gear at the apartment," I said.

"No, by now, the monohorns will be swarming everywhere. They have rules. They delivered something saying I have to show my face at the tribunal in two weeks, and unless they can officially put another piece of paper into my hands, they'll stick to it. So, lynched now, or lynched later: I pick later."

I turned the key and revved the engine. We made it back to the freeway–*sans* bunny hop–and I drove to the one store I knew would be fully stocked with camping gear in March: REI. I eased into a parking lot crowded with people, tables, and harried staff. It was a scratch and dent sale. In less than thirty minutes, we had sleeping bags, a tent, and some funny-looking hats with earflaps. Before I got into the car, I put on my *ushanka*–the hat with the earflaps–and felt the blessed warmth return to my poor ears. Bomber jacket and Russian hat; I was really going to tear up the fashion scene if we stopped anywhere longer than ten seconds.

A short stop for gas, and we were on the road. Sitting in what would normally be the driver's seat, Beth unfolded the map while I tried to navigate yet another intersection without sending the car into convulsions.

"North, to Farmington. We'll get there by late afternoon, early evening."

I'd already looked at the map; I knew the way by heart. Farmington to Moab, to 70, to 80, then Reno, Sacramento, and San Francisco. I'd need to take a detour to get to Ely. It was just a speck on the map, but the key burned in my mind. Was it the same key my father was talking about? As I turned onto the highway, my heart suddenly began to beat faster. This was it. I had two exits to turn back, take the car to my apartment next to the school I hated, and erase the whole afternoon.

And never know my father.

I floored it.

Beth almost lost the map in the wind and quickly folded it up, stuffing it into the glove box. "You crazy?" she yelled. "Do you want a speeding ticket?"

I pushed down on the gas, accelerating the car, and we bumped over the pavement, signs rushing past. I let go of my irrational need to outrace reason, and let the car coast into traffic, a fox hiding among hounds. Just north of Albuquerque, we turned onto a smaller road and drove northwest.

Wind battered the car, and the road rarely curved. Red, sandstone bluffs rose up out of the desert. The land stretched on forever, but the MGB ate the distance in a ground-turning pull for the horizon. We stopped twice along the lonely road: once to put up the rag top—we admitted further defeat since we couldn't even find the top–and once to give the car more gas.

The signs along the road warned that we were approaching Farmington, which was great. My hands were frozen to the steering wheel, and I no longer cared how dorky my bomber jacket and *ushanka* looked. Tomorrow, I'd drive with a blanket in my lap.

The sun sank behind the rocks to the west of us, and the glare on the road made me wish for some sunglasses. I might need them just for the wind. My eyes were dry enough to towel off a whole swim team. And we still had to set up camp. I scanned the road, looking for likely places to camp as we came up on a delivery truck riding in the left lane. Bright yellow letters proclaimed the truck to be Martin's Movers. Wind caught the van and it swerved into the right lane before settling back down in the left.

I pulled into the opposite lane and stomped on the gas. I didn't want to be behind this whale of a truck if it was going to wobble all over the road. Better for the thing to fall into someone else's way.

As we reached the passenger cabin of the van, Beth threw herself sideways in the seat, covering her head with her arms. "Crap!"

"What?" I asked. "What is it?" Some instinct drew my foot off the accelerator, and the MGB drifted back into the backwash of the giant truck.

"That was them," Beth said, still trying to hide under the dashboard.

"Them who?"

"The kidnappers. The trolls from the mall."

An icy chill spread through me, and I whipped the car into a tight tailgate position, out of view of the side view mirrors. In the backdraft of the huge truck, the wind finally relented: it blasted us equally from all sides, seeming to slacken its forward drive.

"Now what?" Beth yelled over the lashing wind.

"We can't follow them forever!"

"They have to stop sometime!" Beth pointed at the truck. "They might have Steve! We get him and head back to the monohorns. We could be done by midnight."

I still wouldn't know any more about my father, but I nodded agreement. It's not like the two of us could take out three trolls. We were outnumbered, and Beth couldn't even manage to fight Mr. June in the parking lot. How could she manage trolls?

As far as plans went, I had nothing better.

"Okay." I nodded. "We can follow them until they stop. Then we sneak into the back of the truck and take it from there."

Beth narrowed her eyes. "And what do we do if there's more than one person in the back of the truck?"

Yeah, and where would Steve sit in this car? It only had two seats, and there was barely enough room for the tonneau cover behind the seats, let alone a kidnapped unicorn. "Let's take this one step at a time. Maybe we can get the cops involved if it's like a big operation or something."

She nodded like a bobble head doll. "Yeah, okay, that sounds good."

"Besides, we might not be able to get in."

"We're getting in."

I stole a look at her.

Jaw set, eyes ahead, the half troll had moved into business mode.

Great. If we did manage to pop open the truck, we'd only be legally stealing, and likely to piss off three giant dudes who healed quickly and didn't mind a face full of fire. The plan was Grade A crazy. USDA certified.

The trolls drove most of the way through Farmington, following the way we were planning to go as well. Just at the north end of town, they pulled the van into a grease-covered gas station. Tumbleweeds rolled by, and I had to bite back the urge to whistle the theme from *The Good, the Bad, and the Ugly*.

Well, they had ugly covered; the only thing left to determine was whether Beth and I were the good or the bad.

I pulled away from the truck, and parked the car on the far side of the service station. The last rays of sunlight squinted out, and the temperature dropped. My skin tingled from the sudden lack of wind on my face. Even the area covered by the giant bandage felt like the hairs had taken on a life of their own.

We slunk around the corner of the service station, and I tried not to think the guilty thoughts of a criminal. After all, I'd already stolen a car today. What would be the big deal if we managed to steal back some kidnapped people?

The fluorescent lights over the gas pumps flickered, and two trolls walked into the convenience store. That left one at the truck. I scanned the area. A troll stood with his back to us, holding the pump nozzle. We darted out from behind a pump and got to the back of the truck.

A padlock held the rolling door closed.

"Fan-*freakin*-tastic," Beth whispered.

"What, can't you just snap it off?"

Beth rolled her eyes at me. "Can't you use your super dragon hearing and listen for the tumblers to click or something?"

I rubbed my finger along the rolling combinations. I could hear them click, even over the wind, but the clicks sounded exactly the same. "Not over the wind." I put my ear to the rolling door and listened for anything. The faint rhythmic sound of breathing drifted to me. "There's someone inside."

"Fine, move over." Beth stepped up and grabbed the lock. She twisted it savagely, and the metal gave way with a *pop*. The sound echoed through the gas station, and the scent of metal rose up, sharp and fresh, like mown grass. Mown metal?

"Hurry up," I hissed.

Beth pulled away the broken lock, but the door latch was bent. "Damn it. Could today get any worse?" She pounded on the door latch, and the handle broke off and clattered to the ground.

"That did not improve things."

"You think I don't know that? I'm going to break open the door."

The troll pumping gas walked around the corner of the van, then stood behind Beth.

I froze, eyes wide. My chest itched with that now familiar burn.

Beth rolled her eyes at me. "What, it's not like I haven't ripped doors off their hinges before."

I pointed behind her, unable to speak past the burning sensation in my lungs.

She swallowed, blinking a few times, then turned around slowly, coming face to face with the troll.

He just watched her, not moving a muscle, which was exactly what he did the last time we ran into this particular individual. I think his name was John. I checked around the side of the van for Baldy and Flame Eater, but they were still inside.

"What are you doing here?" John asked Beth.

"We were just, ah, admiring your truck," I answered.

The troll looked from Beth to me. "Could I have a word with her, alone?"

I met Beth's gaze, but she shook her head and shrugged. I widened my eyes and looked at John then back to her. She nodded, but I hesitated. These guys tried to grab us at the mall, what would he do now? I'd be crazy to leave Beth alone with him. Still, he seemed different from the other two trolls. Beth gave me another curt nod, and I stepped away from the truck. Moving slowly, I sank into the shadows of the self-service propane tank and kept an eye on Beth. I picked up a rock in case I needed to draw some attention to us.

The troll took Beth around to the side of the van farthest from the convenience store, and I watched carefully, trying to focus on the movement of their lips, to no avail. I tried to eavesdrop, but the wind renewed its howling. I caught maybe one word in five, and those words made no sense at all. Something about windswept fires, and blossoming irises. Whatever they were discussing, it didn't sound much like Beth was trying to talk him out of his victim.

The other trolls left the convenience store, and I threw a rock at the van. It pegged off the side of the truck, but they didn't notice. I picked up a second rock and got closer, keeping a car between myself and the other trolls. The second rock hit Beth. She jumped, rubbing her shoulder where the rock hit. Beth searched me out in the darkness, and I pointed frantically at the convenience store. She nodded and said something to John, who then walked around the front and called to his companions. While they were distracted, Beth flew across the pavement to my hiding place.

She slid into the shadows like a baseball player sliding into home, her cheeks flushed pink.

"Sorry, Bob, I forgot the combination again," John said to the bald troll, pitching his voice much louder than when he was talking to Beth. Baldy rolled his eyes in exasperation.

"We aren't going to check on them in public places, John. How many times do I have to tell you that?"

"Oh, yeah. Sorry, Bob. I'll try not to think so much." John did a great impersonation of supremely dumb troll.

The third troll slapped John with a folded up map. "That's right. No one pays you to think. And you're supposed to be the smart one."

John made a show of struggling with the door handle, and if I could see through it, I couldn't imagine how the others couldn't. But then again, there aren't many stories about cunning trolls.

The abusive troll looked at Bob and shook his head. "Why did we bring this moron with us?"

"Button it up, Gary. He's just young, now let's get moving. I want to make the valley by tomorrow night."

They piled into the van, then drove away, spinning the tires in the gravel. We watched them leave, frozen in place. Even after they were gone, we stayed crouched like statues until Beth sighed.

"Do they have Steve?"

"He didn't know any names, but he described someone about right for Steve."

Irises and windswept fires didn't seem like the kinds of things used to describe Steve. "What else did he say?"

She smiled–not the indestructible grin she'd rehearsed for so long. No, this was a real smile. "He said I'm cute."

CHAPTER ELEVEN

Beth craned her neck to follow the van as it drove off. A dreamy smile pulled her lips into a lopsided expression to match John's features.

"Uh, Earth to Beth: he's a kidnapping troll," I said.

"Only to pay the bills."

I raised my eyebrows. "And you know this how?"

"He told me." She met my gaze. "Anyhow, he gave me a map. Apparently, their boss doesn't expect them to make it from point A to point B without losing a few, so they each get their own map." She produced a crumpled bit of paper.

"Should we follow them?"

"Nah, he said they're going to camp at Goblin Valley tomorrow night, so we just have to beat them there." She blinked then focused on me. "Besides, there'll be fewer people at a campground, and maybe more cover." She waved the map.

"Let's take a look at that inside." I pointed to the convenience store; my stomach growled, and Beth's answered. "We need some real food."

Beth gave the convenience store a skeptical glare. "You think they'll have real food in there?"

"You know what I mean."

It was a convenience store with a burger joint from the seventies, complete with checkered flooring and covered in thirty years of insufficient cleaning. The food was dubious, but my stomach wasn't picky. We ordered hot dogs and fries and pretended everything was normal.

"What now?" Beth asked.

I unfolded the map, exposing the destinations circled with dates next to them. Today's destination was Farmington. Tomorrow's was indeed labeled Goblin Valley. "We camp, and get a nice early start in the morning. We beat them here," I said, pointing to the map. "Then we'll have the lay of the land. That should give us an advantage."

It sounded nice when I said it, but I was faking. I didn't know how we were going to steal back the kidnap victim. And really, I wanted to get to Ely, Nevada. Maybe it was a key to some safety deposit box full of jewels. If I were rich enough, I could protect Beth from that crazy pack of monohorns.

We got directions to a KOA campground, and set up camp as the temperature dropped.

The phone in the glove box rang, and I jumped to answer it. I hit the talk button without checking the caller ID.

"Hello?"

"Oh, thank god. Agnes! They have her," my mother said.

"Mom?"

"Allyson? Where are you? Where's your aunt?"

My stomach sank into oblivion. I left home, and I hadn't written her a note. I was dead meat. She was going to reach through the phone and strangle me where I sat.

"No, I'm–"

"What are you doing? Where are you? Is your aunt there?"

"Mom, I'm just–"

"You tell me this instant. What's going on, young lady?"

"Mom, I'm helping Beth," I said, finally getting a full sentence through the maternal freak out.

"Beth? Honey, she's being charged with kidnapping. I want you to come home right now. You shouldn't even be with someone like that."

I scoffed. "Who have you been talking to?" The police didn't charge people without cause. Even I knew that. I'd seen Law and

Order for crying out loud.

"Beth's doctor. He says she has *special* needs. Beth is unstable. Do you need to hear it from him? Dr. Targyne is right here, I can put him on the phone."

"Ah, no thanks, Mom. We don't exactly get along." The image of the unicorn horn crashing through a closet door flooded my mind, except, in my imagination, the horn gored my mother. I swallowed a giant lump in my throat.

"Where are you?" she asked.

"I'm helping Beth prove she's innocent."

She took a breath and covered the receiver on her end. A man's muffled voice came through. I clenched my fist. They were plotting, and they didn't think I was smart enough to figure out what they were up to. My mom had to know I wasn't that dumb, right?

"Just tell me where you are, and I'll come get you." The sugar in my mother's voice was sweeter than a lollipop.

"Is that what Dr. Murdering Bastard asked you to say?"

So much for the adult approach, and right into name-calling. Way to prove you're taking the moral high ground, Allyson.

"Allyson! What is the matter with you?"

"You really want to know what's the matter with me?"

She *tsked.* "Yes. I do."

"You! You're trying to run away from the only place I've ever had a friend. So I'm helping the one person who's ever been nice to me, Mom. I'm helping my friend. And if you can't understand how important that is, then maybe you aren't a very good mother."

Silence.

"And another thing, Mom? Tell Dr. Targyne I'm not that stupid. I'm not telling you where we are, but we are going to rescue Steve. You can count on it." I flipped the phone shut and resisted the urge to throw it across the campground into the desert.

Beth's bright eyes stood out among the murky shadows of the tent. "Um, that sounded bad."

"Yup." I put the phone in my pocket. It buzzed again, but I ignored it.

"You, uh, wanna talk about it?" She didn't know what to say, but I appreciated the attempt.

"The unicorns are trying to use my mother to figure out where you are."

"Crap, I hadn't thought about that."

I nodded. The phone stopped buzzing. And where was my aunt in all of this?

Beth scanned the campground. We weren't the only crazy people in the freezing cold wilderness; an RV parked on the far side had grease smears down the sides, like someone had driven it through a grease storm before it stopped for the night.

I pulled on my dorky hat and wrapped the bomber jacket tight around me.

I had no change of clothes. Beth, on the other hand, had brought her freshly laundered clothes. I had my American Institutions book in my backpack, and that key. I rubbed my fingers across metal in my pocket.

"Come inside," Beth said. "It's warmer in here."

The wind caught the tent, rattling the zippers as I stepped through the door. We didn't talk as we got ready for bed, which, for me, meant I climbed into my sleeping bag. Beth got into some pajamas and slipped inside her sleeping bag, then zipped it up.

"We'll need to get you some clothes or something soon," she said.

"I guess."

"You guess? I'm not sitting in the same car as you after three days without fresh clothes and a shower."

I smiled. "But it's a convertible."

Beth threw her pillow–a wadded up t-shirt–at me. "You're funny, Drake."

"Tell me about being half," I said, quietly.

"What's to know?"

94

The tent lurched in the wind. "I just want to know more so I can plan. Like what can those trolls do? And are they full blooded or halves?"

Beth pushed up to her elbow. "Well, John is at least three quarters."

I smiled. "You like him."

She blushed. "He did say I was cute. It's not like I have to beat them off with a stick, you know? Too many guys at our school are part of the monohorn commune. They wouldn't touch me with a ten-foot pole. They tell their friends, their friends tell their friends. It's a vicious circle."

"I'm familiar with having a reputation," I said.

"Well, you've never had to live with one for more than a few months. I've been the pariah for as long as I can remember. Kindergarten, even. It'd be nice not to be judged is all."

"Yeah, too bad he works for the bad guys."

"Yeah."

The tent shook in the wind.

"I'm sorry. I don't know what it's like to be constantly hated by the same group of people. It's never been that way for me." I waited for my apology to sink in before asking, "So, what do you know about manifesting, and all of that?"

Air whistled between her teeth. "Some of the monohorns don't manifest. The ones who do are considered more important. They have arranged marriages just to increase the likelihood of manifesting."

"And what does manifesting mean exactly?"

"It means that they can actually turn into unicorns. They shapeshift. They can use their horns to do things like heal and clean poison from water, that sort of thing."

"Really?"

"Yeah, why do you think there are so many in Albuquerque? The water from the aquifer is completely tainted. I suspect the old Manhattan project, but they won't talk about it. The only reason half a million people have drinking water is because the monohorns clean it."

"How humanitarian of them. That's not what I would have expected from the same people who routinely attempt to disembowel you."

Beth snorted. She snorted a lot when talking about the unicorns. "Yeah, well, they are constantly under threat of attack. I watched them take out a whole herd of manticores who were getting too close to their territory. They brought out the whole clan. It was a blood bath."

"What's a manticore?"

"According to the monohorns–and I can't confirm or deny this–they are man-sized cats with tails of a scorpion. They can go crazy and kill people. Well, eat them, actually, but you get the picture. There are things worse than unicorns."

"And trolls?" I asked. "They don't really eat goats who try to cross bridges, do they?"

A laugh puffed through her lips. "No, trolls will find somewhere comfortable and stay put. Interrupt their food supply and they can get cranky, but other than that, mostly harmless."

It was my turn to laugh. "And by *mostly harmless*, you mean strong enough to rip apart metal with their bare hands?"

"Don't forget the diminished IQ." Beth fussed with the zipper of her sleeping bag. "Trolls actually make really good soldiers, because of the healing thing. You won't find too many in the actual army though. Too big. They'll only take people up to six foot six or so."

I chewed that thought over. "So, how many trolls does John work with?"

"He said there were about a hundred others."

An army. Great. Whoever was stealing unicorns had an army of trolls. "Hey, Beth?"

"Yeah?"

"I've got a plan. Let's make sure to steal Steve back before we have to face down all one hundred trolls, hmm?"

"Sounds like a solid plan, Drake."

CHAPTER TWELVE

Four Days Before

I woke long before the sun rose, stiff, cranky, and tired. Truth be told, Beth snored. Who'da thunk? A troll snored. I'd have to put out a bulletin.

I popped the top off the driver's side of the MGB and pulled out my backpack. No one was moving about in the campground, so I fished out the Hollywood horror makeup and peeled off the bandage. Shiny scales winked back. I painted the liquid latex on, layer by layer. It gave me plenty of time to really feel guilty about hanging up on my mom. After the third layer, I fished around in my backpack for some notebook paper. I never imagined I'd write a letter– possibly the last letter I ever wrote, if things went badly–on homework paper. Before I found the notebook paper, the knick-knack my aunt gave me poked my hand. I pulled it out of my bag and set it down next to me before finding the paper I wanted to use.

I tried to write, but my words came out angry. If things didn't go well, I might be dead from tangling with trolls. I didn't want my last words to my mother to be angry, so I threw out that page and started fresh. I made peace. I used 'I' statements. I wanted to point fingers, but the image of her reading my letter in about a week, with a coroner arranging to have my body released kept bumping into my head. And even if I didn't die, I wasn't completely sure I was going back. After all, what if there was something too good to leave in Ely?

All my life had been dictated, and for once, I just wanted to do something I chose. I'd never been a cheerleader; I'd never been in the chess club; I played guitar, but I couldn't take music classes at school because I never started at the beginning of a semester. I needed to do something just for me. More than that, though, I wanted to find out what was at that address in Ely. Was it a house, or maybe a deposit box? A mailbox? I turned the little key around in my pocket and imagined the lock that might go with it.

What I wanted was a home, and I wanted more than anything for that home to be waiting for me in Ely, Nevada. I just had to get there.

After the last layer of latex, I dumped some emergency pancake from my school kit over the wound, and critiqued my face. It looked like I was covering zits. Scales disguised as zits masquerading as healthy skin was way better than the alternative.

I folded up the letter and went to the building at the front of the KOA. A nice old man sold me a box of envelopes and stamps, and I tossed the letter in the mail. If things went well, I might actually get home before it got to her, and I could shred it then. And if things didn't go well, she'd have something.

Bright pinks and oranges streaked across the sky as the sun crept over the mountains in the east. The wind had died down over night, and I waited for it to pick up again. Dawn brought wind in the desert.

Back at the campsite, Beth sat at the picnic table, map spread out in front of her. "Bob said they wanted to make the valley before sundown. Goblin Valley."

"Are goblins real too?" I asked.

"How the hell should I know? I've been living with goody-goody two shoes and the narwhal band. I didn't exactly get to go socializing. The monohorns have so many stories about hunting some of the other races into extinction–dragons included–that it's hard to know if they got anything right."

I nodded. "Awesome. So, now we're going to drive out into the middle of the desert and hope the goblin stories are either not true or just exaggerated. So, what do you want for breakfast?"

"Goat entrails." Beth delivered the line straight and waited for me to blink.

"Over easy, or with a side of bacon?"

"Hmmm, bacon sounds good."

"How long are we driving today?" I asked.

"From here to Goblin Valley is, like, three hundred miles. So, five, six hours, depending."

"Depending on what?"

"On how long it takes you to buy some clothes that don't smell like you've been wearing them all day." Beth poked me.

"I smell fine."

"For now."

"All right, I'll buy some clothes. I'm sure they have a Wally World or whatever here."

We broke camp and got directions to the super retailer. I bought a change of clothes, blowing fifty birthday bucks, but I didn't care. Everything would be better in Ely. The more I thought about it, the more I just knew that whatever it was, it would change everything and in a big way. I expected to find a great treasure trove, something Aunt Aggy didn't want Mom to know about. Probably money, then. If I had enough money, I wouldn't have to roam around the country with my mom. I wouldn't think twice about fifty bucks for a pair of jeans, some t-shirts and a sweater. And my jeans at home were too short anyway. Now, at least they fit. I just wish we could have stopped at a Laundromat to wash them. Who knows how many other people tried them on before I got to them?

Clad in my fresh jeans, t-shirt, and my bomber jacket, we got back in the car, hunted down breakfast, and followed a troll's map into the high desert of Utah. Towering sandstone monoliths rose out of the desert, only to shrink into the distance again behind us. The sky was a shade of blue I'd never seen before, more saturated, but also darker. As the elevation climbed, the blue went from pale water to shades of cornflower, almost more than blue.

We stopped for gas in a town with three gas stations, two of which were closed for the season. In that tiny town, we ate tamales and burritos and pretended we liked them as the owner of the gas station leaned over us, explaining that the tamales were real, traditional, and made by his very own grandmother.

I left him a tip for trying so hard. It was the least I could do. I was on my way to fulfill my destiny. How could I not spare a couple bucks for some poor sod waiting out the rest of his life in Podunkville, population two closed gas stations?

The road twisted into the mountains, and the temperature dropped accordingly. Snow dotted the shadows nearby, and rust red cinders coated the roadside. The road wound down again, and all hints of moisture–snow and rain–vanished. Pines were replaced with rock formations, and we drove on.

Following the signs to Goblin Valley State Park, we drove on until we reached the little hut where a woman in a uniform asked if we wanted to camp. Beth handed over seven dollars–way cheaper than the KOA–and we drove to Spot 13. Not the auspicious omen I was hoping for, but there were several large vans and camping trailers in the campground. The crisp air promised a chilly evening, and I set up the tent while Beth scanned for Martin's Moving van.

"What if they don't come?" Beth asked.

"If they don't come, then we always have Pier 22 1/2," I said, for the hundredth time.

The afternoon sky had that promise of adventure, and my legs itched to do something other than sit. My ankle screamed from holding one position the whole time, but my relationship with the clutch was definitely improving. Still, I wanted to do something– smash troll heads or take a hike; I didn't care which. But we lacked the trolls. "I'm going for a walk, wanna come?"

"Fine." Beth growled something about waiting, but we both knew that nothing could hurry the trolls. Either they'd show or they wouldn't.

Walking through the park, we found the hoodoos–funny mushroom-shaped rock formations. The wind blowing through the rocks sent a tingle across my spine.

I nudged Beth with my elbow. "You feel that?"

"Feel what?"

I stood still, calming myself, hoping my heart would stop thudding in my throat, and listened. The wind carried whispered words, soft at first, quickly turning into conversation. I couldn't make out the words, but the mushroom-shaped rocks resembled people–malformed and grotesque, but people nonetheless–with every passing second. They marched toward the end of the valley, in an impossibly slow trek. The wind eroded their faces, weathered their skin, and even their equipment became coated in the dust of this place, camouflaging them.

Beth hit me in the shoulder, and the illusion vanished.

Once again, I stared out over mere rocks.

"Hey, what's wrong with you? I asked you a question."

I blinked, focusing on my friend's face. "What?"

"Hey! Are you going to stand there staring all day or what?" Beth pointed at the top of one rock wall, and the last sliver of sunlight vanished over the edge. I'd been standing there for at least a minute, maybe longer

Or was it some sort of trick, some illusion?

"You didn't see that?"

"Obviously, though I see why people were starting to call you Statue Girl. You didn't even twitch."

"They're real." I pointed at the mushroom rocks. "They're real goblins, Beth, part of an army."

Two tourists, an older man and woman, marched up the walkway, decked in sun-faded hiking gear.

"Could you take our picture?" the woman asked as soon as they were close enough.

Beth took their camera. "I'd love to."

I looked back over the mushroom rocks, but no amount of concentration would bring back the goblins.

The man shook his head, watching the rocks. "They really do look like goblins climbing out of the rock, don't they?"

"Yeah." I sighed. He was just trying to be polite, but he was wrecking my chances of seeing anything. And the sun was going down.

The man turned a mischievous eye on his wife. "There's a story about these rocks."

The woman hit him with a playful backhand. "George, don't you dare."

"A story?" I asked, taking the bait.

He hunkered down and whispered, leaning in to keep the sound from carrying. "They say the rocks here danced in the light of a full moon. If you bring the goblin king what he wants"–he pointed to a particularly tall rock formation–"he'll march his army wherever you want. For the right price, he'll even march his goblins to Hell, but I imagine most of us have no cause to lead an army into the depths of Hell."

Beth chewed on the inside of her cheek. "Huh." She scowled at the rocks. "Why would anyone need to march an army into Hell?"

The man laughed, and if we weren't talking about leading armies of goblins into Hell, he would have been perfect for a sweet Santa Claus. "Pack on a few more years and you'll be more than ready to lead an army to Hell, if for nothing else than to get your friends back amongst the living."

The woman rolled her eyes. "Honestly, George, how do you know their friends will go to Hell, just because yours did?"

George, looked at us and wagged his eyebrows. "I don't know about you fine young ladies, but I'll be back up here 'round midnight to check on the hoodoos."

The woman dragged on his arm. "Don't listen to this old fool. He'll fill your heads with stories."

"A pleasure meeting you," Beth said.

"And you!" George's eyes sparkled, and they moved along the trail.

"Well, what do you think?" Beth asked.

"Sounds like a great story, but there has to be a reason those trolls would risk driving a giant van like that to this place. If their employer has a hundred trolls on his roster, why does he need goblins too?"

"You don't actually believe that story, do you?"

I looked at Beth and pointed at the make-up covering my scales. "You don't actually believe I'm half dragon, do you?"

"Well, you know what they say: if it spits fire like a dragon, has a bad temper like a dragon, then it must be a duck."

"Oh, come on, I have scales sprouting out of my face. And– and"–I pointed at her to cut her rising retort–"when I get really upset or scared, I spit fire. If I'm part dragon, then why not goblins that spend their days as rocks?"

Beth chuckled. "I bet you believe in the tooth fairy, too."

"I do not."

"Santa Claus?"

"I don't have to listen to this." I quickened my pace.

She caught up quickly. "The Easter Bunny? The Great Pumpkin?"

At one end of the campground sat Martin's Moving Van. We both stopped dead in our tracks.

The trolls had arrived.

CHAPTER THIRTEEN

We scanned the campground for any sort of cover, but there was nothing–no trees, not even trashcans big enough to hide behind. Our already pitched tent sat between the moving van and us. Slinking across the road, we made our way to the tent and slipped inside. I racked my brain for ways they might recognize us, but when they saw us in the mall we hadn't been with the faded red MGB. As long as we stayed out of sight, we were probably safe from discovery.

Beth unzipped the tent's window, and watched the three kidnappers. "They're building a fire. And they're roasting kabobs on it."

My stomach growled. "We haven't exactly had dinner."

"You're the one who didn't want to stop." Beth rubbed her stomach. "We could hit up that couple for some food."

"Maybe we can sneak out of the campground after they fall asleep." I checked the road to be sure we wouldn't have to drive past them to leave.

"If they fall asleep, you mean."

"Trolls sleep," I said. "Some of them even snore."

Beth turned away from the window. "And by some, you mean me?"

"I'd rib you more, but there's probably nothing you can do about it."

"I'm sorry. Did you expect a troll to be a dainty sleeper? You look like the dead when you sleep, by the way. I almost poked you to be sure you were alive last night."

I peeked through the window at the trolls sitting around their bonfire, roasting strips of meat on sticks. My stomach growled. "Sorry to worry you."

"Is it one of your dragon abilities?"

"To sit still? That doesn't sound very dragonish to me." I imagined taking a bite of one of the kabobs. They had a whole cooler full of them, and after they finished one, they reached into the cooler and pulled out the next one.

"Try it," Beth said.

"Try what?"

"Do that standing still thing, and see if you can use it to sneak around. Dragons are supposed to have exceptional camouflage."

I gave her the hard sideways stare. "Are you suggesting my super power is standing still?"

Beth put up her hands. "At least you get super powers. I just heal really fast, making me the perfect practice dummy."

"Fine, I'll see what I can do." I slipped out through the tent door, and found a picnic table and eased down behind it.

They had a six-pack of beer, but they didn't touch it. Crouching, I waited. Taking a chance on a nearby boulder, I took a step forward, sliding into a new position. I crept along the campground road for what felt like an eternity, but my thighs didn't scream, despite holding each position unnaturally long. Every action adventure book talked about fatigue, but I didn't feel anything. In fact, slinking along, belly to the ground, using my hands for balance and support felt natural. I focused on the trolls and their cooler. The roasting meat smell made my mouth water at the dream of eating. My stomach demanded food, and they had it.

Standing behind Martin's Moving van, my prey waited. The cooler sat untended, and the trolls launched into a carousing song about a Scotsman and his kilt. Skulking the last few steps, I kept my head below the level of the picnic table. I took a plastic bag from the bench and used it to grab two solid handfuls of kabobs. I didn't have to reach far; the ice chest was full of red meat, top to bottom.

"Did you hear that?" the short troll asked. John looked in my direction, and I froze. I literally had my hands in the cookie jar. John locked eyes with me and arched an eyebrow.

"Hear what?" he asked. I ducked down, and the short troll–I think his name was Bob–looked around. He looked straight at me, but he must have been fire blind. He kept searching the night for the mysterious sound.

"It's time; grab the offerings," Bob said, standing up.

"But we just started eating," the third troll complained.

Bob grabbed him by the collar and twisted it around his fist, lifting the third troll off the ground.

"And now, we're going to meet the king, so I suggest you wipe your slobbering face."

Bob dropped him, and the third troll wiped his mouth on his sleeve. "Jeez, you don't have to be so dramatic."

John grabbed the six-pack of Bud, and they walked off in the direction of our campsite. I watched from under the picnic table, heart pounding, as they walked right past our tent and up the trail to the mushroom rocks.

Seconds after they disappeared, Beth came running up the road. "Allyson," she whispered.

"Down here," I said, hands still wrapped around the kabobs.

"Did you see that?"

"Yeah, do you think we should use their fire, or start our own?" I squirmed out from under the table.

"What are you talking about? They left the van. Let's get Steve and get out of here."

Oh, right, rescue mission first, dinner second. "How about I stand out here and keep watch while you see about breaking out the prisoner?"

Beth looked from me to the bag of kabobs. "Just roast enough for me, too."

Sticking a few kabobs into the fire, I listened as Beth mangled the back door of the moving van. A clank and a screech of metal stole across the campground. I winced as I checked the meat. More metal breaking sounds came from the back of the van, and I hurried. I wanted dinner, but if Beth caused too much trouble, the other campers might mention something to the trolls. The thump of flesh on metal sounded from the far end of the truck. She was going to tear it apart with her bare hands.

I stretched four little sticks across the jerry-rigged spit and went to check on Beth. At the back of the van, the situation was worse than I'd feared. The bumper had three Beth-sized fist prints. "How about stealthy, like a cat?"

"Troll, not feline," Beth said, jabbing her thumb at her chest. She grabbed the door and wrenched. It clattered as it rolled up into the top of the van. "Ah, success."

I gasped as my eyes focused in the darkness.

Lining the walls of the moving van, three sets of bunk beds waited, six beds high. One on the wall against the cabin, and two along each side, eighteen total. Every single one had a person in it.

"Oh no," Beth said.

In the center of the van sat a large rollaway cart, and from the cart, IV lines ran through hooks on poles to the occupants of the van. Something dark pulsed in the IV lines.

My stomach twisted, and the world seemed to tip on its side as I lost my balance. Static ran through my ears, and my eyes blurred. The first wave of it passed over me, receding into memory. When my vision cleared, the drugs pulsed with something more than chemicals.

I'd never believed in such things as magic. But I'd never believed in dragons, either. And without a doubt, coursing through those lines was a vile, repugnant magic that stank like death. I covered my nose, but it didn't help.

"Dear God."

Beth hopped into the back and shook her head. "What the hell do we do now?"

"Call the police." I climbed into the van, careful not to touch any of the IV lines.

"Yeah, 'cause they can stop three trolls and not kill everyone here." Beth looked over the people in their beds.

"Wait, are these guys normal or Kin?"

Beth touched a couple of them. "Kin."

"So then the police really aren't...." My voice died in my throat as a shock drove down my spine.

My breath caught, and my heart skipped a beat. My aunt lay across the bunk on the back wall. My aunt. Worry welled up through me, followed by a sudden need to light someone on fire, or rip their eyes out of their socket. Someone did this to my aunt.

That someone was going to die.

My chest burned, alternating between constricting and gulping giant breaths.

I crossed the metal floor, slipping past the IV lines. I touched her shoulder, and almost instantly, the nausea swept over me.

The magic leaked around the edges, and I was on my knees.

"Allyson, are you okay?" Beth asked. She pulled my hand away from my aunt. Even that small contact had nearly put me under, and they were pumping that stuff into their veins?

Beth put her arm under my shoulders and picked me up. "Shit."

"I'm not that heavy."

She pointed at the bunk above my aunt's.

Steve lay there, peacefully.

Beth pursed her lips. "Okay, help me get them out of the van." She reached forward to pull the IV from Aunt Agnes' arm.

"Wait! What if there's some sort of booby trap in this stuff?"

Beth's eyes grew as she stared back at the IV lines like they had turned to snakes.

"We can't assume anything."

"Okay, so we'll steal the whole van and drive it to the nearest hospital. We can let the authorities sort this out."

"And you think the authorities are going to handle two teenage girls driving into a hospital with a bunch of unconscious–possibly dead–people very well? Not to mention, normal doctors might do more damage than good. That stuff"–I pointed to the IV machine–"is definitely not covered in med school, I'll tell you that."

"Goddamit, this just isn't fair. We've found them! That should be it."

I nodded. "Just think of the story we'd tell when we drive into a hospital. 'We stole a car and just happened to run into these kidnappers, so we stole their car, too.' I mean, they'd lock us up for sure. And who are all these other people?"

Beth clunked her head into one of the bunk supports. "I know, I know. There's no way we can take this to the normals."

"We steal the van and take it to the unicorns. I bet Dr. Targyne would know what to do."

"Yes! I like this plan." Beth hopped out of the truck, and I hesitated. The Kin barely moved in their bunks. The murky magic filled them, slowly killing them.

The cabin door slammed, and Beth came back scowling. "No keys."

"Crap." Why hadn't I thought of that?

Beth shook her head. "Why would someone kidnap all these people?"

It didn't make any sense. If someone wanted to exterminate the Kin, then why bother transporting them across the country to San Francisco? The troll map showed they were headed to the Bay Area, so why did they need unconscious Kin in San Francisco?

And why stop in a completely backwater campground in the middle of the desert?

A plan formed in my mind.

"Okay, here's what we're going to do. You are going to call Dr. Targyne. I don't know if he's a particularly reasonable man, but evidence is evidence. If he doesn't work out, call Mr. June. He's already cracked over Steve; I bet he'll go outside the monohorn chain of command to get his son back. I'll follow the trolls and figure out what's going on." I tossed her my aunt's cell phone, and hopped out of the van.

"Allyson, are you sure about this?"

"No." I walked back to the fire and tossed my makeshift tripod into the flames. My stomach hurt too much to eat. And we needed more information. "Stay here and call the doctor. I'm following them."

As I passed the MGB, I wished for a minute that I could just hop into the sleeping bag and take a night off. But that was *my* Aunt Agnes in there; one of only three constants in my life: Mom, music, and Aunt Agnes, who always showed up at birthdays no matter what part of the country Mom and I happened to live in.

I followed the path into the mushroom valley, moving slowly, trying to do some sort of dragony stealth thing. What I wouldn't give for Harry Potter's cloak.

The hoodoos came into view, and this time, I wasn't imagining it–they were moving.

And they were goblins.

At the far end, three trolls sat around the base of a large rock. Nestled in the large rock sat a scraggly creature with a stone crown to match the surrounding rocks. He had a beer in each hand, and one on the armrest. The rest of the six-pack lay at his feet.

Melting into the shadows of the rocks, I perked up my ears. Maybe dragons really did have some super powers. Even over the noise of the shuffling goblins, their conversation carried to me.

"Your master asks too much," the goblin king said.

Bob rocked back. "We brought the offering," he said, holding up his beer.

The goblin took a drink. "Your master thinks beer will be enough to gain my army?" The goblin king tilted his head toward Bob and took another drink. "Your master is a fool to think I would like this piss." He threw the bottle on the ground just in front of Bob. The bottle shattered, spraying beer and glass into the trolls. A gash across Bob's forehead knit together as I watched. The blood barely made it down his face.

Bob wiped at the blood and shook it off his hands. Bright red globs fell to the ground, lost in the dust. "So you're refusing to join the Stein team, then?"

"I'm not a filthy mercenary, not like you trolls. You have no honor, whereas my kind created the world you know." He popped the top off a second beer and took a swig. He threw the second bottle at Bob. "Tell Kurt he'll have to do better than trolls bringing me Bud Light. I want to meet his dragon, and he'd better have a nice gift." The Goblin King absently waved the trolls away and took the third bottle, bit the neck off in his stone teeth and tossed the beer to a nearby goblin.

The trolls stood, storming away from their failed recruitment.

As they made it to the edge of the hoard of goblins, the king yelled over the din. "And next time, boys?" He waited for the trolls to turn around before rattling the cardboard six-pack of beer. "Bring enough to share!"

The goblins around the king roared with laughter. He handed out his remaining bottles to the two largest, and the other goblins looked on hopefully. "Idiots," the king muttered, loud enough for the trolls to hear.

As the trolls headed my way, I checked my hiding spot, but there was nothing better. I stood as still as possible and prayed they wouldn't notice me. I focused on thinking rock-like thoughts. John looked right at me and winked.

He was way smarter than the average troll.

CHAPTER FOURTEEN

I waited in the shadows, praying Beth had moved everything and locked up the van. When I knew they wouldn't be able to hear me, I slunk back to camp. I felt like a lizard, not a dragon, eavesdropping and stealing stuff. My stomach growled. The shock of seeing my aunt had worn off a little, and I seemed to have a cavernous pit instead of a stomach. I really hoped Beth had thought to bring the kabobs back to our campsite. I slithered back to the tent and slipped between the door flaps.

In the half light, Beth knelt by the sleeping bags, rolling them quickly. "We can't stay," she said, tying her sleeping bag with a vicious yank.

"Now what?"

"Dr. Targyne wanted me to stay put. I don't think he believes me. He's sending a team."

"Fantastic."

"Yup." Beth moved from her bag to mine and quickly rolled it up. I scanned the inside of the tent for anything I could do to hurry along the process and yawned.

Beth looked up at me. "Don't do that. We need to move."

"Oh, come on, it took us all day to get here, it's not like they'll just appear out of thin air," I said, indulging in another protracted yawn. My mind produced an image of unicorns flying into the campground. The thought sent buckets of cold water down my spine. They did have magic–could they...?

"Can they?" I whispered.

"Can they what?"

"Fly here?"

112

A half twitch pulled at Beth's mouth. "No. And the monohorns can't teleport yet, either. Currently, that resides in the realms of Star Trek and video games. But they are ridiculously well connected. One phone call, and the closest set of unicorns is headed our way. We may have less than an hour. Probably more like two, but not long enough to sleep here."

"Damn, do they know what car they're looking for?"

Beth snorted. "Dumb, not stupid. I didn't tell them we were driving in a highly conspicuous red convertible. I did tell him about the moving van."

I helped Beth move our sleeping bags and camping mats to the trunk, and we hastily disassembled the tent. As I unsnapped the tonneau cover, an envelope fell from the cover into the car. I fished out the envelope. It was addressed to Beth and had a stick drawing of a bouquet on it. I handed the envelope to my friend.

"What's this?" she asked.

"I don't know, but if you're ready to go, we should put some distance between us and here." I pulled the rest of the cover off and stuffed it in its customary spot.

Beth climbed into the passenger seat and tore open the envelope. Flipping open the glove box for light, she read quickly.

I jammed the key into the ignition and turned the car on. "You ready, or should I wait before you pull out the map?"

Beth looked at me with the guilty semblance of a child who'd been caught swiping cookies. "Sorry." She brought out the map, and stuck it under the reading light. "Just head toward that big freeway; we can stop at a rest area or something to figure out what to do next."

I pulled out, and we started down the dark winding road. "Who's the letter from?"

"John," she said with a sigh.

I tried not to make gagging noises. "Does he have anything useful to say?"

"I don't know, I had to stop reading it," she said.

If John had said anything important, I wanted to know. "How did it start?"

Beth was quiet. I stole a glance from the road to look at her; she kept her gaze dead ahead, not wavering toward me at all.

"How did it start?" I nudged.

Beth smiled then frowned almost as quickly. "A poem."

I drew breath to laugh but stopped. She was serious. I looked at her again. She stared at the road, unable to make eye contact with me. She *liked* the poetry. Beth had said she didn't have to beat the guys off with sticks. And John liked her. He liked her a lot. In her shoes, I could see how she might really like being liked, even if it was by a troll. But then again, Beth was half troll. How did she identify herself? Did she feel trapped in two worlds, torn? Or did she feel like a troll living in a human world?

And, shoot, who wouldn't want a little poetry?

But a love poem from a troll?

I concentrated on the road, and we drove on in silence. Rocky outcrops loomed in headlights every time the road bent. I lost track of time, but the moon had moved by the time the road wound its way out of the rock monoliths and into more typical desert flatlands. In the distance, the headlights of cars speeding by on a highway made a trail of light. When we got there, the road hitched up and over the interstate, and I turned onto the westbound lanes. Trucks ruled the roads at this time of night, and I just tried to stay out of their way.

It seemed a small slice of forever as I drove, eyes sagging and thinking about falling asleep. Beth hunched down in her seat to get out of the driving wind, and after a few mile markers, she snored. I took the next exit with a gas station for trucks as well as a diner with more dirt than paint on the walls. The parking area was huge, and I pulled the MGB up alongside a barbed wire fence at the edge. Pulling my *ushanka* as far down as possible, I closed my eyes and tried to sleep.

"Hey," Beth said, thumping me in the chest. "Get up."

I blinked my eyes open. I couldn't have slept for more than a couple seconds, but sleep-sand caked my eyes closed. Rosy light stretched across the eastern sky, and the wind sweeping through the car bit through the seams of my jacket.

Beth pointed at the diner. "Monohorns."

"How many?"

"I saw two, but there could be more."

I nodded. "Wait here." I hopped out of the car and headed for the diner.

"What are you doing? Get back here!"

"Hide," I hissed over my shoulder.

"Crazy dragon," she muttered.

I smiled. Crazy or not, we needed to know what the unicorns thought they were doing here.

The diner doors opened with a creek when I pulled the handle. The place was stuck in a time warp. The Formica counters had that sparkle from the fifties, the seats were redone into seventies orange, and the linoleum tile had more chips than whole tiles. Even the waitress wore a light blue frock with a frilled apron.

At the front counter, a man and a woman stood holding out a picture of Beth. They both wore the black suits of FBI agents in movies.

"Any information would really be useful," the woman said to the waitress.

"I'm sorry," the waitress replied. "I just didn't see any teenagers last night."

"We think she might be traveling in a moving van," the man said.

The waitress shook her head and shrugged. "Sorry."

The woman drooped, but the man nodded. "It's okay." He handed the waitress a flyer. "If you see her, please call. It's really important."

The door opened behind me, and the smell of moisture washed over me. It was so out of place in the desert that I stopped. The weather hadn't suddenly changed, but three men and a woman blocked the whole entryway of the diner. They wore leather vests and chaps, and their bare arms bore tattoos. All of them had tattoos of gryphons standing on hind legs, forelegs raised as if to attack. The tattoos on their right shoulder were like an old fashioned coat of arms. Feathers braided into their hair made them look part gryphon themselves. Each of them had a gun, and the man in front held a shotgun.

The dusty scent of feathers swept into the room. Feathers, fog… were they flying creatures? Kin?

No, their tattoos weren't random. My eyes widened at the realization. Gryphons! Did they work for the unicorns, too? I slipped back into the tiny waiting area between a glass counter and a candy dispenser with Chiclets from long ago and a decade far away. I turned my attention to a musty old stack of newspapers.

The lead gryphon racked his shotgun, sending a menacing *cah-clunk* through the diner, yanking my gaze back to the situation unfolding. The waitress's eyes honed in on the gun and she backed away. The two unicorns spun around to face the gryphons.

"I told you not to come into our territory," the gryphon said.

"It's an emergency, Reggie," the woman said.

"Like when my son disappeared?"

The unicorns both backed away, and the waitress fled to the kitchen.

"Now, hold on, Reggie," the male unicorn said. "That was completely different."

"Different how? You called my son a runaway. And now, here I see you showing flyers up and down the interstate of two runaways, a girl and a boy. You assholes only care about your own?"

"I'm sorry about your boy."

The gryphon pointed his gun at the unicorns. "Sorry isn't good enough."

The gun roared, filling the diner with an explosion. Fire lashed out from the tip of the barrel. The unicorns fell into a heap of tables and chairs, and flyers flew into the air. I let out a startled scream, and the smallest gryphon glanced over at me, but looked away quickly, unfazed by my presence.

Climbing out of the tangle of chairs, the male unicorn wiped blood off his cheek. "I've had enough of you feather-headed bird brains, Reginald."

Reggie racked the shotgun once more, sending a spent shell flying through the lobby. It clanked on the ground as he pulled the trigger. Shots blasted into the unicorn, and he staggered but kept his feet.

Reggie looked at the gryphon with white streaks in his hair. "You said silver shot should do it."

The unicorn shifted, and a spiral horn grew out of the man's forehead. His skin slowly morphed to white and sprouted fur. His tail was like a lion's, long and thin with a tuft at the end.

I tried to melt into the tiny lobby area desk, hopeful they might be too distracted to notice one little dragon.

The unicorn leveled his horn at the gryphon and charged. Reggie put two more shots into the unicorn before it skewered him in the navel. The older gryphon pulled a knife and sunk it into the unicorn's neck. A sound halfway between a whale's song and a dying horse squealed out of the unicorn, and he tossed aside his victim.

"I guess knives will have to do." The female gryphon pulled a long knife from a sheath on her chaps. She stepped toward the unicorn, and slashed viciously across his neck. A deep red gash opened up, and he sank to the ground, spilling blood across the linoleum floor. He morphed back into a human, but blood continued to gush from his neck. I had no idea if it would be fatal, but there was enough blood to be worrisome under the best of circumstances.

The female unicorn jumped between the gryphon and her prey. "Stop! We didn't come here to fight; I came to catch a kidnapper. Just let us leave, and we'll get out of your territory."

The biker chick shot a look over to Reggie. He knelt on the floor, bleeding heavily, and gasping in pain. He gave a curt nod. The gryphons stepped aside, and the female unicorn collected the injured man over her shoulder and hobbled out of the diner.

The uninjured gryphons descended on their leader, laying him down in the entryway of the diner.

The woman looked back at me. "Well, aren't you going with your friends?"

"I'm not with them," I said.

"Then do something useful."

"Do you want me to call 911?"

She turned her glare on me. "Don't be daft, kid. You're like us. Get some real help."

How does everyone know but me?

I launched myself out the door and ran across the pavement. I saw no sign of the unicorns, but Beth was already getting out of the car.

"What happened?"

"The unicorn gored a gryphon. They're still inside," I said.

Beth sprinted past me back to the diner. I followed, but my throat closed. I didn't know if I was about to have another incendiary regurgitation, but I didn't want to spit fire in another room with automatic sprinklers. Then again, the diner didn't look like it was exactly up to code.

Inside, Beth knelt in front of the biker gryphon. "Lay back, I need to take a look." She pulled up his leather vest, and her face darkened.

"Are you an EMT?" the gryphon woman asked.

Beth shook her head. "I've got a lot of experience with unicorn wounds."

The waitress burst out through the swinging kitchen doors

carrying a first aid kit. She handed the case to Beth. "Those other two were looking for you."

"I know," Beth said. "They think I did something I didn't."

The grey-streaked gryphon stared at Beth. "What's going on?"

"Give me your knife," she said.

The older gryphon handed over his bowie knife, and Beth took the giant blade. In her hand, it looked well proportioned. Beth turned the blade around and poked the palm of her hand with the point. Bright red blood with a hint of green welled up in her palm, and Beth made a fist and squeezed. Blood dripped from her hand into the wound.

"What are you doing?" the gryphon asked.

"My blood will heal him," Beth said.

News to me!

"What are you?" the female gryphon asked.

Beth didn't answer, but Reggie moaned, drawing everyone's attention back to him. Almost instantly, color returned to his face. He coughed and tried to sit up, but Beth put a hand on his chest. "Stay put, it's not a cure all."

The waitress in her blue dress stared on, eyes wide and hands trembling. "Maybe I shouldn't have called 911."

"Can we move him?" the older gryphon asked Beth.

"In about a minute, sure," she said.

If I were the waitress, I'd have called the cops. Of course, if she called 911, there'd be cops, EMTs, and fire fighters speeding down the highway this very second. How far away were they? Considering my aunt was in the back of a moving van, I doubt she reported the car as missing, but I didn't have an actual license.

I grabbed Beth's arm and pulled. "We've gotta go."

She stood up reluctantly, then stopped moving. Woodenly, as if she weren't in control of her own actions, she reached down to the floor and picked up a flyer. Beth's indestructible smile beamed up at us from the page. Beneath her face, handwritten in marker, the words 'Please help us find our daughter' scrawled across the paper.

I cocked an eyebrow at Beth as she followed me out of the diner. We made it back to the red car, and I slid into the driver's seat. As I turned over the engine, sirens wailed out on the highway, getting closer. Luckily, we sped away without any hint of the usual bunny-hop start.

CHAPTER FIFTEEN

Three Days Before

Driving down the interstate, a pack of motorcycles came up behind us. I put my hand on Beth's head, and she hid under the dashboard. The Harley Davidsons with chrome everything roared past us. The main bodies looked like painted teardrops. I knew nothing about bikes except the ones painted in neon went really fast. These were all maroons and blacks. I scanned the crowd for Reggie, but I didn't see him. After they passed, Beth peeked back up from under the dashboard.

"Well?" Beth asked.

"I can't tell if they're Kin just by looking."

"You'll learn," she said. "If we live long enough."

The gas gauge sat on the empty line, so I pulled off at the very next exit with a gas station. "Why is it that the only interspecies reactions are shooting, stabbing, and kidnapping?" I asked, pulling the car up to a pump.

Beth shrugged. "There's a lot of reasons. I mean, heck, even old stories about dragons and unicorns said they did nothing but fight with each other."

"I don't like it. I didn't choose to be their enemies."

Beth snorted. "And you think most Americans chose to be hated by extremists in the Mid East?"

"That's different," I said.

"Yeah, how?"

I opened the door and pulled down the gas handle. I didn't have an answer, but it seemed like there should be one. It just didn't make sense. We were all hiding from the normal humans. Why not band together in our exile?

"You need to understand, the battles between these people have been going on since before the birth of Christ." Beth turned her hands up in placation. "Hell, most of these battles predate human civilization. It's no wonder they hate each other."

"That doesn't mean we shouldn't try to change things."

She nodded. "You got any brilliant ideas, I'm all ears. I'd love to put this behind us. Don't forget, I'm a member of a kill-on-site group."

"That's racist," I said.

"Speciesist if you want to get technical." Beth sighed. "I know you want to do something, but we need to think about survival. I don't think anything's going to change just because a couple of girls go and chase down some kidnappers."

Reggie's words echoed through my brain. *'Like when my son disappeared?'* Odd that the reason the gryphons were willing to stand up to, essentially, sword-wielding unicorns, was because of a slight when a child had disappeared. Of course, after seeing what the unicorns had done to Beth, I was willing to bash some unicorn heads with little provocation myself.

I went into the convenience store and searched for something suitable for breakfast. I gave the man thirty bucks for gas and bought Pop Tarts and beef jerky. It wouldn't quite fill the tank, for the car or for us, but we'd be in Ely by noon. We could have a feast after I picked up my inheritance, or whatever awaited me in Nevada. I dropped my hand into my pocket, and curled my fingers around the key.

Back at the car, I tossed a package of pastries to Beth and started the gas pump. She tore into her food while I stood there waiting for the gas to finish. "So, you gonna change the world, Drake?"

"Maybe," I said, more because I didn't want to admit she probably had a point.

If everyone hated each other for some slight from two thousand years ago, no wonder they were at each other's throats now. How do you convince a people to forgive murder?

The short answer? You can't.

"What about you?" I asked. "I didn't know your blood could heal people."

Beth scowled into her Pop Tart. "I can't just heal anyone, but I can heal gryphons."

"What about dragons?"

"Maybe."

"Humans?"

"Only the halves."

"What happens to humans when you give them your blood?" The words fell from my mouth, and I wished I could take them back. Images of some human frothing in bubbly death washed through my mind. Did troll blood melt normal people?

Beth's features fell for a minute, confirming my fears. Then a smile broke across her face. "You should see your face, Drake. My blood doesn't kill humans, it just doesn't cure them."

I punched her in the shoulder, but she kept laughing. I finished up with the gas and got in the car. The engine turned over with a hum, and I wished the antique car had a real stereo. The MGB roared onto the road and ate the miles of freeway without complaint. The brown scenery fell away with little change, flat valleys and the occasional mountains. The road to Ely broke from the main freeway, and I turned the car into the desert in earnest. The two-lane road wound through deep valleys along gullies, and signs warned of the imminent threat of cattle. Clearly, this wasn't the golden brick road.

A cow stood in the center of the road. I stopped the car, and the black-horned devil stared back. I honked, but the cow went back to chewing cud.

"Well," I said to Beth. "Can't you do anything?"

"What, like, wrestle it to the ground?"

I snorted. "It would still block the road. Can't you shoo it or something?"

Beth looked at me over her sunglasses. "I vote for 'or something.'"

"It's a cow."

"Which means you could spit on it and have your own personal barbeque."

My mouth watered at the thought, and I shut the door on images of grilled steak. "Right, barbeque." I stepped out of the car. I waved at the cow, but it didn't budge. "Oh, come on, how many roads do you think are between here and Ely? And you're blocking one of them."

The cow stared back, looking even more disinclined to move. I jumped at it in the most predatory fashion I could manage. I could spit fire for crying out loud. "I eat your kind!"

Beth's laughter bounced off the canyon walls like rolling thunder.

I turned back to her, a haughty retort on my lips, but a cowboy riding down the valley wall caught my attention. For a moment, I couldn't quite make out the horse and the rider. He flickered in my vision, like an image fading onto another image. A chill swept down my back. The flickering image coalesced into a creature with the torso and head of a man fused to the body of a horse.

I bent my knees, ready to spring into action.

He tipped his cowboy hat at me. "Ma'am." He trotted closer, and I stood my ground, unsure of what to do next. He tilted his head toward the bull in the road. "That boy giving you cause for trouble?"

I stood back up, trying to hide the fact that my heart pounded in my chest. "He's blocking the road."

His eyes snapped to the bull. "Geeyup!" He lunged at the cow.

The bovine yelped a plaintive moo and cleared the road.

"What's going on here?"

He raised an eyebrow at me. "Pardon?"

"What are you?" I asked.

The cowboy-horse thing narrowed his eyes at me then at Beth. She slunk down in the car seat. "You ladies ought to be careful when you run into strangers." He pointed at Beth. "There are many who would kill a dragon on sight. No one wants to give the thief more fuel than he already has."

"What thief? Why dragons?"

He trotted closer. When he got close enough, he held out his hand to me. He flickered between a horse with rider and the man-horse fusion, but when we shook hands, the flickering stopped at man-horse fusion.

"Name's Darian, and I am a centaur."

"Allyson Takata."

His eyes went wide at my name, then softened with sorrow. "I knew a Takata once. She went missing long before you were born. A pity. She had some fine ideas, but that was a long time ago." He drew the corners of his mouth down as if forcing the past away. "Someone should have warned you 'bout the thief."

"I've never even heard of the thief. We're trying to find a kidnapper."

"The thief is worse than a kidnapper. He steals the powers of dragons, turns them. Makes them dark." He took his hat off, and fanned himself despite the chill in the air. "Your kind tried to wipe him out, but all it did was fuel the fire. Now, folks is so scared y'all'll join over that I heard some idiots in Cheyenne went and skinned a boy thinking he was dragon."

My breath failed me, and my heart beat so hard it hurt my chest. "Was he?"

"Does it matter to the boy? Anyhow, you'll need to be careful. I saw a van full of trolls not more than an hour ago."

"How come you're not scared of me?"

He chuckled. "I got hit by a falling tree once, that don't mean the trees are out to get me." He snugged his hat back onto his head and squinted at the rest of his herd. "Ole Fern's at it again. Good luck ladies."

And without any other warning, he cantered off after a cow half way up the far side of the valley wall. I stood there watching, hoping he'd come back, but the centaur rounded his cattle up and disappeared over the ridge.

"I don't think he's coming back."

I slammed the door. "I wanted to ask him more questions. Have you ever heard of this thief?"

Beth shook her head.

We drove on in silence, winding through the steep valleys. I kept my eyes peeled for any more cowboy-centaurs, but there were none. Despite the brooding sun, the temperature did not range above damned cold, and I was more thankful than ever for my ridiculous hat and mismatched jacket. The hazy sky kept it from seeming like a real desert, but the vegetation was sparse. We rounded some grey rocks, and Ely, Nevada lay in the distance. I'd never been more excited about finding a tiny town in the middle of the desert. I almost let out a yelp of joy at the sight of it.

On the outskirts, we passed the hotel-casino combinations found in most of Nevada. Despite the chill air, one of them had a rushing waterfall out front, an odd decoration for the desert. When we stopped at a red light next to the water fountain, the clean scent of water drifted through the air, a welcome contrast to the salty dust of the desert. I pulled out my scrap of paper while we waited for the light to change.

"What's that?"

"I need to make a stop."

"Are you kidding? We have to catch that van. I told Targyne the kidnappers were going to Ely."

"What? You told them where we'd be going?"

Beth held up her hands. "How else are we going to get their help if they don't know where the truck is going to be?"

I sighed. "So they know where we are, and the trolls might be expecting us too. Great."

"Well," Beth blushed, "only one troll."

"What?"

"John said they usually stop for lunch at some hotel here."

"When did he say that?"

Beth held up her troll poetry.

I pursed my lips, and instantly an image of my mother pursing her lips took over my mind. I smoothed out my facial features. "Fine, we'll find this hotel, or whatever, and you can grab a bite to eat with the kidnappers." The light turned green, but there was no one behind me. I didn't drive on.

"Hey, it's not his fault John got mixed up with these guys," she said.

"Then whose fault is it that he kidnaps people?"

"It's not like you even have a clue what you're talking about. You've only known anything for, like, what, four days? What the hell do you know?"

I stared back at Beth. "Right, so where is this place you want to check for your boyfriend?"

Beth scowled. "He's not my boyfriend."

"Whatever, lead on."

Beth pointed, and I turned into the intersection.

Ely consisted of one lawn–brown from the winter–in front of the city hall, one library, and a row of dilapidated bars. At the end of Bar Row, the only multistory building sat waiting for the rest of the town to grow up around it. It had been waiting for a long time. A cowboy in vintage neon lights and chaps hung on the corner. It looked like it might have once actually moved, but had since fallen into complete disrepair.

I parked in a paved lot off the main road and kept an eye out for the moving van, but I didn't see it. Still, I watched for any sign of kidnappers. If this was a usual stop, maybe they had a better place for stashing the van while they gambled and drank margaritas. I grabbed my book bag, just in case this place had a bathroom or someplace I could freshen up a bit. I stuffed a T-shirt and some underwear into the bag. Two days of road grime and no shower had done nothing for my complexion, not to mention my aroma. Brass numbers clung to the sides of brick buildings. I checked them as we walked past, whipping out the piece of paper with the address on it. They matched.

I stopped on the sidewalk.

"What is it?" Beth asked.

"This is too easy. The only place you want to stop in this town in the middle of nowhere is where I needed to stop too. Don't you think that's weird?"

Beth looked up and down the street. "Usually, I'd agree, but there ain't nothing else here. *This* is where it's at."

I gave the street a broad look and had to agree. The old hotel seemed to be the only place open for business, let alone of actual importance. But now that I stood feet from my destination, I hesitated. Could this really be it? And what was it? This was something from my aunt, right? This key had to unlock something really important; otherwise, why the secrecy?

Or maybe she'd just been in a hurry. Had she known she was going to be kidnapped?

For a moment, my visions of treasure melted into secret messages and conspiracy theories. But what sort of secret would my aunt want to tell me, and why in such a roundabout way?

No, this had to be some sort of inheritance, something from my father. Maybe he had it delivered for my birthday. This had to be his gift to me for my birthday, right? Maybe fifteen was a big deal with dragons.

We walked in through the doors, and the wave of stale cigarette smoke rolled over us. An empty row of slot machines rang their little bells at us, hoping we'd play. Under the stench of smoke and vomit, there was a pulse in the air, a desperation. People came here with their dreams and left with worries.

I scanned the early afternoon crowd but didn't see anything—kidnappers or monohorns. The key practically burned in my pocket. Somewhere in this building was the lock it would open. My whole destiny, behind one locked door.

Strolling through the wild place, a waitress dressed in a corset and puffed up skirt stopped in front of us. Under the makeup, she could have been as young as fifty.

"Can I help you?" she asked.

"Yeah, I ... uh, do you guys have, like, a front desk or something?"

She pursed her lips. "Aren't you a bit young to be getting a room with your girlfriend?"

My eyes bulged, and I blushed. I turned to Beth, prepared to smooth ruffled feathers.

Beth stood straight, peering down at the waitress. "And what's it to you where we spend our money?"

The waitress backed up. "Don't get your drawers in a twist with me, missy. If you wanna room, the front desk is through there to your right. And don't get lost. I can't have kids on my floor."

We followed her sparse directions through the casino to the front desk–which wasn't actually at the front. A statue of John Wayne stood to one side. A man with more grease than hair stood behind the desk. He wore an old style shirt and vest, like a card dealer in the Old West.

Of course, this place had the stuck-in-time thing going for it, so why not a card dealer from a saloon?

"May I help you ladies?" he drawled.

Beth and I just stood in front of him, deer caught in the headlights. Beth gave me a firm shove in the center of my back, and I stumbled forward. "Well, get on with it. I'll see if I can find John."

The card-dealing front desk attendant pointed at the mannequin and favored Beth with a nod. "Mr. Wayne's right there, ma'am." The effigy of John Wayne stood poised to wink.

I slapped my key down on the front desk.

Upon seeing the key, he drew his head back, as if the scrap of metal might bite him. "Oh," he said, then nodded solemnly. "Come with me."

129

He flipped up a false counter piece and pulled the façade inwards, making a door through the seemingly solid front desk. He pulled open another hidden door within the mailboxes in the wall, and we walked into a room with an actual vault door.

My heart kicked up a notch. It was really going to be this easy. After all, who knew I was even coming? And it wasn't like there was ever going to be an army trying to stop me. I was just one kid. Who would even care?

The card dealer shut and locked the door behind me before turning to the vault. A spiked wheel handle and a dark grey metal door completed the ancient bank's Old West feel. The lacquer on the door stank of age and oil, but there was no mistaking the smell of steel, and lots of it. Standing next to the wheel, the dealer looked more the part of a bank teller than a card dealer. He stood between the door and me and turned the knobbed handle.

When the door opened, he led me inside. The quiet in the room blotted out the rest of the world, cutting out all sounds and smells. This was the sort of place psychopaths would hide bodies. Or worse, soon-to-be bodies. I shivered at the thought.

The teller held his hand out. "The key," he said.

I laid it in his palm, and he turned it over.

"Ah, an old customer." He walked along a bank of drawers.

Each one had a place for two keys. Safety deposit boxes. My hopes jumped, startling my heart into fluttering like a bird. There could be deeds in these boxes, cash. More keys to more boxes.

He bent down and stuck my key into a hole before putting a key from a giant key ring into the other hole. He turned them both and pulled out a long thin metal box. He pulled a shelf out from the wall of drawers and set the box down. Discreetly, he stepped away so I could view the box in what limited privacy the vault offered.

My heart pounding, I flipped back the front half of the metal lid. It clanged back, startling me. The room seemed to swallow sound, but even my breathing was loud. I tried to calm down and search the box, but there was nothing inside. I picked it up, and something slid from the back to the front. A ragged black book the size of my hand clanked to the front of the metal drawer. It was rubber-banded shut, and on the dog-eared front cover were two dragons twisted together in a Celtic knot.

I checked the rest of the box, but except for the ratty journal, it was empty.

"Is that all?" That couldn't be all. This was supposed to be my inheritance, my fortune, the answers to why I'd never met my father, not some cheap, dingy diary. A diary? This couldn't be it. There had to be more. There just had to be.

"Is something missing? Has there been a theft?" he asked.

Just of my dreams. I grabbed the book and turned toward the door. "No," I said. A lump lodged in my throat, so I didn't try any other words.

He didn't comment on my lack of chatter, just carried on in his same professional manner. "Are you finished with the box?"

"Yes."

He locked things up and handed back my key. It seemed to mock me. I was such an idiot. I read *Great Expectations*. What was I thinking?

CHAPTER SIXTEEN

I followed the banker to the front lobby, clutching the book. How could I be so stupid? My inheritance? Yeah right. I checked my pocket, and pulled out my cash: a twenty, a five, and some ones. Why had I bought those clothes in Farmington?

The clerk held up the false counter for me, and I stepped through. I didn't want to open the book here. I had no idea what might be inside, and if it was a bunch of lewd pictures or something, I didn't want my blushing face caught on the casino's security cameras. Of course, I had enough latex makeup on for any blushing to be completely hidden… at least on one side of my face. Damn scales.

Recap: I ran away from home, chased kidnappers with my best friend—in a stolen car—and all of it for a stupid, worn out journal.

A man in a black suit jumped in front of me. I stepped back on instinct, but his fist slammed into my chest. Air exploded from my lungs, and pain shot through my limbs. He watched me sailing through the air calmly, as if he punched teenage girls every day. I crashed into the mannequin of John Wayne. Thousands of pieces fell to the ground as I crashed to a halt.

"Not John!" the desk attendant screamed.

My lungs ached for air, but I couldn't draw a breath. I panicked. Could lungs collapse? I lay stunned, trying to breathe, and Dr. Targyne walked toward me, nodding. Another unicorn, dressed in a black FBI suit, stood behind him. They had that clean, polished, special agent look about them.

"Goddamned dragons ruining the whole bloody planet," he said. "Traitors, every last one of you."

My head rolled from side to side as I looked for help. The desk attendant had his hands to his mouth as if trying to hide the fact he wanted to cry about his life-sized doll.

John–the troll, not the mannequin–struggled to keep his hand over Beth's mouth. She fought back, but John had her pinned. Behind them, Bob and the third troll slunk toward the nearest exit.

That asshole wrote her poetry, and now he's kidnapping her!

My lungs burned with the need for oxygen, and agony clawed up my chest.

Dr. Targyne's eyes grew wide as his gaze settled on my hands. "What's this?"

The other unicorn stared for only half a second, before leaping on me. He punched my cheek, and my head slammed back into the broken mannequin. Air surged into my lungs, and he tore the book free from my hands.

Fire erupted from my mouth, burning my teeth as it rushed out in angry gouts of superheated death. The smell of ammonia filled the air. Flames slammed into the unicorn's face, and his hair caught on fire. Screaming, he dropped to the carpet, slapping his head with his hands and the book.

Just as I sat up, Dr. Targyne kicked me in the jaw. My head snapped back and hit the ground again. Something sharp dug into my side; I'd forgotten I had my backpack on.

Darkness swirled in my vision; I fought to keep my eyes open as the pain in my head surged, my heartbeat thundering away in my ears.

I didn't hear them anymore. I scanned the room with blurry vision, but they were gone. When my head hit the ground, I must have blacked out. How long had I been unconscious? Seconds? However long, it was enough. The unicorns were gone. John still struggled with Beth, but the other two trolls were already through the door. Beth's arm came free, and she elbowed John in the face.

John wrenched her hand back. "I'm just trying to help!"

"Stop helping me!" Beth stomped on his foot, and he released her. In a flash, Beth raced to me.

John looked from me to the exit, then swore. He threw down the crash bar and disappeared into the noontime sun.

"You okay?" Beth asked.

"He took it," I said.

"What? What did he take?"

"I don't know. A book, I think. It was mine." It was mine, and I needed it like I needed water when I was thirsty. The book was part of me, an extension, and someone else had control over it. It might be part of a broken dream, but it was still mine. The fury stoked the fire inside, and my stomach cramped on the roiling pain in my gut. I would be sick soon.

Beth's face dropped into a stone mask. "Those jerks steal everything."

With one hand, she pulled me to my feet and propelled me toward the door. She threw it open, and I looked around. Bob and the other troll lay on the asphalt of the parking lot in a lake of blood. John stood over them, but he didn't look worried, just angry. "They took the truck!"

"Which way?" Beth asked. John pointed. I was having a hard time following the conversation, and my brain refused to catch up. Beth dragged me to the car and dropped me into the passenger seat. My backpack caught, and for a moment, I thought about taking it off, but Beth started pressing against my pockets, and I returned my attention to her.

"Come on, Allyson, I need the keys."

I reached into my pocket and gave over the keys, but I had to focus on not throwing up in the car.

Beth rammed the gearshift into reverse and floored it. No bunny-hop for Beth.

What the hell? "You didn't tell me you could drive."

"You never asked." Beth threw the shifter into first and peeled out of the parking lot, barely missing John and the other trolls.

Already, the two on the ground were showing signs of life. Maybe gunshots couldn't kill a troll.

I had to grab the roll bar to keep from falling out of the seat as Beth took the corner too fast. The tail end of the car swung out in a dangerous arc, and Beth slammed the accelerator just as the squealing tires were pointed in the right direction.

"There." I pointed at the disappearing van.

The engine roared as Beth drove it past its happy place before shifting. The car briefly let up as she jammed the shifter into gear and floored it. The acceleration pushed me into the seat, and I pulled on the seatbelt, not bothering to take off my backpack.

Bikes roared to life along the road, pouring out of the side streets. They filled the road behind us like an angry mob of bees. The sharp clean scent of water filled the air, like clouds or fog.

Clouds. They were gryphons. The MGB stayed ahead of the bikes, and the truck rushed into view.

"Now what?" Beth yelled.

"Just get me close enough to get inside."

A small part of me gawked at my words. Get inside? How would I do that? Fly? Not unless these scales suddenly turned into wings. But a deeper part of me uncoiled with the need to get back what was mine. They had my aunt. They had Steve. They had the book. And, no matter what was in that book, it was mine. I wanted it back. My lungs burned, so I knew I'd have a weapon, if only I could keep from actually puking until afterwards.

By the time I could easily read the writing on the van, we were already well out of town. Beth tore up the two-lane desert highway and pulled to the right of the van, driving on the shoulder.

I undid my seatbelt and climbed onto the seat. I watched for an opportunity to grab the truck, or somehow get into the cab, but there were no handholds. The van swerved toward us, and Beth dodged to the right. The tires hit the bumps on the side of the road, rattling my teeth. The burned unicorn rolled down the window. He held a gun in one hand, and the van veered toward us again. As it swerved, my muscles bunched, and I leapt with every scrap of power in my legs.

By luck and chance, I sailed through the open window into the lap of the gun-toting unicorn. A shot rang out in the truck, and at almost the same instant, a bullet hit something in the cab. I twisted onto my back and kicked the burned unicorn in the head. My book bounced on the dashboard. It popped into the air as the speeding van hit a bump, and I caught it.

"Get her out of here!" Dr. Targyne yelled. He threw a punch at my head, but he was distracted by trying to keep the van on the road. All around, motorcycles with angry gryphons swarmed. Another gunshot hit something in the cabin.

The doctor ducked. "Shit! They're shooting!"

The burned unicorn dropped an elbow into my gut, and I slammed my heel into what I hoped was his crotch. He moved under me, grabbing the waist of my jeans. Wind whipped into the cab, and he yanked me toward the door. As I slid across the unicorn, I caught the edge of the door, clinging for dear life. Pavement sped by with nothing between me and the ground that would tear me to pieces at this speed. The MGB roared up next to the van, but it was too far away to reach.

The unicorn kicked my sternum, and the spasm rolled up my arm. I couldn't hold both the book and the car. The doorframe slipped through my fingers. The world slowed as I fell to what was certainly my death. I swiped out for anything, but the kick had propelled me away from the van. I unleashed a stream of fire at the unicorns, one last hurrah before I died of road rash.

I tensed as the air rushed around me, and then my calves hit something hard. I fell into the passenger seat of the MGB, feet dangling over the door, head practically in Beth's lap.

"Gotcha!" she said.

Adrenaline pumped through my body, and I unleashed a triumphant scream. Take that, stupid monohorns! I pulled my legs into the car, and Beth sped ahead of the now smoking van. "You're awesome!"

"I know," Beth said, her indestructible smile lighting the way. She shifted again, pushing the car's engine dangerously, but the more distance we had, the better.

A gun fired, and the tire exploded. We slammed into the dashboard, and the car fishtailed dangerously. Beth fought for control, but we spun out into the sagebrush on the shoulder. Clouds of dust swirled in the air, blocking the road. The ever-present desert wind cleared the dust, and the sand rolled off the windshield in sheets. The car had come to a stop facing the moving van.

Flames leapt from the side of the van. It sat in the sandy shoulder of the road, the unicorns desperately trying to put out the fire. The swarm of gryphons drove past–would that be a flight? A flock? A wing?–followed by two Porsches speeding up the interstate.

A bullet rang off a nearby rock. Then I heard the gun shot.

"Are they shooting at us?" Why did I ask stupid questions like that?

Beth slouched down behind the steering wheel as another bullet pinged nearby. "What do you think?"

My response got lost in the roar of Harleys as the gryphons came to a stop around us.

"What are you waiting for, an invitation?" Reggie yelled. "Get on. Hurry!"

I popped open the door, and ducked down like I'd seen people do in movies, but really, what did that do other than concentrate my vital organs in one area? Beth beat me to the back of Reggie's bike, but another gryphon waved me over.

I stuffed the book into my backpack as I dodged over to the bikes.

"Hurry up!" the nearest one yelled, but I made sure to zip my backpack shut.

I swung my leg over the back and clutched the bike. Before I could find the pegs for my feet, the bike took off, rumbling beneath me. I leaned in close, and mimicked his body movement. The bike pack roared down the highway. The silver Porsche tore up the road behind us, and gunmetal gray flashed from the driver's side of one of the cars.

As we sped away, the unicorns made some headway on the fire in the moving van. A knot in my chest released. My aunt wouldn't be burned to death by *my* fire.

But we were still running, and my aunt was back there, in that van. My aunt and Steve, Beth's only hope at redemption.

The motorcycle pack split, and the second pack fell back while the rest of my group flew down the road as fast as their bikes could go. The engine burned my legs when they touched the side, putting me in the awkward position of trying to hold on without touching anything. The silver car caught up to the rearmost part of the bike pack. One of the bikes tumbled end over end, and the car broke free of the group.

The whine of sports bikes tore through the air, rising in pitch. I whipped my head forward and saw three racing motorcycles, red, yellow, and orange. The riders wore leathers and helmets to match the bikes. The three spun around in front of the gryphon pack at a crossroad, skidding to a halt. The pack stopped.

"Get on the red bike, quick," said the gryphon driving my bike.

I jumped down and dashed the two feet to the other bike. The rider bent over the handlebars, keeping the engine warm as I flung my leg up and over the back. My butt barely hit the seat before he gunned it. I had to grab his waist or fall off the back, and the bike just kept going faster. I stole a glance behind us. The pack broke up going in all directions. Beth, clinging to the back of the bright yellow bike, sped down a different road.

I struggled to turn my head forward against the drag of the wind. I could only open my eyes to slits as the wind pummeled them, and tears streamed down my face. My hair whipped around wildly. I couldn't afford to let go of the rider–pilot, really, considering how fast we were going–to fix my hair. The desert blurred by, and I just closed my eyes and leaned into the biker. I concentrated on keeping down my paltry breakfast, but I'd breathed fire. I would be sick soon. We quickly outdistanced the other bikes. The engine roared as he pushed it to some ungodly speed.

After what felt like hours but was probably more like five minutes, he turned down a badly paved road and stopped the bike behind a barren hill. Turning his head toward me, he flipped up the visor of his helmet, revealing eyes the color of the sky.

My heart skipped.

"Fix your hair, it keeps hitting me," he said.

I didn't trust myself to speak, so I nodded and pulled my hair back and started to braid it.

My stomach did a barrel roll to the right.

I kicked my leg over the back of the bike, but I missed and nailed him in the back. I fell in the dust, but the sickness took command of everything else. I turned away and heaved. My body had lost control.

He pulled off his helmet and set it on the seat as he got off the bike. "Are you okay?"

When I was certain I could keep my stomach in check, I turned back to the gryphon. He had short, curly blond hair, and a lean build, enough muscle to be athletic, but not so much that he would be mistaken for a body builder.

Puking in the dust, and that's how I meet the hot guy?

I hate you, world.

He held out a hand and helped me stand, looking me over, his brow furrowing as he took stock of my less than stellar condition. I didn't know what to say. Thank you? Sorry?

He tilted his head to the side and reached out to touch my face.

I jerked back, whipping my hand up to the latex shield I'd created. Somewhere along the way, the cover-up had started to come off. My scales were visible.

I pressed my hand over my cheek. "Crap!"

He smiled. "It's okay, the first molt sucks for everyone."

"Molt?"

139

"Yeah, my first set of feathers scarred. It was worse than chicken pox." He pulled off his glove. Rows of dots scared the back of his hand, like ostrich hide. "See?" He put his glove back on and narrowed his eyes. "So, if you don't mind my asking, what are you?"

"Dragon." My eyes widened a little… I'd never told anyone that before, yet I answered without hesitation.

"Dragon? I didn't know there were any left."

"I didn't either. Well, not until, like, four days ago." I shrugged an apology for my ignorance.

"Oh, man, you didn't even know? Harsh." He held out his hand. "I'm Felix."

"Allyson," I said, putting my hand in his.

He pulled my hand up and kissed it. "M'lady," he said, with a lopsided smile.

I blushed, but couldn't think of anything to say.

Felix cocked his head toward the road. "We'd better go. I think I hear a car."

I turned my head to listen, and heard it too. "How far do we have to go?"

He shook his head. "Not far, but we have to leave a lot of false trails in case someone is trying to find us. You ready?"

CHAPTER SEVENTEEN

I clung to the back of the motorcycle and tried not to think about how I was clutching the racing suit of a really hot guy. And he could really ride a motorcycle.

The landscape sailed by, but the sun touched the horizon before he pulled off the paved highway and drove up a steep dirt road. It switched back up the side of a mountain, twisting between trees, until we came out at the saddle of the mountain. A slice of the sun still illuminated the land, lighting up the valley and the rows of mountains north and south.

The golden-red light caught in the grey rocks, casting the land in pink. Felix stopped and flipped up his visor to watch the sun go down. We said nothing, just sat in the crook of a mountain watching the sky. When the sun disappeared behind the horizon, my stomach growled.

Felix turned around to meet my gaze, his blue eyes crinkled at the corners. "I guess we should get you some food. All the stories say hungry dragons are dangerous." He winked and kicked the bike forward to get started again.

The road went up along the ridge of the mountain and into a large stand of pine trees. Log cabins huddled under the canopy of giant trees like a logging camp, complete with people tending barbeque pits. A group stacked wood against a cabin, while another fixed a roof. Around a giant stone pit, a horde of men and woman roasted a side of beef, and the garlic and herb spices filled the air. My stomach roared its approval of the coming meal.

I hadn't eaten since earlier that morning.

Felix drove through and parked at a central building with metal siding and large roll up doors. The inside was paved in smooth concrete. Bikes of every color, style, and creed lined the walls. There were racks for holding motorcycles, but most of them sat around the wall, kickstands in place. One sat in a rack in the center. The front tire fork was twisted like a giant had squashed it in its hand. Felix stopped and backed it into a slot in a row of motorcycles. These bikes had sponsor stickers. It wasn't just a racing suit he wore. He raced bikes for real.

The engine cut, and the garage went quiet. I put my foot down and slid off the bike. My legs felt shaky from the adrenaline and riding all afternoon. Felix kicked his leg over the handlebars and pulled off his helmet.

"You race?" I asked like an idiot.

He smiled. "Yeah, I'm still qualifying for circuit, getting points and sponsors." His face darkened. "We had a team." His eyes flicked to a bright green racer down the line.

"What happened?"

"They didn't come back; they just disappeared."

Steve's face flashed through my mind, as Reggie's words floated back across my thoughts. *Just like my boy,* he'd said. Was Reggie's son hooked up to an IV somewhere like Steve and Aunt Agnes?

"We need to find out what happened," I said.

Felix unzipped his jacket and headed for the bay doors without a word. I followed, not knowing where else to go. My hand went to my cheek. Crap, did I have any makeup in my backpack? I pulled my hair out of my jacket and unbraided it, letting it fall over my face; black hair and shadows might do the trick. Then again, these people had children in feathers—would they even flinch at a couple of scales?

I wound my fingers through my hair. Better safe than chased down by a gryphon motorcycle gang.

Felix strode through a Frisbee game, pausing just long enough to avoid the flying disc. I had to jog to keep up, but I did not want to be left alone in this crowd of strangers. Not that I knew Felix any better than the rest of them, but I felt like I'd bonded with him while racing through the desert roads, evading raging unicorns.

My backpack bounced as I jogged, and whatever was at the bottom jabbed my side again. He walked up to a large building, at least three stories high, built in a rustic log cabin style. Tree trunks held up the vaulted roof on an oversized porch, and three large balconies fanned out from the second and third floors. A group of people sat in chairs on the porch, hair disheveled and skin sand blasted. From the dirt and the sweat streaks, these had to be some of the bikers.

As we walked up the steps to the porch, Beth emerged from a sliding glass door. "He's awake," she said to the bikers sitting in a circle.

They sagged with relief, letting out long sighs. Two stood up and headed back inside.

"Beth?"

"You're back!" She crossed the porch and scooped me up in a bear hug that should have broken ribs. "I was getting worried."

"We had to loop around the mountain to get back," Felix said.

"Your Pop's inside, Felix." A man from the circle said. "He's with your uncle."

"What's wrong?" Felix shot through the door, leaving me on the porch with Beth.

The others watched him go, then turned back to me. "So what's all the hub bub? What've you girlies done to rile up the unicorns?"

"It's complicated," I said.

They roared with laughter. "It's unicorns, girl. Of course it's complicated."

Before I could think up a proper retort, Reggie stuck his head out. "Beth, why don't you bring your friend inside? We need to talk."

Thank God. I didn't want to talk in front of the peanut gallery. Besides, what would I say? The unicorns think Beth kidnapped someone so they want to kill her, but really it was those other trolls, not Beth? Oh, and my father might be trafficking unicorns? I'm sure

143

they'd be real understanding. The gryphons might be entertained by the mix up, but those unicorns were shooting real bullets.

And I'd seen the damaged bike. Someone was probably in the hospital. No one was going to be in a forgiving mood. I followed Beth inside, keeping my head down so my hair would hide most of my face. Candles lit the lodge. A woman wearing a khaki uniform with patches on her sleeve and a broad brimmed hat sat on a couch. Next to her, a man wearing camouflage and combat boots with a trucker hat fiddled with a knife. He stopped playing with the knife to peer at some papers on the coffee table. Two men in racing leathers hovered near the roaring fireplace. Everyone looked up as we came in, their gazes on me as I walked through the lounging area.

"Is she really a dragon?" someone whispered.

Reggie turned on his heel. "Shut it! She's a guest."

Crap, they hate me, and I haven't even done anything!

Well, nothing except get someone riding a bike hurt.

Did they hate dragons for some ancient slight or war? In the diner, the gryphons just opened fire on the monohorns; what would they do to a dragon?

I raised my hand to my face to cover my scales.

Beth grabbed my shoulder. "Come on," she hissed.

We walked down a hall and into a huge room. A vaulted ceiling rose above the bed, and a cedar headboard with twisted branches extended up the wall. The bedspread matched the painting on the wall, and a little statue sat on the bedside table.

Felix perched on the edge of the bed, holding the older man's hand. There were bandages over most of the man's skin.

"You brought her in?" he asked.

"I couldn't leave her outside for the vultures," Reggie said.

"That's probably better anyway. Safer."

I wanted to wave a sign that said *I'm in the room.* Instead, I crossed my arms. "Is there a problem with me?"

"Only that you're the daughter of a traitor," the man on the bed said.

Felix looked down sharply. "What are you talking about, Dad?"

His father pointed at me. "That's David's girl. Can't you see it?"

Felix looked up from his father, meeting my gaze. His eyes narrowed.

Paralyzed by those sky-blue eyes, my brain choked on the information. *My dad.* They knew my dad.

And they hated him.

Felix's jaw clenched. He looked at the ground. His whole body tensed as he took a deep breath. When he looked up again, his face was set in a stone-like mask.

"I didn't know David was a dragon," he said, forcing the words through clenched teeth.

"You knew my father?" They were the wrong words, but my world was spinning out of control. How could these people know the father I'd never met? Not even once. It was so incredibly unfair.

Reggie cocked an eyebrow and huffed out a puff of laughter. "No, I didn't know him. I just thought I did."

I held my tongue, but my need to know twisted through my gut.

"Snakes shed their skin," Felix said.

Did he just compare my father to a snake?

Reggie shook his head. "If only he'd been a snake. Snakes can't change their stripes."

Felix shot me a glance from the corner of his eyes before turning his attention to his father. "Can we trust her?"

I blinked. "I don't understand. What happened? What aren't you telling me? And what the hell is going on around here? Who are you people with your secret hideaway and your motorcycles and guns and 'oh, you're a traitor's daughter?' I've never even gotten a birthday card from him!" Drained of words, I tried to catch my breath. Deep in my gut, the burning sensation raged to life.

Silence held for a few heartbeats, then Reggie and Felix's father both roared in laughter, heads tossed back. Stupid gryphons.

Reggie had to wipe a tear away from his eye he laughed so hard. "She sounds just like him, too."

Felix's father let out a deflating 'ho, ho, hah,' and my face jumped from hot to nuclear.

"She does." He turned to focus on me. "It's your father we have issue with, not you, girl."

Felix furrowed his brow.

"My name is Allyson. And why would you even bring me here if you hate my father so much?"

"Careful, girl, you're running hot, and unless you're a phenomenal liar, you've never met your father. We aren't fools. Lying bastard isn't a genetic trait like scales," Reggie said pointing at my face.

My cheeks burned, which probably only made the scales stand out more. "You knew?"

"There aren't that many dragons in the world. I thought I recognized you at the diner. That's when I called in back-up," he said nodding to the man on the bed. "Dragons and unicorns can get pretty volatile."

"Volatile?"

"They wouldn't hesitate to kill a dragon if it was in their way," the man on the bed said. He looked at me and shook his head. "I'm Giuseppe–Joe for short–and you've met my brother Reginald." He turned back to Felix, who still avoided my gaze. "Help her get some food and settled down for the night, we'll talk in the morning. And try to keep your trap shut. The place'll be crawling with rumors soon enough."

Felix stood, frowning, then pushed past Beth and me. "This way."

Beth turned to follow him.

"If you can spare some more time, Bethany, I'd like for you to stay," Reggie said.

I met Beth's gaze. She raised an eyebrow at me, and I shrugged back. Her lips pressed together into a thin line and she gave me a watery smile before squeezing my shoulder. In anyone else, that would have caused a broken bone, but I guessed dragons were hard to break. My shoulder stung from her squeeze as I followed Felix back out to the lounging area.

"How's your father?" the ranger woman asked Felix.

"He'll be okay. I didn't know troll blood worked like that."

The woman nodded, then gave me a piercing look, leaning closer to Felix as she held my gaze. "Is she…?"

Felix looked away. "We're not supposed to talk about it."

The ranger nodded her head. "She is, then. I'll come with you."

"Thanks, Aunt Bea, but that's not necessary."

"And you know just how to make a girl feel comfortable surrounded by a mob of bikers?" She waited for an answer, but Felix rolled his eyes. "That's what I thought. Go see if your father has any orders for the clan. I'll take care of the girl."

Take care of the girl. I might as well have been a horse that needed to be fed and watered and groomed. Of course, the conversation was whispered. Maybe they thought I couldn't hear them.

Felix turned back to look at me. His brow tightened, and the muscle in his jaw twitched. His eyes focused on something past me and he studied the floor, nodded, and patted his aunt on the shoulder before turning to go.

What happened to the guy who teased me about being a hungry dragon? How could knowing who my father was change that, especially when *I* didn't even know my father? It's not like my dad was some sort of Hitler or anything.

Well, at least, I hoped not. I guessed my father could be—I knew less about him than I did about our last landlord.

"I'm Beatrice." Felix's aunt held out her hand.

I watched Felix retreat for a second longer before turning back to Beatrice. I shook her hand. "Allyson."

"Pleased to meet you," she said, then leaned in. "Whatever you do, try not to mention your father or your last name. There are some hard feelings around here."

"What happened?" I asked.

"I'll tell you after we get you some food. I doubt that feather-headed boy took the time to give you so much as a cracker."

I shook my head.

Laughing, she winked. "Boys."

Yeah, boys.

She led me outside. Around the fire pit, gryphons laughed at jokes as they piled their plates with salad, bread rolls, and barbeque. Kids chased each other, squealing as part of their games, and mothers tried in vain to pull children to some of the picnic tables to eat their dinner.

"This," Beatrice said, waving her hands to indicate the whole encampment, "is the Aerie. The big house is the Lodge."

"Everything looks really new," I said.

"The old Aerie burned down almost eight years ago."

"That's terrible."

She glanced back at me over her shoulder, but we arrived at the roasting pit before she could say anything else. My stomach rattled my ribs with its grumbling. The smell of the barbeque made my mouth water, and I couldn't wait to eat. Beatrice sliced a thick piece of meat off and plopped it onto a plate, then piled potatoes and salad on one side, and topped the whole thing with a bread roll. She thrust the plate into my hands. "I'm sure you'd rather eat in private, so we'll head over to the unused cabins."

Holding a plate of barbeque was torture. My stomach demanded attention, but she kept walking through the camp. I barely heard what she said as we walked, so focused on making my feet go forward and not falling into my food.

"The fire killed the matriarch and her daughter, so the clan went to her daughter's husband, as she had no other daughters." Beatrice kept walking while talking, as if giving a tour at a park. I hurried to keep up, but I didn't want to spill my food. When we were far enough away from the fire pit that only the occasional gryphon kid was around, she stopped, gazing out at the last streaks of color in the sky.

The pines broke, opening up to a ledge of rocks sticking out over a cliff. Wind whistled through the trees, making the needles moan.

She turned to me, blinking expectantly. "The man who started the fire was named David."

David. My father.

Beatrice nodded slowly.

A cold stone fell into the place my stomach occupied. My father had started a fire that killed gryphons.

All my life, I'd dreamed about who my father was. In some dreams, I'd make him a member of the military, fighting for our nation. I tried careers on my father like dresses on a paper doll. I'd imagined he worked for the CIA for the longest time, and that was why Mom and I moved all over the place. I never once imagined he'd be anything but some sort of hero. In my mind, he was always saving the day or keeping the world safe from harm.

Never had I considered the possibility he'd be anything but a great person.

And he was actually an arsonist?

But if he was a dragon, maybe it was an accident.

"A lot of people died that night. The fire was huge; it made the headlines. You can still see the scorched area from airplanes." She gazed into the darkness. "The matriarch's daughter died. She was Felix's mother." She turned and started walking again.

I followed, scared to ask any questions. And this was why Felix suddenly hated me. My father killed his mother.

Over her shoulder, Beatrice said, "I just thought you ought to know, seeing as how there are some strong feelings here about that night. I'd hate to see you bear the brunt of a crime not your own."

She stopped in front of a camping cabin like the ones at KOA. "Here you go. Flashlight'll be inside. See you in the morning."

And with that, Beatrice left me standing in the middle of the woods with a bunch of people who hated me because my dad had killed their pack leader.

My father was a murderer.

CHAPTER EIGHTEEN

I fumbled with the tray of food and found the doorknob on the cabin. Inside, the flashlight sat on a ledge next to the door. The cabin had four bunks and a table, with screens for windows. It wasn't likely to be warm. One of the bunks had a sleeping bag on it. I slid my backpack off and set it down on the bunk.

After fiddling with the light, I found the lever that turned it into a lantern and set it on the table. And to think, I ended up stuck on top of this mountain because of some stupid safe deposit box.

The book!

All the riding around on motorcycles and talk about my father had made me forget about it. I pulled out the tattered tome, and as an afterthought, fished around to find out what had been poking me in the back all day. The plastic knick-knack caught the light from the cheap flashlight, and almost sparkled. I set it on the table next to my plate, then took a bite of the barbeque before it got cold and clammy.

Too late.

Holding a piece of steak in one hand, I slipped the rubber band off the cover and opened it to the first page.

This book belongs to:

David Takata

I almost dropped my steak. My Dad's journal. My heart raced. I put down my food and wiped my hand on my jeans. I could clean them later. This might have all the answers to the questions I've been asking since I was four.

Turning the book over in my hands, I took a deep breath. It smelled vaguely like piñon and dust. My hands vibrated with the knowledge that this had belonged to my father. My father had held this in his hands. As I opened it again, I held my breath and I started to read.

At first he wrote about normal things, well, normal for a dragon. Flying and breathing fire–he didn't seem to suffer from the puking problem, but I'm only half. I skimmed through an entry where he wrote about my mother and accused my maternal grandmother of being racist. Apparently she didn't think a sweet Irish girl should be marrying a Japanese boy.

I wondered what she would have said if she'd known he was also a dragon.

The more recent entries were about a sword. He called it the Kornus Blade, but when he was being derisive or peevish, he called it the Narwhal Horn. It read like the travels of the Knights of the Round Table, searching for the Holy Grail. They never found the sword, and as they hunted for it, more people died. He hunted for it with gryphons, unicorns, and dragons. They needed the weapon to kill someone, though he never wrote down the name. They called him the Magic Thief.

An envelope fell out of the journal onto the table. Bright red wax sealed the envelope with the same symbol as on the cover of the journal. I picked it up. The seal glowed, and fire sprang up from the paper. I dropped it, and the flames extinguished. I touched it again, and the fire leapt up. I jerked my hand back, but where the fire had burned me, tiny blue scales covered my skin. I blinked at my hand, expecting something to change, but the scales just winked back in the flashes of light. Was I completely covered in scales just beneath the skin?

And how exactly did I get back to looking human? The monohorns and the gryphons could do it, why not me?

Still, the fire didn't burn my scales, so I picked up the envelope. Again, it popped into flames, and I opened it with one hand. I didn't want both hands to look like I had a run in with a D&D illustrator. A piece of paper fell out with a cloud of dust and the sharp smell of oregano. I picked up the paper with my scaled hand. I'd need a glove for it. Good god, I'd be like some 80s pop artist, wearing only one glove.

The paper appeared to be normal, and when I picked it up, it didn't try to torch off my hand. I unfolded it.

Dear Allyson,

I hardly know what to say. If you're reading this, then I'm almost surely dead. I don't expect you to forgive me. I know that you and your mother have had a hard life because of me, and I'm sorry. I'm not sorry I had a daughter, just sorry I can never be your father. I have fallen on dark times. We all have. My only hope is that Agnes has found a way to unleash the sword. It is our only hope.

Even now I can feel his will taking over. Never let a human touch the sokra *on your head. It's awful to feel them in your thoughts. If you hear nothing else, heed this advice: nothing is as terrible as an enemy in your* sokra. *By the time you read this, I will be gone, and I must ask you to do something terrible.*

Allyson, if I'm not already dead, tell Agnes to kill me. She won't want to, but I won't be me. She'll need to put the blade through my heart. She'll know which one. You must help her. She has been groomed for this fight her entire life. I've instructed her to give you this letter when you're old enough to help. That means she's probably standing right there. Give her a hug for me, please; she'll need it. I'm just sorry I can't be there to help. I'm sure this will be hard, but if everything Agnes has told me is true, you're as strong as your mother. You, of all of us, can do this.

I now have the information we need to take out our enemy, and that's why I've written this letter. His name is Kurt Stein, and he stole something from my great grandfather, your ancestor. He stole your grandfather's memories, forcing him to share his mind through his sokra. *All the knowledge of dragons passed down through thousands of years–magic, power, everything–he stole it. Now, Kurt has me, too. The other dragons are trying to kill him, but with the power of our ancestors flowing through him, he is invincible. He has taken other dragons, and with each one, his power grows. He can wield the magic of dragons. Kurt has an army of trolls, and no force the gryphons, unicorns, centaurs, or even the giants could assemble will stand the might of a troll army. Kurt has them enthralled.*

He used your grandfather's blood to make a spell to bind the trolls. They are not usually so violent.

He keeps the spell going through the blood of other Kin: the gryphons, unicorns, and even a phoenix. I wish I could tell you about your family and teach you to fly, but I'm sure Agnes is taking care of all that. I love you so much, and I've tried to protect you, but I've never managed to protect anyone. When Kurt first took me, he learned where a flock of gryphons lived. They had been my friends. I burned down the Aerie to keep them from Kurt, but he captured so many. I tried to warn off Hazel, but Kurt took her too. I don't know how much longer she can last, but I check on her, lying in that bed, her life sent to feed the very spell that holds me.

Kurt must be stopped, and the first step is to take me down.

Tell Agnes to kill anyone who stands between her and Kurt, especially me. Armed with the Kornus Blade, she can kill him. This is the moment everyone has sacrificed for. This is what we've all worked for. Do not falter at the finish line for me. Tell Agnes. Tell her everything. Remind her of my wishes. I'd rather die than remain in the thrall of a wizard.

I wish I could say more, but he grows near and I lose my will. Good luck.

I love you.

Your father,

David

My hands trembled and I dropped the letter onto the table. Confirmation in my father's own handwriting. He lit the Aerie on fire. On purpose.

My stomach twisted into knots, and I felt the fire rising in my gut. My father was a murderer. When I'd seen the letter, I'd hoped. My heart had soared with that hope. Now, it rolled in the embers of a dying dream.

He did it to save people from whoever this Kurt person was.

How could I help my Aunt Aggy now? She was on her way to San Francisco in a moving van, unless the unicorns had her. Would the unicorns kill her? Was it worse than if the trolls managed to steal the van back? And what about the sword? Where was the Kornus Blade?

153

Kornus, narwhal, there was something just at the edge of my mind, not quite making sense. Wasn't a narwhal a whale? The image of one flashed before my mind. It was my biology textbook from when I lived in Vermont. The whale was in a tank, at some place like Sea World, and a bright white horn struck out of the water, pointing at one of the handlers in a wet suit. People used to kill the narwhals for their horns. Was the Kornus blade made of narwhal horn?

Then the memory of Dr. Targyne's horn missing me by the width of a piece of paper flooded through me. It had sizzled with power and magic. What happened to a unicorn's horn when they died? Could such a thing be made into a sword? It would make a lousy sword. The horn of a unicorn spiraled, wobbling back and forth like really thin soft serve.

Just like that stupid knick-knack Aunt Aggy gave me.

I almost fell off the bed reaching for the chunk of Lucite.

It was way too small to be an actual unicorn horn, but I held it up to the light. It looked just like a unicorn's horn in miniature. A soft, golden glow came from the tiny sword. The Kornus Blade.

How could it be that small?

Magic?

My aunt had found the sword, but it was useless like this; a toy.

I searched the giant plastic—well, it couldn't be plastic—but it was no good in this form. Did Agnes know how to free the sword? I paced back and forth holding the thing in my hand. The smell of burnt paper from the envelope still filled the cabin. I waved my hands through the air to disperse the smell as I paced.

Could I break open the encasement? Would that set it free? Would it grow to full sized when it was set free?

I sat down on the bunk, thinking. If it broke, then I'd have nothing to fight whoever that Kurt Stein guy was. And my Dad wanted to kill him. He's going to start a war, but with who and for what? I stared at the chunk of plastic. If I couldn't get it out, the sword was as good as broken.

I looked for something to smash the plastic into, but only the table was nearby. I took the statue in my burned hand. If I was going to bloody my knuckles, I didn't want to expose any scales on my good hand. Holding the miniature sword high over my head, I smashed it down into the corner of the table. It dented the table with a terrible thud. My plate rattled, and I thought for sure I'd broken the sword. I pulled it up to see if I'd chipped anything, but there wasn't a scratch.

I scowled and smashed it down again, harder this time. Nothing. I beat the knickknack into the table as hard as I could. I pounded until my arm got sore.

The door burst open and Felix rushed inside, one hand on the doorknob and one hand on the door frame, eyes wide as his gaze quickly flicked around the room. His breath came in heavy gasps. "What's going on?"

I held the encased blade in one hand and stared back. "I, uh, well–"

"What's that?"

"None of your business." I hid the knickknack behind my back.

"What happened to your hand? And what is that smell?"

"That's none of your business either. And who just barges in on someone?"

He let go of the door and held his hands in front of himself, palms out, in a gesture of peace. "I thought you might be in trouble with all the banging."

"What?"

"It's just, you know, the smoke?" He focused on the ground, scuffing the toe of his boot across the floorboards.

"I don't understand, and no one explains anything." I threw my arms up and looked at the ceiling for a moment; the top of the cabin was actually a canvas tent. I looked back at Felix. He looked anywhere but at me, and his gaze fell on the letter.

"That's private," I said, snatching the paper from the table. "Haven't you heard of privacy?"

"I'm sorry, okay?" He ran his fingers through his short blond hair. "Can we start over? I thought you might be hurt, and it smells like fire and, well, worse."

Then it clicked. My eyes widened. The scent of something burning where it shouldn't be would probably set the whole herd of gryphons into a frenzy. "We can start over, just so long as you tell me what's going on."

He smiled, extending his hand, but when I reached out to shake on it, his gaze dropped to my newly exposed scales.

I sucked in a breath and yanked my hand back.

Felix quickly met my gaze, then thrust his hand into mine before I could slam it into my pocket.

"Look," he said, still gripping my scale-covered hand. "If you want to figure yourself out, you're going to have to accept the fact that you're a dragon, no matter how human you look."

"I'm half human," I said. Dumb, like clinging to a sinking raft. *Oh, I'm not all big bad dragon; I'm only half.*

"And half dragon. If you have more than about an eighth, you can manifest, though some people are stronger at it than others." He shook his head, and feathers sprouted, replacing his face and hair. A hooked beak took over where his mouth had been. Only his eyes remained the same, though the feathers were nearly the same golden color as his hair. He shook his head once more, returning to his human form again. He grinned. "It just takes practice."

"Holy crap!" I covered my mouth with my hand. "Uh, I mean, that's pretty amazing." I rubbed the scales on my hand. "I found out about this, like, four days ago. And then the letter." I shook my head, turning away from him.

"What letter?"

"My dad wrote me a letter."

Felix tensed. "I thought he died in the fire. That's what my father said." He took in a breath and nodded. "But if he was a dragon, he probably got out alive."

I flopped onto the bunk. "Yeah, it seemed like it was written after the fire." I stuffed the statue and the journal into my backpack, then zipped it shut. "Who was Hazel?"

Felix's face drained of blood. "Where did you hear that name?"

"Why, who is it?"

"Was it in that letter?" His eyes were wide, crazy.

"Are you going to explain anything?"

He took a deep breath and closed his eyes. "Fine, ask away."

"Who's Hazel?"

He sighed, his features pinched. When he spoke, his voice was hoarse. "She died. I'd rather not talk about it. Next question."

I chewed the inside of my cheek, but decided not to contradict him. "Who's Kurt Stein?"

Felix squinted, tilting his head, his eyebrows knitting together. "He's a racing sponsor. Our biggest, actually. Dad invited him up here to see the garage. We can get more money if Mr. Stein knows we can use it. That's why the shop is so clean right now. Usually, it's half disaster, half organized chaos."

"He's coming here?"

"What's the big deal? He's a money guy from San Francisco."

"What does he do?" I asked.

"Some sort of investment banker, why?"

"It can't be the same guy."

"As who? You're not making any sense, Allyson."

I jumped up and paced the floor again. I walked past the battered table four times before Felix grabbed my shoulder. "What aren't you telling me?"

"It's not like I know if it's even true."

"Why don't you tell me, and I'll be the judge?"

Was this some elaborate hoax? It felt like walking home with Steve all over again. But that hadn't been a joke. I took a deep breath to steady my head and ease the rising fire.

"In the letter, it said Mr. Stein was raising an army of trolls."

He laughed. "That's ridiculous. How could anyone control an army of trolls, let alone a room of them? They're not the brightest bunch, no offense to your friend."

"She's only half," I said, automatically.

"You're pretty hung up on half and whole."

I shrugged. "It seems important to acknowledge the human component. Besides, those trolls were way stronger than Beth, and she crumbles rocks in her bare hands. And just think about it, an army that heals before it dies of a gunshot wound? Can you imagine?"

His brow furrowed, and he shook his head. "He's an investment banker, not a James Bond villain."

"Everyone needs a hobby."

Felix rolled his eyes. "Oh come on, he's been a sponsor for years."

Fire burned in my lungs, rolling through my chest. "Oh, yeah? How long?"

"I don't know exactly. Four or five years, practically forever."

"Before your cousin disappeared?"

His body tensed, and his eyes hardened. "What are you saying?"

"I'm saying this guy uses people like us to fuel his army-controlling spell."

He tossed his head back and laughed. "Spells? You think there's magic, too?" He cackled with mockery.

My stomach cramped, and the burning need to set the world on fire danced up my torso. I ground my teeth instead. Finally, he made a show of stopping his laughter. He was enjoying my discomfort, and I wanted to punch him. But I was the daughter of the devil as far as they were concerned. I couldn't give them the satisfaction.

I held his gaze, willing him to listen. "Last week, I would have laughed just like that if you'd told me you were a gryphon."

He clenched his jaw, and a muscle jumped along the side of his face. "I only came here to tell you my father wants to see you at first light. Good luck with that." He spun around and slammed the door.

I sprinted after him into the night.

158

"Wait! Damn it, you didn't explain anything." I jogged to catch up, but he had a head start. Most of the crowd around the fire pit had already turned in for the night, and it was just me chasing some boy I barely knew through the trees. The forest ended, and the night sky opened up over the ledge before me.

Felix jumped off the edge.

"No!" I sprinted to the edge of the rock and searched through the darkness for him, expecting to find a broken body in the ravine below.

As my eyes adjusted, Felix flew away against the starry night sky.

CHAPTER NINETEEN

Two Days Before

My mind conjured images and visions of what the gryphon bikers would do to the daughter of a traitor, keeping me awake all night.

On top of being the daughter of David Takata, I'd now also accused some beloved bringer of money of kidnapping their people.

Yup, they'd fry me for sure.

And every time I thought about Felix leaping off that cliff, my stomach twisted into rabid ferrets. Did he jump to get away from me, or had it been an invitation to follow him?

My hand was covered in scales instead of skin–another thought that kept me tossing and turning. The edges of the skin had scabbed over, but I had no clue how to make it grow back over my hand. I searched my dad's journal for clues on manifestation, but of course, he was all dragon and probably learned how to look human as an afterthought.

I turned my hand over and studied it in the dark. The more I watched, the more my scales glistened, like they were drying; the more air they were exposed to, the shinier they became. As I watched my hand in the scant light of the moon, I could almost imagine my whole body covered in the sapphire gems.

I cut those thoughts from my mind and turned on the flashlight.

In my backpack, my emergency makeup waited. If I couldn't sleep, the least I could do was cover the scales on my face. If gryphons didn't like dragons, and only a handful of people knew what I was, I should try to keep it that way. Stupid secrets. Besides, makeup was normal. I could use some normal.

I put on my shirt and pants before I pulled out the tiny compact, setting it on the table so I could see my face. I painted the latex on with a tiny brush like they put in finger nail polish. As I waited for it to dry, I couldn't shake the feeling that I was painting on a mask, and Felix said I should find peace with my dragon half.

But it was easy for him to embrace his gryphon side. He was born into a community of gryphons, surrounded by them. They even had a special camp in the mountains. I'd found out I was a dragon days ago, and my aunt, my only other contact with dragons, had never once mentioned it.

I should hate Felix for running off without answering any of my questions. But if I hated him, why did I scream when he went over the cliff? I just couldn't pin down anything about him.

The latex did the job well, filling in the cracks between my scales like skin. I added another coat to be sure, but it was practically overkill. And then, of course, I only had my touchup foundation, not the pancake I used at home.

Did I ever get to go home? Not Albuquerque, but would Mom's next job be the one? The one where I'd get to join the drama club and build up some extracurricular activities to put on my college applications?

Dawn colored the sky, and I found myself eyeing last night's dinner. I needed to eat something. Anything. And if it was already light out, then I needed to go find Felix's father so he could tell me all about being a cranky, old, fire-puking betrayer.

I tried to calm myself with a few cleansing breaths, but it only stoked the fires still rolling in my belly. It didn't seem fair that Felix could just fly away. I'd told him what I knew, and he still hadn't explained anything.

When I stepped out of the cabin, the cold mountain air bit at my arms, but I didn't go back for my jacket. No one else was up yet. At the stone fire pit, the ashes from the previous night's barbeque blew in the soft breeze. Through the trees, I spotted the garage and the Lodge, and made my way to the log cabin of doom. To the west, the rocky ledge where Felix had flown away taunted me. Had he come back last night, or was he curled up on the cliffs in his feather-headed form?

A gryphon flew overhead, landing on a balcony of the Lodge. It hit the wooden deck with a not-so-subtle *thunk*, turned to look at me, and opened its beak. I expected a squeal or a squawk, but instead, he spoke.

"Meet me on the rocks," he said.

I recognized the voice from last night as Felix's father, Joe. I nodded, and the gryphon took to the air in three pounding wing beats. When I got to the rocks, my previous suspicions were confirmed. The boulders jutted out over a steep cliff, more than a hundred feet down to the first ledge. I stepped back from the edge. When I turned around, Felix's father stood behind me, and for a wild second, I wondered if he was going to try to push me off.

I dropped into a crouch, and the fires surged within me.

His leather vest tightened as he laughed, and his whiskers curled. His beard mimicked the shape of a gryphon's beak. Still, his laugh was hearty; it had none of the mocking Felix had last night. "You startle pretty easily for a dragon. Aren't your kind supposed to be stoic, calm, and wise?"

"Uh, no?"

He laughed again.

"Look, I don't mean to be rude, but if you brought me out here just to mock me, then why don't you round everyone up and get a good solid laugh out of the way."

"No need to get your feathers up," he said, then sighed. "You remind me of better times."

"Before all the kidnappings?"

"It seems I've been bad luck for my people." He hobbled over to me. "And I wouldn't try to push you off a cliff. You'd just fly back and bake me on the rocks. Only fools toy with dragons."

"I don't know how to fly."

He looked down at me sharply. "That's a shame. Is that why you wear so much makeup? To hide what you are? Or, just to hide yourself?"

"You sound like my mother."

"And where is she?"

I deflated in a sigh. "Worried sick about me in Albuquerque. I didn't want to tell her anything because the unicorns were spreading lies about Beth and me. They want to kill Beth because they think she's working with me and the other trolls to kidnap their people."

"Well, first things first." Joe handed over a cell phone. "Call your mother. I won't have her worrying, seeing as how the first thing the unicorns will do is leave her in the dark."

I held the phone, but I didn't want to make the call. I certainly didn't want to call my mother in front of this grizzly gryphon biker gang leader. I thumbed the number in and Joe walked away, pretending to give me privacy.

It rang and I prayed she wouldn't pick up. I could leave her a message. Yeah, that's what I'd do, a message. *Come on, come on, go to voicemail already.*

Mom never picked up the phone for strange numbers.

The line clicked softly and I deflated.

"This is Catherine."

"Mom?"

"Allyson? What's going on?"

"Mom, I'm..." *I'm what? Okay? Am I? What am I supposed to say?* I have a letter from Dad and he wants Aunt Aggy to kill him with this special sword, but I can't get it out of its casing. Oh, and I need to stop an army of trolls because I think they're kidnapping people and making the unicorns crazy. Do you know anything about magic? Because these gryphons are completely worthless on that end.

"Honey, where are you?"

That stopped me. I didn't really know. "Uh, somewhere in Nevada, I think."

"Are you hurt?"

Only my pride. "No, Mom, I'm okay. I'm with some people."

"Who?"

"Um, that's sort of hard to explain."

A brief silence hung on the phone. "Try me."

The steel in her voice traveled up to my defiance switch. "Fine, Mom, I will tell you the truth. I'm currently camped out in the center of the base camp for a huge biker gang. Think Hell's Angels but with gryphons instead."

I drew breath to keep going, but my mother cut me off. "Are you with Hazel?"

"Who's Hazel?" I asked.

Joe locked eyes with me.

"She was a friend of your father's. I was supposed to go find her if things ever got crazy."

I looked at Joe, and he watched me intently. They thought everyone from the fire died. But in the letter, my dad said he watched over Hazel. Was she still alive?

"Someone took her, I think. She isn't here. Did you want to talk to Joe? He's in charge now."

"When are you coming home?"

"I don't know, Mom, but you need to be careful around Dr. Targyne. He's not all together truthful." *But not to worry, Mom, he's a terrible shot.*

"Just come home, and we'll sort it all out. Please, Allyson, just come home."

The thought of home swept through me. Sleeping in on Saturdays and watching stupid movies. Eating TV dinners and messing around on the Internet. But somewhere in San Francisco, my father was working for one Mr. Stein. Soon, Kurt would have my aunt, too. What would he use his army of trolls for? Could he conquer the world?

Or did he just need to conquer my father?

"I'm sorry, Mom." I kicked a rock chip at my feet and it sailed over the edge of the cliff. "I can't come home. I have to find Dad." I pushed the button and hung up the phone.

Joe watched me, his mouth open.

"I think that went well. Next?"

Joe shut his mouth with a snap and took back his phone. "What games are you playing at, dragon?"

"I read it in a letter."

He held up his hand. "Don't say anything else. My people have keen ears. We should go somewhere more private."

I looked around, but we were alone. The rocks were bare, but there were trees nearby. "Where?"

He pointed across the valley to a peak. The mountain on the opposite side of the flat-bottomed valley looked a long way off.

"It's not like I can fly."

Narrowing his eyes at me, Joe nodded and smiled the kind of smile better suited to Santa than a biker gang leader. "I'll give you a lesson." He walked to me and put a fatherly arm around my shoulders. Together, we walked to the edge of the cliff. "Feel that wind?" he asked, holding out his arm.

Air welled up from the edge of the cliff, lifting stray hairs. I put my hand into the wind. "Sure, I feel the wind."

"Good, that'll help. Just don't fly into any rocks and you ought to be fine."

He shoved me in the center of my back, and I fell forward into the empty air. Wind tore at me as I plunged over the edge. Time slowed, and vivid details jumped out at me. The rocks below were layered and grey, and even as I tumbled through the air, I spotted sea shells imbedded in the same surface I would splatter across if I didn't figure out how to fly in two nanoseconds.

Fire rushed from my lungs with an overwhelming taste of ammonia, and I blew out a fireball, setting my shirt ablaze. The flames ate away at me, licking up my sides, fuelled by the rushing wind. Almost as suddenly, my burning clothes peeled away. A second set of arms unfolded from my shoulders. Air caught around my flapping arms.

Wings! I had wings!

Air scooped into my wings, but they couldn't stretch out like I'd imagined. It was like trying to run in a pair of really tight jeans.

With one last tear, something snapped free, and my wings sprang open.

I flapped frantically, and at the last minute, I veered away from the rocks. My claws scraped across the fossil-filled stone, and I pushed out into the air over the valley. The wind rushed around me, and I flailed desperately. My wings knew more than I did, however, and they carried me away from the cliff and spiraled down.

Joe flew next to me in his gryphon form. "Now, flap your wings to stay aloft."

I drew my wings down, and the surge yanked me to the left. With wings to catch the wind, the air suddenly had substance, like water, but it rippled around me unexpectedly. A tiny tweak of my wing sent me veering toward the ground, but I recovered before I hit dirt. I climbed through the sky until the air was cold, and we soared across the desert valley. I was free of gravity.

The distant mountains grew less distant, and Joe spiraled down onto the rocky crag at the top. He shouted directions, but the wind stole his words away before they reach me. He cleared the landing spot and watched expectantly.

I swooped down toward the mountaintop. The rocks rushed up at me, and I had a second of panic. If I missed, I'd brain myself on the rocks. If I made it, I'd brain myself on the rocks. I scooped my wings and curled up at the last minute. I'd lost a lot of height, so I pounded the sky with my wings, circling around for another try. As I came up again, I spotted a pile of feathers curled into the rocks just below the summit. Before I could think about remembering to say something, the peak came at me again. I back winged, scooping the air and flapping hard. I caught the edge of a boulder with my back leg, and I curled my toes over it, clutching tight. My claws squealed against the rock's surface, but held. I folded my wings back, and the airstream lost its purchase on me.

"Not bad for your first molt!" Joe yelled over the wind.

"Is that how you train all your children?"

He laughed. "No, just the ones with talent."

I blinked, but I had a desire to scratch my scales clean on the rocks. I sank to my belly, and moved across the stone to ease my itching. I wanted to roll like a dog but felt like that might somehow be considered rude. Instead, I surreptitiously smoothed my elbows along the rocks as though sweeping away stones and dust. The rock beneath was polished smooth, and as I pushed aside a pile of sand, I found a half buried scale the size of my head. It was dark blue and dull. The luster of it had faded in the sun, and one side was cracked.

"Your father came here often."

"This is his?"

"Yes. I come here and think about back then, and wonder what went wrong." He looked back toward the Aerie for a moment, before he turned his blue eyes on me. "So, tell me what happened. I've never heard his side of the story."

"I've never met him, you know that?"

"I do." His words came out in a puff of air that twitched up the feathers on the back of his head. "No flying creature would leave their children without knowing how to fly, not even a dragon. That, more than anything, tells me you've never met your father."

"How do you stay hidden?"

"Luck and tales. We don't fly during the daytime very often, and there's a risk."

"What if the government finds you?"

"There're no laws against being a gryphon. I studied law for a time. I even passed the Bar some years back."

The idea of the leather clad biker wearing a suit and buried in books made me laugh. A gout of flame escaped my snout. Joe ducked out of the way, smoothing back his feathers to keep them out of the fire. I snapped my jaw shut, and smoke tricked from my nostrils in lazy trails.

"You need to learn control," he said, feathers slicked back hard against his body.

"Sorry."

"Don't say you're sorry. Do the deed; learn control. You'll puke less after."

I felt something like the heated flush of blushing. "You know about that?"

"Your father complained about it."

"Did you know him well?"

"I knew his mother." His eyes searched the sky for the past, and I wished he could hand me his memories. Then he sighed, and, finding the sky empty of old friends, he turned back to me. "You're not the first dragon to sun on that rock."

"What was she like?"

"Your grandmother?" A laugh escaped his beak. "She was fierce, refined, beautiful–for a dragon–and motivated. She wanted to bring all the Kin together. She thought if we worked together we could overcome our differences and learn how to live with humans. In the open and everything. After she died, your father took up her cause for a time. That's when I knew him. He was like a darker copy of her, stormcast to her sunny day."

I held my breath and waited for more straws of my family to fall from the gryphon's beak. The wind moaned through the rocks, and the desert seemed like a very lonely place, full of terrible dark secrets. How could they live here? There was more life in Albuquerque, and that was full of dead lawns and dormant trees.

"I'd like to hear what you know of that night. It has long haunted me," he said. "I thought he was like his mother, and I've often

168

wondered if my folly was in trusting him as I believed in her."

"All I can tell you is what he wrote in the letter."

"I'm all ears."

"He said that he lit the fire because Kurt Stein knew where the Aerie was. He was trying to clear people out. His letter said Stein had captured Hazel, but she was growing weaker."

Joe closed his eyes. A deep keening noise rose from his throat, and I tilted my head.

"What did the letter say about Hazel?"

"It said she was weak, and being drained. He said he checked on her frequently, but Stein was using her blood to fuel a spell."

The feathers on top of Joe's head shot up like a cockatiel's. "Spell? What spell?"

"A spell to control the trolls and my father."

Joe hopped to his lionish feet and paced. "But what does an investment broker need with trolls?"

"In his letter, my father wrote that Stein had stolen my grandfather's memories."

Joe stopped pacing, his eyes wide. "Stein is the thief?" He looked back and forth, as if checking the sky for this evil figure. "We have to go, there's no time to lose."

"Wait!"

At the sound of Felix's voice, we both turned to the cliff's edge.

Felix hauled himself up over the edge, claws scarring the rocks in his hurry. He mantled his golden feathers. "What about Mom? Did he say anything about Lucia?" Felix's feathers glinted in the sun as they stood up and smoothed down like a dog perking his ears.

"Damn it, boy, we have more important things to do."

"More important than Lucia?"

Joe snapped his beak. "We have to move everyone. The whole clan. Today."

Felix's eyes darted from his father to me. "Did he say anything about Lucia?"

I shook my head.

Joe fretted, caught in his guilt. "I gave him directions to the shop. We have to hurry."

"I'm going after Mom and Lucia," Felix said.

"No. You'll help your clan, not chase dreams. There's no way to know if she's there, or even still alive."

"What if Jessie's with them?" Felix asked.

Joe stopped, and the tension that held his body reminded me of a bow, poised to shoot. "There was no mention of Jessie or Lucia. And the only–only!–mention of your mother said she was weak. That letter could have been written years ago." He curled his neck, tucking his beak into his chest, before shaking his enormous head. "No. We have a responsibility. We have to move the clan. Besides, where would you look?"

"Pier 22 1/2," I said.

They both looked at me as though surprised to see me still here. I shrank down to the stones.

"Felix, you don't know what you're talking about. The thief is very dangerous. Even if you went, you would have no way to defend yourself."

Felix ruffled his feathers. "I'd be going with a dragon." He pointed a paw at me. "She breathes fire!"

"She's just a girl, and the thief has power over her kind. Dragons don't come back." Joe turned to me. "It's what happened to your grandmother."

My mouth went dry, and the cruel desert wind stung my eyes. My grandmother. "She fought?"

Joe's brows drew together. "She thought we could change the world." He shook his head. "When the thief took her, she fought. The fire scorched the ground. So many people died."

Felix narrowed his eyes. "We're not trying to change the world, Dad. I just want to save Mom, and Jessie, and Lucia."

Eyes pinching shut, Joe shook his head. "No! He'd steal her, and then you'd just be fighting everything. We have to protect our people."

"But Dad–"

"No! I've been down this road before. We are going to protect the people we have." His breath came in a deep gulp, his voice cracking. He coughed, and when he spoke, he pitched his voice low and hard. "You have a duty to the clan. We will protect our own. And that's my final word. I forbid you to leave, even after we move the Aerie. I won't lose anyone else."

Felix wilted.

Joe pointed a claw at him. "Get back to the Aerie and start the preparations. I'll warn the centaurs." Joe looked at me for a minute. "Go with him, Dragon, and don't do anything stupid."

I nodded. Don't do anything stupid left plenty of room to do something dumb.

"Yes, sir," Felix said, and we watched as Joe stepped into the wind.

"We should go." Felix turned to me.

"I thought you didn't believe in magic."

Felix shook his head, his feathers flashing in the sunlight. "I don't care about magic. I just want my mother back."

CHAPTER TWENTY

I have a plan," Felix said, as we landed on the rock ledge at the Aerie. "Just be patient and help out."

He shifted to his human form, still wearing his racing leathers from the night before, then strode toward the trees.

I cleared my throat, but it came out as a deep growl.

He cast a glance over his shoulder at me. "What?"

"I've never turned back," I said.

"Oh." His eyes grew wider. "Oh. Ah, why don't you wait here and I'll be right back."

"I thought I wasn't supposed to let people know I'm... you know." I pointed at my head with one giant blue talon.

He blushed bright red and took off his jacket. "Okay, right. Well, just think of your body the way you remembered it from before. Like, the feel of sheets, or a bath, or something really human." Felix focused on the ground as he spoke.

I scowled, but nothing was ever as simple as remembering something. I thought of a time I cut my leg with the razor. That had to be the least dragonish experience of my life. I couldn't imagine a mere razor blade taking out these scales–that would require something more like a katana. I closed my eyes and envisioned the razor rash, and my balance shifted as the world tilted.

Dizziness took me, and cold rushed over my skin, sending waves of shivers across my body. I staggered, balancing on my toes for a second before the spinning sensation stopped. My long hair tickled across my back.

Goose bumps pricked up all over my skin.

My completely *naked* skin.

"Aaaaghhh!" I squeaked as I folded in half, covering as many important parts as possible with my arms. My cheeks burned, and my heart pounded in my chest. I had never been fully naked in the locker room, let alone standing on a picturesque ledge.

In front of a hot guy.

And for the record, screaming while naked only increases the number of people who actually look. In this case, just the one person. His eyes briefly met mine, and his cheeks flushed scarlet. He looked away, but couldn't hide the grin that spread across his face. Making sure to avert his eyes, he took a couple steps toward me and held out his jacket.

I slipped into it quickly.

"The first time's the worst," he said.

"Your clothes came back with you."

"That's because I didn't burn mine off as I manifested. You did."

My cheeks burned. I wanted to hit him, but he'd given me his jacket. It covered just enough for me to not feel completely exposed, but the hem of his jacket was barely long enough to cover all the girly bits.

He gave me a sympathetic smile. "I'll walk you back to your cabin, okay?"

I nodded, scanning the surrounding forest. Plenty of startled eyes peeked out from the trees. This hadn't been as private as I'd hoped. Great.

Beth trotted up, out of breath. "You okay?"

"Fine. I'm fine. I'm just standing in the middle of camp naked."

"Well, actually, you're wearing a jacket, so it's like wearing a really short dress." Beth winked.

Felix hid his mouth behind his hand.

"I can hear you snickering, gryphon," I said.

"I'm not snickering–much." He turned to Beth. "If you can help Allyson back to her cabin, I should get to work. I'll come see you later." He gave Beth a pointed look. "Both of you."

"All right," Beth said, confused, but going along with it. We watched as he took off at a run. "What's eating the Bossman's kid?"

"We should wait until we're indoors," I said. "But the short of it is that they're going to move the Aerie."

"No kidding?"

"Long story."

"And the story about how you came to be naked with the hottest guy here? Is that a long story too? I didn't even see evidence of kissing. I expected more from you, Drake."

I glared at her, but Beth appeared impervious as she held open the door to my cabin. "So," she said. "Do you have any other clothes with you?"

"My jacket and a pair of underwear. I thought I might get a chance to use the facilities back in Ely. Everything else was in the car."

"Which is parked on the side of the road collecting parking tickets and bullets," Beth said, pursing her lips. "If you're okay here, I'll see if I can round some up."

She took off before I could say anything else.

I sighed, looking around the sparse cabin. In the last twenty-four hours, I'd been shot at, flung from a speeding truck, taken my first flight, and been found naked in the forest with a guy.

Before I could pace a hole in the wooden floor, Beth came back with Beatrice. She wasn't in her ranger outfit today, and she had a stack of clothes over her arm.

"How's the air?" she asked.

The image of the world sailing by beneath me leapt into my mind. "Great!"

Beth cocked an eyebrow, and Beatrice smiled.

"Well, I hope you had fun, but it sounds like you stirred up a whole hornet's nest of trouble," Bea said.

"I didn't mean to."

A mischievous smile spread across her face. "They'll probably tell naked dragon stories for a decade."

"Oh, right, that. I'd thought you meant the, um…" I remembered Joe had asked his son not to talk about some of it, but what parts? "So, what'd you bring?"

Beatrice winked. "Don't worry, I already know more than I should." She dropped the pile of clothes on the bed and handed me a pair of boots. They were combat boots, but they looked to be in my size, the black leather softened by wear and age. The rest of the clothes looked normal, t-shirt, jeans, and a sports bra.

"Take care, you two. And, Beth? If something comes up, good luck." Bea tossed a small set of keys to Beth.

"Thanks again. I hope this won't, you know," Beth said.

"It will, just try not to damage it, okay?"

"I'll be careful when I can."

Beatrice gave me a hug. "I hope everything turns out well for you, little dragon. And if the shit really hits the fan, you're welcome in my home. Both of you." She stood up straight, her eyes misty. "Don't be seen."

And then she disappeared out of the cabin and into the bustling masses of gryphons running back and forth through the camp.

"What was that all about?" I asked.

Beth inspected the keys in her hand, then put them in her pocket. "We got to talking last night, and we have a lot in common."

"Like?"

"Like we both hate unicorns, and the unicorns took your aunt's car, so we needed a ride to San Francisco. She said I could take her bike."

I blinked at Beth. "You know how to ride a motorcycle?"

"Sure. The monohorns like to show off, and they have me wash them and park them." Beth pawed through the clothes. "So, what's the real plan?"

"I'm not sure, but Felix has something in mind. Do you see any socks in there?"

Beth handed over bits and pieces as I dressed into someone else's clothing. The jeans were a little too big and the bright yellow t-shirt with the words "Oh, yeah?" across the chest was at least a size too small. Though, in truth, even tight, it did nothing to accentuate my tiny boobs, made smaller by the second hand sports bra–but still a million times better than naked.

I pulled on the black boots last, and we headed out into the bustle of the Aerie. People were shuttling things to the cliff where others were flying away with loads of stuff. At the food pit, a table strained under the burden of enough sandwich fixings to feed an army of gryphons. Groggy gryphons with cups of coffee directed traffic, and children bustled to stay out of sight, lest their lack of a job qualify them for the next round of 'go fetch it.'

Beth and I made sandwiches before offering to help. For the rest of the morning, we schlepped boxes either to the cliff or to one of the trailers. By lunch, all children under the age of ten were missing from the Aerie. I caught sight of someone flying off with a toddler in his claws and knew that they were protecting the littlest people first. My respect for the gryphons continued to climb throughout the day as they worked tirelessly.

The plan was to break down everything except the Lodge and the garage, which they'd lay some booby traps in before leaving in the morning, taking all the drivable things. By mid-afternoon, centaurs came with a herd of horses, and the heavier things were strapped to the pack animals. It took less than two hours to secure all the loads, and by the time we saw the backsides of the horses, my hands were practically rope burned from tying all the bundles down.

Beth and I sat in a group of tired gryphons, eating another round of barbeque as the sun set. They'd built a bonfire out of the papers they weren't going to move, and some people roasted marshmallows. It was just like camping, except they didn't have to hunt for the firewood.

A gryphon produced a battered guitar and started to sing. My hands twitched to get the feel of something so normal as a guitar under my fingers.

When the first song ended, he passed the guitar to the right, and so it went around the circle. People who didn't play called on people who did, but the guitar continued its journey until it landed in my hands.

The instrument was bigger than mine, but tuned. Racing stickers covered the back, and someone had plastered the rampant gryphon symbol across the front. I strummed a chord, then slapped my hand onto the strings when I realized what chord I'd strummed.

I couldn't sing *My Father's Eyes* here.

I played the very next song in my mind, the one my aunt gave me for my birthday.

As my fingers played across the strings, the firelight winked back from the eyes of the others. I tuned them out and played my aunt's song. I filled the air with each note, and drove away all thought of panic and fear. For a few brief minutes, I filled my world with music and failed to exist in any other way. When the last note faded, I felt them take the breath they'd been holding.

Felix stared at me, jaw hanging open.

I blushed, then passed the guitar to the next person.

Felix stood. "It's late, and we all have an early morning. We should get some rest. Sunrise will come too soon." He paused and looked directly at me. "And tomorrow is going to be a very big day." He widened his eyes very slightly at the end.

The gryphons started to split away from the dregs of the fire, but some remained. I knew how they felt. I never slept the night before a move. At least, I couldn't sleep the night before a move if I knew it was the night before a move. We'd moved the same day a bunch of times.

Then again, maybe I didn't know how they felt. This had been their home for eight years, how much harder was it to move after eight years rather than eight months?

Felix smiled at me and winked. "I'll see you bright and early."

What are you planning?

Oh crap, play it cool. "Uh, yeah, I like dawn here. Nice view."

A smile caught on his lips, and I realized he must be thinking about this morning with me naked on the cliff. I blushed and swung at him.

He ducked out of the way, laughing. "I'll be around," he said, and headed off, catching up to someone else leaving the food tables.

We left the fire pit and went straight to the cabin. I didn't know where Beth stayed last night, but I was glad to have her near me tonight. It would make sneaking away easier if we didn't have to go hunting for Beth.

"What was that all about?" Beth asked when the door closed.

"We're leaving tonight. Probably sometime after midnight," I said. I rolled clothes into tubes and laid them in a pile next to my backpack.

"How did you get that out of what he said?"

I dumped my backpack out on the bed, and tried to figure out what I could leave and what I needed to take. "He had that *I'm not telling the whole truth* look in his eyes."

She picked the Kornus Blade out of the pile of clothes from my backpack. "Isn't this that thing your aunt gave you?"

"Yeah, but I can't get the sword out."

She turned it in her hand. "That's because you're not a monohorn. Only the touch of a unicorn horn can break their little stasis-shrinky-things," she said. "Is this the Kornus Blade?"

"What? How do you know about the Kornus Blade?"

"The monohorns. It's made from one of their horns. They have pictures of it in their history books. They made it as a gift to all humanity, but it wasn't much of a gift. More like 'here, do it yourself if you want to kill dragons.'" She held out her hands in exasperation. "*So* unicorn."

I choked and sputtered. "Dragon slaying? Seriously?"

"Oh yeah, dragons are really tough. I mean, look at what you've been through, and not much besides a unicorn horn can actually injure a dragon. The Kornus Blade is supposed to give someone the power they need to actually kill a dragon."

The Kornus Blade stared back at me from its magical casing. No wonder it almost killed the table. "So, how do we get our hands on a unicorn horn?"

"I'm sure Dr. Targyne would love to let you use his," Beth said.

I barked out a laugh. "Right after he skewered me with it."

"Why did your aunt give you a dragon killing sword?"

I sat down in the pile of clothes. "I'm not sure. Maybe to hold it? Maybe she thought I was friends with the unicorns or something." I shook my head as it occurred to me. "My aunt is supposed to use this sword to kill my father."

"Oh, crap," Beth said.

"Yeah, crap is right." I tipped my head back until it hit the bunk bed post. "I have a sword I can't use, an aunt who can't wield it, and a father I don't want to kill."

Beth nodded her head for a moment. "So, how are we going to fix it?"

"I have no idea." I stuffed clothes and books into my backpack.

"I guess we wait for your boyfriend to come up with a plan?"

I flushed. "He's not my boyfriend," I snapped, but the thought of him made my heart race.

"Sure he's not," Beth said, drawing out her words. "And I sure didn't catch you naked with him either."

My face burned, and I snatched the Kornus Blade from her. I stuffed it into my backpack and zipped the whole thing shut. "All things considered, you might want to get some rest." I pointed at one of the bunks.

"Thanks." She smiled. "Don't mind if I do. It'll be nicer than sleeping on the couch at the lodge." Beth stretched out across a bunk while I made a show of getting into my sleeping bag. By the time I arranged myself, Beth snored.

I didn't think I'd be able to sleep, but before I knew it, someone knocked on the cabin door. My eyes shot open and I scanned the room. It was blacker than the inside of a closet, and Beth's snores rattled the floorboards. The knock came again. I jumped out of bed to get the door before he tried to knock again.

Felix stood in the moonlight, dressed in his racing leathers. "We have to move quickly. My dad drank with the others, but I don't know if he's sleeping."

"He's gonna freak when you're gone."

He sighed, deflating. "I know. He reminded me of his decision three times, but those are our people Stein has." His jaw tightened for a second. "He told me about the fire. I think he knows I'm going."

I nodded and squeezed his shoulder. "Thank you. I don't think I could do this alone."

He nodded, then pointed his gaze at Beth. I stepped back inside and shook Beth awake.

"Huh?" she asked.

"Shh," Felix hissed from the door. Beth got up, and I slung my backpack over my shoulder.

"What's the plan?" I asked.

"We're going to take a couple bikes and get out of here," he said.

"Walk them out, so it's quiet?" Beth asked. "I don't want to be rushed, I've never ridden Bea's bike."

Felix's eyes went wide for a second and then settled too normal. "Yes, *exactly*. We'll walk them out." He bit his lips, as if he could bite the lie out of his words.

She didn't notice as she fiddled with her shoelaces. "Good, just like the *Sound of Music*."

Felix and I both looked at her.

She shrugged. "What, I like the classics."

"Come on." Felix led the way to the garage.

We walked quietly, and all through camp, gryphons in their feathered forms lay sleeping here and there. A group of people had camped out on the rock ledge, probably to keep Felix and me from flying off. But there were no gryphons in front of the garage.

Inside, the garage had an unnatural silence; my footsteps didn't echo like in most large spaces. The room swallowed sound.

Felix went to the red bike and walked it over to the rolling garage door. He pushed a helmet at me. "Put this on and be ready to move."

Beth struggled with a dirt bike on the far wall and retrieved a red and white helmet that matched the bike. She brought the bike over and pointed at the person-sized door and held her hands out like she was judging the size of a fish.

"They aren't going to fit through the door," Felix whispered. "I've tried. Allyson, you're going to have to pull up the doors, then jump on behind me, fast. You got it?"

I nodded and went to the chain next to the bay door. The chain ran up to a winch above the door. These doors made a terrible noise, like a thunderstorm in a metal barrel.

Beth's head whipped around. "You said we were going to do it like they did in *The Sound of Music.*"

"Don't you remember that scene where they race motorcycles through the alps?" Felix asked.

"There wasn't a scene with–you're not?" Beth asked, but she hastily stuffed the helmet onto her head.

"Now," Felix whispered.

I yanked the chain, drawing it down, hand over hand as fast as I could. The rattling chain clanked, and the metal slats of the door banged up the tracks. Felix kicked the bike starter and revved. The rolling door came to a stop at the top with a slam, and Beth kicked her bike to life. Without hesitating, she sped off into the night. Felix grabbed my arm as I jumped, tossing me onto the bike behind him, and we flew out of the garage after her. Trees zipped past, caught in our tiny cone of light for less than a second.

If Felix made a mistake here, we were dead.

We caught up to Beth in no time, and we led the way down the mountain. The road flew by, tree, tree, cactus, sagebrush.

At nearly halfway down the mountain, the engine sputtered and died. We coasted downhill, before Felix put his foot down, sliding the rear wheel out to the side.

"What's wrong?" Beth asked as she pulled up behind us.

He pushed a button on the handlebars, and the engine gave a sad gurgle and choked to a stop. "My Dad must have had someone siphon off the gas." He jammed the kickstand into the ground.

"Bea thought he might." She turned to the back of her bike, where two red cans were strapped down. "Will this be enough?"

Felix looked at me. "Is it?"

I leaned back. "Why are you looking at me? I don't know anything about motorcycles."

"But what's the plan?"

I froze. I thought I'd given him enough information to make a plan.

"Uh–well–I mean, plan sounds so formalized."

"You don't have a plan?"

"I know about as much as you. Something is happening at Pier 22 1/2 tonight. We go there, we might find out what."

"What are we going to find at this pier?"

"If we're lucky, my aunt and a unicorn." Then we'd have everything we needed to take care of my father.

"If we're not lucky?" Felix asked.

"My aunt and a unicorn."

Felix exchanged a look with Beth before they both cocked their heads at me.

"In the letter my father wrote, he said the only way out of being controlled by Kurt was to kill him. He gave my aunt a special sword to do it."

Felix's white eyes shown through the darkness.

My eyes stung, and I couldn't hold his gaze. "I guess you'd like that plan."

He put his hand on my shoulder. "Allyson, if your father is being controlled, then I know who needs to have a special sword stuffed through his heart, and it's not your dad."

"Still begs the question, is this going to be enough gas?" Beth asked holding up the tank.

Felix nodded. "We'll just be a little more conservative until we get to a gas station."

I checked my pocket but I didn't have much money left. "How much money do we have?"

Beth shook her head. "Not much. I had to abandon it in the car. I have a couple twenties, but that's it."

"We don't have to be crazy. If Dad thinks I'm about to run out of gas, he won't be in much of a hurry to send anyone out for us."

"Wouldn't he be worried Beth might have come too?" I asked.

"Nope," Beth said. "He's offered me protection against the unicorns."

"Then why are you coming?" I asked.

"Honestly, Drake, you'd get lost without me. Besides, I can't let the damned monohorns have access to my trust fund. Those bastards have enough money as it is."

"I'm glad you came, Duke City," Felix said.

"Duke City?" I asked.

"Yeah, it's what they call Albuquerque. Like New York is the Big Apple and Hollywood is Tinsel Town." He pointed at Beth like she was the embodiment of all of Albuquerque. "Duke City."

Beth play punched him in the arm, and Felix winced. I knew from experience, those play taps hurt. "That's for lying to me." She hit him again, a little harder, and he hissed. "That's for profaning *The Sound of Music*."

"Come on, Duke, we haven't got all day."

Beth smiled. "I kind of like Duke."

CHAPTER TWENTY-ONE

The Day Before

My legs and butt burned with fatigue, but the rest of my body ached from the cold. Snow rimmed the mountains around Reno.

We had to stop often as we rode through the snow and ice corridor, riding in short spurts between truck stops, and all the while, the sun kept marching toward the horizon.

My stomach hurt. I was leading my friends to their death. Joe had tried to warn us, but Felix was determined. The unicorns were going to kill Beth, so it was lead my friends to their death and do everything I could, or watch them die in other ways.

Even with the frequent stops to warm our fingers, we made it to Sacramento by six in the afternoon. We bought gas, and I lamented once more the loss of the MGB, with all of Beth's money. It didn't solve problems, but it sure made things comfortable. We found a taco truck with burritos for a dollar each, and turning out our pockets, we came up with just enough money in loose change. We bought three stale burritos and ate them on a log next to the bikes.

Wolfing down her burrito, Beth looked at the bike, now transformed from cool toy to giant torture device. "I wish we still had the car."

"Me too. I guess we'll have to clear your name so we can get it back for my aunt."

"And the bullet holes?"

"I'd forgotten about the bullet holes. But that's what body shops are for."

"Someone shot at you, and you forgot about it?" Felix asked.

"Honestly, flying totally overrides everything that happened before."

Felix smiled, as if remembering something. "It's better than anything. Racing is a close second."

"I hate races." I turned away, pretending to study my hands. I especially hated racing to a city where a bunch of trolls were going to be waiting.

"That tells me you've never been prepared. To win races, you have to train, and hard. My family has a long history of bringing home trophies, so when we go to a race, we have a game plan. Everyone knows their role, and there's a whole team of support."

Beth snorted. "What, it's not all about the talent?"

Felix scrunched his lips to the side but kept chewing. "I'd be lying if I said talent didn't factor in. But the truth with racing is there are three things that have to meld together to win every race: the bike, the prep, and the talent. Without one of the three there's still some hope; but let's face it, if you're racing on a bad gearbox, there's not a lot you can do about it." He took another bite.

Beth grinned. "Well, we've got the bikes and the talent. Two out of three ain't bad. How are we going to win?"

I shrugged. "Pier 22 1/2 and pray, I guess."

Beth stuffed the rest of her burrito into her mouth, and swallowed without chewing. "Then what are we waiting for?"

Felix stood and offered me his hand. I took it, and he pulled me up. He seemed to be handling the grueling endurance race better than Beth and I, but he'd probably trained for it.

As he prepped to kick start the bike, he turned back to me. "Prayers are great and all, but in a race, we always have a plan."

Before I could think of an answer, he kicked the bike to life, drowning out any chance of talking.

Through the tangle of freeways and overpasses, his words haunted me. The clue we chased was so thin. If there was no one there, Beth would have to spend the rest of her life running from the unicorns.

But if they were there, I'd have the sword, my aunt, and hopefully Steve. Could we use the sword on Kurt? Would it work on him?

The sun set over the bay as the Pacific Ocean came into view. Light reflected off the world, and even my bones ached. The road twisted closer and closer to the water until the Bay Bridge rose in front of us.

Fog puffed up in great rolls of doughy clouds, swallowing one end of the road as it stretched across the waters. The telltale towers of the Golden Gate Bridge poked through the fog, spanning the gap in between the distant mountains.

We rode over the water and took the first exit. Buildings rose to our left, and the piers, more like warehouses, stood on our right. Gaps between the buildings gave us a view of the water, reflecting the light from the city. The façades were painted white with bronze numbers over the arch. Some of the bay doors had been replaced with solid walls and man-sized doors. Others were blocked by cyclone fencing.

Pier 22 1/2 squatted between two white façades, an afterthought compared to the other piers. A two-story building stood on top of a badly paved parking lot. Red paint around the trim of the white building flaked in places. A red shield painted on the front doors said SFFD.

Oh great, not only would we be trespassing, but it'd be trespassing through a fire station.

Around the building, cyclone fencing kept the unkempt lawn from invading the parking lot. I scanned the parked cars behind the fence, but no Martin's Moving vans, so hopefully they hadn't beaten us. They could have beaten us easily–we'd spent a whole day moving the gryphons.

We parked the bikes behind a sign and hopped the fence into the parking lot. Beth stepped up to the door and crushed the handle. "It's always polite to come in the front door."

"I wasn't really thinking about our manners," I said.

186

"Now what?" Felix asked.

There wasn't a 'Kidnapping Trolls' sign with an arrow. Fire equipment and boxes filled one side of the building, and the faint smell of fish clung to the cement floor.

Two moving vans were parked farther down, but these trucks didn't have any scorch marks up the sides. So either they got the truck repaired in a day—unlikely considering the fire—or these were different trucks.

I nodded toward the truck, and Beth walked up and crushed the lock in her hand.

"Damn, Duke, you're good at that," Felix said.

Beth gave him a half smile. "Yeah, muscle and blood, we trolls have all kinds of uses."

"You're more valuable than your muscle and blood," I said.

Beth cocked her eyebrow.

"What, I'm not saying it isn't useful, I'm just saying it's not *all* that's useful."

Beth opened the door. Inside, rows of bunks lined the walls, but no Steve and Aunt Aggy. "Crap."

"I don't understand," Felix said.

I looked from Beth to Felix. "It means they're kidnapping lots of people."

He scanned the rest of the warehouse. "Then where are they?"

I shook my head. "I don't know. This is where my dad said to meet him, but I'm not sure he was actually talking to me, or just lying to someone else."

Felix grew still except for his fists, which clenched and shook. "You mean you don't actually know if anyone is going to show up?"

"It's the best I had to go on. My dad called my aunt, and I picked up the phone. My dad was on the other end, but Stein came in. My Dad said to meet at Pier 22 1/2 and, well, here it is." I pointed at the bunks.

He shook his head. "Where are they?"

Beth put a hand on each of our shoulders. "I know I'm not usually known for my great plans and all, but why don't we search the place? If that doesn't lead to anything we can find some good hiding spots and wait for midnight."

"Why is it always midnight?" Felix asked.

I yawned. "To keep the children from finding out?"

"It's pretty cliché if you ask me," Beth said.

We searched the place, but other than hoses and boxes, there wasn't anything useful. We made a sort of nest out of the hoses.

I pointed at Beth and Felix. "You guys should sleep. You've been driving all day, and it's hours until anything is supposed to happen."

Felix scowled, but he yawned. Grudgingly he made himself comfortable.

Beth laid down and started snoring in seconds.

The waiting stretched on with only the sound of water lapping against the pier to keep me company. I jumped when a rat scuttled through the boxes. My pulse hammered in my throat, and I tried to take deep breaths to calm the burning in my lungs.

Beth and Felix slept like the dead. As I watched them breathing, Joe's words filled me with dread. *Dragons don't come back.* They didn't know how dangerous this could be. My father wrote a letter explaining how to help my aunt kill him—giving me permission to help her.

My stomach twisted at the thought. There had to be another way, a way to free him.

I could protect my friends though. If there was an opportunity to keep them from getting hurt, I had to take it. This wasn't Beth's fight, and Felix—well, if I found my family, they could help me rescue his.

I jumped when the doors rumbled open, nearly falling.

A battered moving truck drove in. Black char marked the cab over the windows, and it smelled like burnt plastic. Three trolls sat abreast in the cab. John sat in the middle, stiff and keeping his arms to his side. The trolls piled out and immediately opened the back of the van.

A flash of silver from by the door distracted me, but John and the other trolls pulled out their first victim. They laid people out on stretchers, and John rearranged an arm or a leg. My heart leapt when they pulled out my aunt. She still wore her clothes from days before, and her limp body hung lifeless. They wouldn't have brought her all this way if she was already dead, would they?

Outside, boards creaked, and one of the bay doors opened to the dock. Outside, boats strained against their moorings. Two boats were covered in reflective paint and bright red markings like fire trucks. Ropes squealed and wood moaned as the boats rolled with the water beneath.

A man in a business suit stood next to the door. He was Japanese with long black hair hanging from a ponytail at the nape of his neck. I recognized the hair; it was mine.

My father.

David Takata stood less than thirty yards away. For a second, he looked straight at me. He searched my hiding place, and the scent of piñon wafted through the warehouse.

I held my breath, and everything except my father fell away. His nose had the same curve as Aggy's. His ears were the same shape as mine. Then he turned, and I inhaled. My heart pounded in my chest.

A hand slipped over my mouth, and someone pinned my arms in place. "My apologies, Miss Takata, I had assumed you were with the trolls," Dr. Targyne whispered. Something sharp pinched my arm, and the world quickly swam out of focus. "But I can't risk them catching you, too."

Of course, the silver at the door had been a unicorn slipping in.

Oh good, a unicorn. Now I can get out the sword.

Everything went black.

CHAPTER TWENTY-TWO

The Day Of

A murky nothingness swam through my thoughts. I wanted the oblivion, but something urgent rattled in my mind. If I didn't get up in time for the first bell, Mom would kill me. A dark room flickered into view, and the world shifted, disorienting me.

Then it came back to me in a rush.

That son of a monohorn!

I was buried in thin layer of hoses. Someone had hidden me.

Dr. Targyne?

He'd said he couldn't risk me being caught, but what was he doing here? And what happened to his gun-toting goons?

I pushed up out of the loose debris and scanned the room. No one else was here. My aunt, my father, Steve, all of them gone while I'd been knocked out by Dr. Targyne's drug. *That slimeball!*

And why was keeping me on the sidelines so important?

Leaping down off the pile of hoses, I fell. My face smashed into the floor. Pain shot up through my chin, and I rolled over with a groan. What was I thinking, jumping after a sedative? Maybe that stuff took out a bunch of brain cells, too. My limbs were slow and heavy.

The smell of my father lingered. I pushed through the door on the dockside, following the scent. It was strong enough to follow across the water.

The SFFD lettering left nothing in question, those were fireboats. If I stole one, someone might get hurt if there was a water fire.

And my burning lungs suggested fire would fly before the end of the night.

If I wanted to follow, I'd have to go as a dragon.

I dropped my backpack and threw my jacket to the pier. If I died, I wanted the cops asking very uncomfortable questions about my whereabouts.

Taking a deep breath, I focused on how it felt to be a dragon. Impervious to cold. Thick air, like swimming. Even my vision was sharper as a dragon. Most of all, as a dragon, I wanted to bask in the sun all day. I poured my consciousness into that feeling of baking in my blue, scaled hide. My skin shivered with the change, and the world felt fifteen degrees warmer. Air poured into my huge lungs, and the world of smell opened up to me as if I'd never had the pleasure of tasting the air. My view shifted several feet up, and my claws sank into the wooden decks.

It worked!

I chuckled and smoke wafted from my nostrils.

I had whiskers like an Asian style dragon. My head was easily taller than the tops of the doors, and I fell onto my front legs. My long, slender body tapered off to a very long tail. My wings were more what would be called a European dragon's wings, jutting out from just behind my arms—now front legs. A ridge of scales traced down my back, and I flicked my tail to watch the scales move.

With my giant claws, I peeled open my backpack to look for the Kornus Blade. I grabbed the lump of plastic in my claws and slipped into the water. It parted around me like a silk dress, and I slithered through the ocean.

With a roll of my tail, I zipped through the water after the boat carrying my father. The smell of dragon wafted across the water, easier to follow than a trail on the ground. Steam rose from my nostrils, but fog choked the bay, whisping off the water.

The boat came into view, and I dipped lower in the water. With only my eyes and nostrils above the surface, I crept alongside the boat.

The tugboat sat low in the water with Bob at the helm. My father and John stood in front of Beth and Dr. Targyne. Beth's hands were cuffed behind her back in thick metal manacles. John stood stoically, but he shot covert glances at Beth.

John leaned over and shook something. With a groan, Felix stood up, his hands also bound behind his back. He launched himself at my father, trying to bash him with a head or a shoulder, but my father dodged aside easily, a well-trained martial artist. When Felix missed, he fell to the deck.

Looking down, my father *tsked*. "Honestly, must we act so human?"

"Where's my sister? Where's my mother?" Felix asked through gritted teeth. He collected himself and stood again. His face burned red, muscles tight and eyes blazing. "Why didn't you come back? We needed your help."

My father's face froze, and he blinked. He took a breath, closing his eyes. Pain pinched his features, but then something else stole across his face. The snide mask of indifference swept over his features. "That was a long time ago. Perhaps I could arrange a meeting with your mother. Would you like that?"

"Where is she?"

"You'll join her soon enough."

Dr. Targyne stepped forward, drawing my father's attention. "What are you doing here, David? What happened to your crusade?"

At the unicorn's words, my father looked out over the water—the opposite side of the boat from me. "Things change, Aaron." He watched the water for a moment and nodded to himself. "But some things stay the same."

"Did you ever even love her? You goddamned hypocrite," Dr. Targyne said, but my father ignored him.

It felt like something dark swam through the air and changed him. My father turned to John and pulled out a gun. It flashed silver, and he held the gun up to John's head. "I do believe you've lost faith."

"I—I don't know what you're talking about," John stammered. "I followed orders and everything."

"But you've been thinking, causing too much trouble. I can't have that in my operation." He turned to Beth. "We're expanding, you know, but I simply can*not* stand disloyalty."

The gun barked in his hand three times, and John staggered. My father pushed him over the edge of the boat with a lazy hand. John's rigid body did a half flip over the far edge of the boat, belly flopping into the bay with a splash.

"And you think a gunshot wound will hurt him?" Beth smirked.

"No. But drowning certainly will. Full blooded trolls don't float, and they still need air like the rest of us." He narrowed his eyes at Beth. "Do you think he can tread water with three holes in his lungs?"

The color drained from Beth's face. She went to the railing, but my father held a gun to Felix's head. "He doesn't regenerate so easily, does he?"

Beth froze, but I slipped beneath the surface.

John sank through the murky water like a brick. I grabbed him around the waist in my clawed hand, swimming as far as away from the boat as I could before breaking the surface. John gasped for air, blood running down his face in rivulets. Sprinting through the sea, I headed for a spear of rocks just up ahead. The precarious heap sat near the base of a bridge. Keeping low in the water, I swam for the shore, hoping no one on the boat would hear us. I kept one eye over my shoulder, watching the boat, but the fog swallowed it.

I threw John onto the shore. "Do you know where they're going?"

He coughed, gurgling water. I dragged my attention away from the sea. He nodded, still coughing. Water drained off John in a pink pool of blood and muck. He bent over coughing, and soon, the whole beach was covered in troll blood.

Apparently trolls had rather a lot of blood to bleed before they died. He spit up a bullet, caught it and set it down on a nearby boulder. Waves smashed against the rocks, dripping more salty water into the mix and washing blood from the beach. Mist rose from the rocks and the soaking troll, and I waited.

"Well?" I said.

"You can eat me"–he coughed and hacked up more blood–"if you'd like, but I–I was only trying to help."

"How is kidnapping her helping?"

He spit another bullet onto the rocky shore. "You still mad about that?"

"Surprisingly, I stay moody about felonies for weeks on end."

He coughed again, but this time it sounded much clearer. "Look, I only grabbed her to keep her from letting the unicorns know she was there. How was I supposed to know she'd react like that? I didn't mean to make her mad. I love her."

The word pulsed through me. Love. He *loved* her. He'd met her three times and he loved Beth? "How do you know? Everyone says teenagers are idiots. How do you know you're in love?"

"The first time I saw her. I looked at her, and the world snapped into focus. I'd seen my other half, and it broke every spell they put on me."

My tail slapped the water in a nervous twitch. "Tell me about this spell."

"It's simple, the dragon controls the magic, and Mr. Stein controls the dragon."

My heart pounded against my chest. *Power over her kind.* Joe had said as much. My father had said it, too, but I hadn't wanted to believe it.

"What do you mean, control?"

"I don't know how, but whenever they meet, Mr. Stein kisses Takata's forehead, whether he's in his dragon form or not. The dragon said it renewed the bond." John squinted at me. "You look a lot like him. I thought all the dragon families were different."

I ignored him. "So, you got sight of your true love and it broke the spell? What kind of spell is it then?"

"I was invested with dragon blood, it helps with, well, you know." He pointed at his head and smiled. "The others, like me, were imbued with other tributes, loyalty from the gryphons, and well, other stuff from the unicorns."

"So they just want all these people to make blood?"

John shook his head. "No, the magic needs something of life. The investments are just an aside. The real spell binds us to obedience. Mr. Stein runs it, but it doesn't work without life."

"What about Takata?"

"He does everything Mr. Stein tells him to."

The letter made more sense with each passing second. My father would rather die than be controlled.

"How do I break the spell on the dragon, true love?"

"No, there's something different with the dragon. Trolls break loose all the time, but none of the dragons do." John watched the surf. "The dragon's spell sustains Mr. Stein. I heard them talking about it, and that's why they need so many people. One dragon can only give Stein so many years, but all the dragons he has working for him know magic."

"How many?"

"You hear talk, but we have transfers from Montreal, Miami, Seattle, and I met a troll from London."

"You're just full of good news."

He shrugged. "Would you rather I lied?"

"Where are they headed?"

"There's a bunch of ships moored in the bay near Vallejo. They call it the Ghost Fleet."

"How far?"

John took his bearings, spotting the bridges. "An hour, even when Takata uses his magic to make the boat go faster."

I closed my eyes. "Right. How do I free Takata from Mr. Stein?"

John scowled at me suspiciously, like a school kid when they knew the answer, but thought the teacher might be tricking them. His eyebrows pinched together. "You kill him."

CHAPTER TWENTY-THREE

My stomach heaved.

I'm gonna puke right here.

Then ice cold water pumped through my veins. His words bored through me. Kill him? There had to be some other way. *Kill him?* The Kornus Blade cut into my hand as I squeezed. Kill him? What the hell kind of answer was that?

Only the one he wrote about in the letter, idiot.

Oh God, I can't do this.

I sagged onto the rocks. No father-daughter dances, no letters, no secret inheritance, just the Kornus Blade and a journal. *You kill him.*

"You okay?" John asked.

"No." I never told people the truth when they asked that question. I always said fine. I'm fine. I'm always fine. My stomach heaved again, and I wondered if I could puke as a dragon.

John grabbed my face by the whiskers and pulled me around so I *had* to look in his eyes. They pierced me with the wild intensity of a man gone half mad. "Look, I don't have time for you to have some moral crisis on Angel Rock. We need to get to Beth. Stein always shows up when there's a big delivery, and this shipment is huge. Not all of us can just break free of the controls, and Stein could have her forever."

"What's the deal with Stein?"

"He's the head honcho, and he's smart. He has bases all over the country. If you take out one, his whole power base isn't interrupted, just weakened. And if he enthralls Beth, she'll be locked in. For. Eh. Ver."

"What about you? Could you be enthralled again?"

As I asked the question, Joe's words slipped through my mind again. *Dragons don't come back.* Could he take me?

Too late now, everyone was already too far in to back out now.

John nodded. "It was the shock of seeing Beth that broke me out of it, but if he put it back on me, I'd be a slave again."

I didn't have to kill my father. I had to kill Stein. Cut off the head, and the rest of the machine would fall apart. Maybe I could break my father free. Maybe seeing me would do it for him. Rescue Beth, kill Stein, that was a plan I could get behind; way better than the kill-the-father-you've-never-met plan.

"Get on," I said.

John swung himself up behind my head and sat on my neck. The water splashed around me as I dove back in, careful to keep John from slipping off. I passed under the double-decker bridge and made my way through the bay. Even through the fog, John knew the way, pointing me around corners and through bridges. We passed an oil refinery on a hill, covered in pipes and flaming towers. Through the fog, the flames diffused to eerie, flickering ghosts, a fitting landmark for a ghost fleet. When we came to three bridges in a row, John tugged on my eyebrows, which, as a dragon, were big enough to be the handlebars on a gryphon's bike.

"That's it, there." He pointed. Looming up out of the ocean, rows of steel grey ships sat in the bay. "It's the Ghost Fleet. Derelict boats from World War II, just sitting there."

"And no one goes on them?"

"No one but us, that's how they keep the people hidden. And, if push comes to shove, Takata can take off with the boat, and move the whole operation."

The smell of magic, like ozone and loam, wafted from a boat in the middle. Even through the fog, my father's scent lingered on the water.

John leaned forward to whisper. "Just get me next to the boat, and I'll do the rest."

"No. I'm coming too."

Rust stains ran down from the portholes. These ships hadn't seen a new coat of paint in over fifty years. A patrol boat cruised by, motoring right past us. I waited until I couldn't hear the engine before I continued on to the fleet.

We approached, following the wisps of magic undulating like ribbons in the breeze. Our target loomed out of the water, larger than the others, with great cannons pointed over the bow. The cold metal slipped beneath my claws as rusted chips of paint sloughed away. The rotting paint covered something else, something darker. Slime and foulness poured through my soul. Evil, if such a thing existed, lurked here.

The rusted metal curled in my claws, and a piece of the ship broke away. I swapped it into the claw still carrying the Kornus Blade before climbing to the deck. I crept over the edge, setting the broken bit down. John hopped off, hitting the deck with bent knees that swallowed sound. Quiet, strong, nearly indestructible–trolls were definitely not how the Grimm boys described. We scurried across the deck, staying low, in case a military patrol came by.

John led the way to a door with a wheel instead of a knob. "I don't think you'll fit," he whispered.

I nodded and dredged up my most human moment ever, standing on the edge of a cliff naked. My blue scales receded, and the brief moment of magic blocked out the putrid feel of darkness around me. It was like stepping through a waterfall only to wallow in a gritty mud bath on the other side. Shivering, I stood on the deck. John raised an eyebrow at me and moved to take off his jacket. It was soaked through as well, so I shook my head. At least this time I still had on my shirt and pants.

Without so much as a scrape, the wheel on the door spun open. The floor beyond the door was polished marble, and varnished panels of oaks lined the walls. I gulped, suddenly very conscious of my soggy stature, but John went in. Clutching the Kornus Blade in its useless state, I tiptoed down the hall behind John. He led me to the belly of the ship.

At the bottom of an immaculate staircase, a door opened onto an enormous room. Beams overhead stretched across the expanse. The curved walls matched the shape of the boat. This was the hold, and only a sheet of metal separated this warehouse from the water.

Open space stretched out to the left, but cubicles filled the area to the right of the door. The partitions made a labyrinth, but instead of desks, each cubicle held a bed. I did a quick count of the cubicles. If they were all filled, there were over a hundred people lying in hospital beds.

On the opposite side, the new victims were laid out on stretchers in a neat row. My father and two trolls stood across from Beth, Felix, and Dr. Targyne. Extra trolls stood around, some wandering up and down the cubicle maze, but many stood with Takata, guarding my friends. John and I slipped into a cubicle as a troll wandered down the hall.

"Now what?" He hissed under his breath.

More than a hundred people laid on beds in the belly of this ship, all of them Kin, and all of them nothing more than batteries for a spell. How the hell could I save two hundred people from my father?

John's words echoed through me. *You kill him.*

No, I kill Stein.

The Kornus Blade seemed to sense my thoughts and pulsed. I just needed a unicorn. My aunt was supposed to use the blasted thing, but if I had an opportunity to kill Stein, that was my primary target.

"I need a unicorn and a distraction."

John pointed. "There's a whole row. I can wake one up. What do you need?"

"The horn."

John nodded. "There's a station at the center of each row. Inside, you'll find a sort of toolbox of drawers. The purple mixture wakes them up. Just push it into the thing here." He pointed at the tubing running into the arm of the person right in front of us. "We keep a bunch in case of emergencies. I've got your distraction."

I made a grab for him, but he slipped past and walked into the main area as though on a stroll after lunch.

I dove back behind the cubicle barrier, peeking around the corner.

My father focused on John, and I ran for the row he'd pointed out.

A giant toolbox on wheels sat in the middle of the corridor, and I searched the drawers between frantic checks for other trolls. Nothing was labeled. I scrambled through the drawers until I found one holding eight needles filled with a purple liquid.

"John!" Beth cried out. I peeked over the top of the cubicles. John strode toward Beth, Felix, and my Father.

My father's eyes narrowed, watching John before sparks of magic flew from his fingers to the troll. "How did you get here?" he asked.

John's step faltered, and he fell to his knees, shaking.

"Answer me." My father's eyes widened. A deluge of bright orange magic flooded John, and he gasped.

"It was a dragon." He gasped, struggling for air. "She fished me out of the water."

A deathly silence stole through the ship, as he froze. "She?"

I dropped below the cubicle wall, but if my father could smell me half as easily as I could smell him, the gig was up. *Crap, where is Stein?* I had to have him to break my father free.

I shook as I slipped into the nearest cubicle. A woman with platinum blonde hair lay there, unconscious. I fumbled with the IV line, pushing the concoction.

"Find the dragon!" My father yelled. "Hurry, before Mr. Stein–"

He was cut off, and the sound of a scuffle came from across the room. I focused on pushing the purple liquid into the IV line. How long would it take for her to wake up and manifest? The seconds stretched into an eternity, and a gun fired twice.

"Come on, come on," I whispered.

Then the woman sat bolt upright and screamed. The blood-churning wail echoed off the sides of the ship.

So much for stealth.

I bolted from the cubby and dashed down the aisle. Ducking into the first cubby in the next row over, I hid. Trolls ran past me to get to the screaming unicorn, and I waited. Checking the corridor first, I ran in the other direction, listening for other trolls in this rat maze.

"I don't need another victim," Takata said. I peeked over the wall, and watched as my father shot Dr. Targyne in the gut. Beth shouted and rammed my father with her head. He stumbled back, and Felix rushed him, hands still tied together. Beth broke her manacles with a roar. The gun bounced away from Takata, and Beth grabbed it. She turned and emptied the clip into him.

My breath caught in my throat as Beth pulled the trigger.

My father shifted into his dragon form, ignoring the bullets as he changed. He grew, magic wrapping around him as midnight blue scales rippled over his skin. His tail and body moved like kelp in the tide. His short, powerful legs were separated by thirty feet of a slender, powerful body. His head was the size of two school buses stacked on top of each other, and his hind legs had talons like a rooster–a rooster the size of a T-Rex. Right in the center of his forehead sat a giant sapphire, his *sokra*.

He stood over Beth and chuckled. His voice rumbled through the hull. "Only one thing can stop me, child." He loomed over her as if deciding something, then fast as lightning, his head shot down and he took her into his mouth in one bite.

"No!" I leapt from behind the partition and ran for the fight.

John, closer to the action, jumped and grabbed Takata's muzzle.

As I ran, a giant claw hit me. The scaled hand batted me out of the air like a cat toy. Time slowed as the wall of the ship rushed up. I twisted, flipping in midair. I struck the wall arm first, and pain exploded through my body, radiating from my left arm. The world fuzzed out as the searing jolts of electricity zapped through me.

My vision blurred, and I hit the deck.

The world reeled. I was going to pass out.

I blinked my eyes and shook my head, focusing on the pain radiating from my arm.

Blood dripped from the dragon's mouth. He rolled his tongue around like he was trying to pick something from his teeth. Beth tore at his mouth with her bare hands, ripping great gashes in it, but it was a losing battle. If she made one wrong move, he'd swallow her whole.

I tried to roll onto my back, but lightning shot through my arm.

"Stay down," Dr. Targyne whispered. Not far from me, he laid on the ground, panting and clutching his side. Felix had been knocked out not far from the doctor. Dr. Targyne inched his way toward me, pulling himself along by his arms. A red streak of blood trailed behind him.

Takata shook his head, and John sailed through the air, crashing through the cubicles on the far side of the room. Half-walls flew up in a rain of troll debris, and out of the wreckage climbed more trolls. My father swung his head around like a dog, and Beth sailed across the boat, smacking into the metal hull.

"Manifest," I said to the doctor.

He narrowed his eyes at me. "Why?"

With my good arm, I held up the Kornus Blade for Dr. Targyne to see.

White bloomed around the edges of his eyes. "*You* have it."

"Hurry up."

He nodded and steeled himself. His face tightened and drained of color as he gasped, shifting. Halfway through the transformation, his cry became an equine squeal. His back was bent and twisted, a mangled ruin of muscle, fur, and bones, but his head and neck gleamed in brilliant white. He tipped his head down to the lump of Lucite and touched it with his horn. The Lucite lump melted away from the blade. A silver light flashed through the room, and I dropped the tiny blade.

When I looked back, the curling blade pulsed like a beating heart, flashing silver. It grew, twisting to full size, maybe even too big for me. I took the blade in my right hand. It hissed, burning my palm.

"The feeling is mutual," I said, standing. I tucked my bad arm against my ribs, but pain shot through me, threatening to blanket the world in darkness again.

My father roared, and I felt something rip, not in me, but something in the world, as if I'd been wearing a tight suit and it was being unzipped. It made the world feel unseated, as if all of reality would slip and fall. I searched the room for the source of this new threat, and found it standing at the door next to the cubicles.

On the far end of the room, a man stood. His clean suit and shiny shoes would have been at home in a fancy bank, not standing on the deck of a ship. His hair was combed to a perfect balance between youth and power. But around his designer clothes, streams of magic radiated out from him like the aurora borealis–if the northern lights were all sickly orange and putrid green.

And the threads of magic ran from my father to this man in a suit.

With all the players present, the whole picture unfolded in only too much clarity. My father passed power from the victims to this man standing on the stairs. There was only one person he could be: Kurt Stein.

He surveyed the room with a cool eye, as if a rampaging dragon was perfectly normal. Then he smiled, inhaling like the world had just given him the gift of a great and beautiful day. Black tendrils of magic shot out from his body, searching the room for targets. One wrapped around Dr. Targyne and another found Beth. I jumped clear of the grasping magic. Beth screamed as the power of the dark spell curled around her, draining her life force, binding her to Stein.

He was using magic to suck her life away, and I had no idea how to stop it.

Power ran from my father to Stein, supporting the spell siphoning away Beth's very soul. My father. John's words rang through my head. *You kill him.*

It made sense now. My father was Stein's tool. Stein had immeasurable power at his hands, and my father had no control of his actions.

You kill him.

Even as I dodged another swipe from Stein's magic hands, I hesitated. This was my father. My father. The one who'd hidden from me, who set the Aerie on fire to make the gryphons run before Stein captured them. But as I watched, power flooded from my father to Stein, and I could sense the unconscious Kin weakening as Stein demanded more.

My father was distracted with sending power to Stein, and I took advantage of the free shot. I swung the Kornus Blade and caught him in the cheek. A piece of scale the size of my head fell from his face and pierced the deck. I swung again, but he pulled his head back and away from me.

John skidded to my side and held his hands in stirrup. "Time to fly."

Without thinking, I put my foot into his hands and tensed for the jump. John bounced me into the air, and I pushed off his hand into a flip. The shock of sailing through the air jostled my arm, but I held onto the sword. Landing on the bridge of my father's nose, I thrust the sword down. It tore open his flesh, parting the scales, but it skipped off the bone beneath.

He roared; the deafening sound vibrated through my bones. I brought the sword down again, and my father's scream rattled the hull of the ship. When I pulled out the blade, the wound knit back together, just like a troll, only stained in the black magic of Kurt Stein.

It was like trying to take down a bull with a toothpick. I'd spent so much time debating if I *should* kill him, I never considered if I *could* kill a dragon.

The size of a watermelon, his *sokra* winked in the light from between his eyes. *Never let anyone touch your* sokra.

He shook his head, and I fell to his nose. I scrabbled to catch the edge of a scale, twisting my arm. Below me, the ground threatened to break me should I fall, and if I made a mistake, my father would try to eat me. The world reduced to a bucking pile of dragon scales. I wouldn't get another chance to end this. He stopped for a moment, and I pulled myself up, wrenching the Kornus Blade free. In the same motion, I launched myself toward the *sokra*. The blade cleaved the air.

The sword crashed into the gem. Like a breaking window, the *sokra* resisted for a moment before sundering under the pressure, shattering the world into splinters, and bits of the gem pelted me.

Memories—not my own—crashed through my mind. I watched through someone else's eyes as my mother gave birth. I saw my aunt playing with a whale. I watched the fire burning down the Aerie. I sat beside a woman with wild golden hair who looked like Felix. An older man yelled at me, and my mother threw a glass of wine at my feet. I walked through a forest of impossibly tall, slender trees, as elves danced through the hidden places of the world. I saw caves and warehouses, all filled with Kin, unconscious and fueling spells.

The memories came faster and stronger, until I was lost. Finally, I saw a young woman with black hair wielding the Kornus Blade, drenched in water and blood, and I recognized her. She was my daughter, and she had come to kill me. Profound pride swept through me. My daughter had taken up the fight; Stein would die for his treachery. I could pass on the torch. The nightmare had ended.

I snapped back to myself, gasping for breath—gasping for me—and my father's body fell to the ground. We hit the deck like an earthquake. I tried to tumble away, tucking my arm, but I wrenched my shoulder and smashed my elbow.

All around me, magic unraveled. Like a thread only partially cut, the power curled, ripping away from the order of the spell. My father was dead, and the magics woven together by his life sundered in an instant. The Kin were free, but my father was irrevocably gone.

At the end of the cubicle maze stood Kurt Stein trying desperately to catch the ends of the spells as they unraveled in front of him. He was why my father had fallen. The fire blazed inside me, spilling from my mouth when I screamed. Kurt peered down at me, sneering. Already, the trolls looked confused. The binding spell had broken with my father's death, but clearly Stein still had command of magic. Some trolls muttered, looking from Kurt to me.

"I'm going to kill you!" Flames poured from my mouth as I screamed. My world contracted to Kurt and my unreasonable need to stuff my hissing blade through his heart. I sprinted across the floor.

Kurt slipped into the nearest cubicle. I followed blindly. When I rounded the corner, he stood poised over a unicorn woman, knife ready to strike. Like a snake, I lunged out with the Kornus Blade and knocked the knife aside.

A black fist of foul magic slammed into my chest, knocking me down. I kicked out with my flailing leg. I hit the floor, and my already injured arm snapped like a pretzel. Screaming, I slashed blindly with the blade into the air above me. The sword ripped through something more solid than air, and a severed pile of black tar fell to the ground.

Kurt yelled.

I slashed again, but the dark magic wrapped around the tip of the blade and wrenched it from my hand. The hissing blade soared through the air over the edge of the cubicle behind me. I swiveled my head back to Kurt, who now stood over me, black tentacles of magic extending out from behind him. It handed his knife back.

"Who do you think you are, child?" he asked. "Do you know who—"

Beth launched over the side of the cubicle and tackled Kurt, interrupting his introduction. They crumpled into a pile. "Get the sword!" She wrapped up Kurt's arm, but he hacked open her leg with his knife. Beth's scream pierced me.

John leapt over me to wrench the knife away from Kurt and took a steel blade to the face. "Go," he yelled over Beth's screaming.

I jumped to find the sword, but a black rope of magic wrapped around my throat like a whip. Where the dark magic touched my skin, filth rained down on my soul, as if I ate tar. The putrid magic seeped into my very being, and I turned to face him again. Kurt held Beth in two of his black tentacles, and three tentacles struggled to keep John at bay. Kurt looked only at me. Fire rose in my throat, and I spit at him in rage. I was every shred a dragon, and that thing had my friends in its filthy claws.

Rage fueled my transformation, and I unleashed my fire.

Kurt smiled as my fire splashed aside, harmless.

I blinked. How could he just–

Dragons don't come back.

I pulled my head back, but I couldn't move. Jerking away, my scales tore under the magic collar. He meant to capture me.

I've just traded him one dragon for another.

I dug my talons into the deck and tore the metal between my claws. My struggles cut off my breath, tearing the skin, but it held me fast.

Kurt chuckled. "Do you know what I do, child?"

What happens if he touches my sokra?

The moment the question crossed my mind, a memory flooded to the surface of Kurt touching my father's. He thought he had known some magic that could guard him, but he'd been wrong. In that moment, my father's mind had been open to Kurt, and Kurt broke the warding spell, invading my father's mind completely. He'd failed to protect himself, and he'd given the thief another weapon.

I snapped back into my own mind, reeling from the intensity of the violation and failure in my father's memory. Cold panic stole across my heart. My claws rent holes in the metal decking, but I couldn't break free. Twisting my head back and forth, I threw myself against the bonds, but Kurt walked forward, calmly claiming his prize.

An eagle's screech sliced through the air, and Felix dove at Kurt in full gryphon ferocity. He hit the mage like a bird of prey, sinking his giant beak into Kurt's shoulder. The blackness dissolved, freeing me. Beth and John fell to the ground, suddenly released. A ball of green light flashed outward, and Felix flew through the air like a rocket, slamming into the ceiling. He fell, a lifeless ragdoll with wings, and crashed into a row of cubicles, leaving a trail of destruction in his wake.

I ran for the Kornus Blade, tucking my broken leg up. The pulsing white blade stuck out of the bulkhead.

"Stop!" The word rang through me, and I whipped around to face Kurt again. My tail brushed the hissing sword, and through the scales, it stung.

Kurt strode toward me. Wind howled through the cavernous hold, but it didn't ruffle his hair. The damaged, cubicle walls fell down in the gale, and trolls braced themselves against the winds. Despite the detritus in the air, Kurt's gaze never left me. I was captivated. I sat back on my haunches and curled my tail around my feet like a cat. I couldn't move

"That's better," Kurt said, looking me over.

My tail twitched at his words, as if my *tail* knew I should be running for my life.

"That's it." His calm words were better suited to coaxing a wild animal than conversation. Petrified, I watched him, and he never broke eye contact, swallowing me in those great basilisk eyes. "You are a pretty one aren't you?" He put a hand on my shoulder, and I shuddered at his touch.

My tail twitched into the Kornus Blade, and that pulsing monohorn blade sliced into my scales. Pain seared through me, jerking me free for a breath. Kurt had a hand on my shoulder, and his other hand reached up to touch my forehead.

He was going for my *sokra*.

With my claws, I wrenched the Kornus Blade free from the side of the ship. In a squeal of twisted metal the sword slipped free, and I sliced blindly upwards, holding Kurt's gaze. The Kornus Blade cut through bone and muscle with the same ease as a knife through soft serve. Kurt's hand fell to the deck and he stared into my eyes, disbelief warring with rage and fear.

His spell broke. The wind stopped, and debris fell to the ground around the hold.

I plunged the Kornus Blade into his chest.

The world tore open, and a hole broke in reality just behind Kurt. I flinched away, pulling the blade with me, but Kurt fell into the black hole of darkness, flashing a smile as he fell.

The hole collapsed on itself, and a wave of force blasted outwards, flinging me backwards like an insect. I smashed into the hull of the ship, and metal screamed and sheared in the impact.

He was gone. Kurt was gone.

Water sprayed up around me. Where I'd smashed into the wall the metal had cracked and torn. Water drenched me in a fresh layer of salty cold.

Because today just wasn't challenging enough, now the boat was going to sink.

CHAPTER TWENTY-FOUR

After

I stood there, holding the Kornus Blade in my dragon hand. The sword was designed to kill my kind, and it throbbed. Water shot out from the holes in the metal, pouring down my scales to the puddle at my feet. Back by the cubicles, Beth picked herself up out of the debris of cubicle bits. She bent down to help John up, but he wrapped her in a kiss. I looked away. Kurt's left hand lay severed on the deck at my feet, and a band of silver encircled one of the fingers. I looked back up at Beth and John. Anything was better than severed body parts.

When they parted, Beth radiated a blazing beam of pure power and confidence.

Some kiss.

She jaunted toward me, and I found myself keenly aware of the fact that cold seawater sprayed over me while I stood there doing nothing.

"Hey, Drake, you can't fit through the doors like that," Beth said.

I shivered into my human form, and pointed at the severed hand with the sword. John produced a plastic bag from somewhere, and wrapped up the hand, careful not to touch it. "What do you want me to do with it?" he asked.

"Burn it," I said, only half joking.

John raised an eyebrow. "Can't we use something like this to track him, you know, if he doesn't die?"

Beth looked from John to me. "He isn't dead?"

I shook my head. "He was a really powerful mage. I don't think he'll die even from a Kornus wound."

Beth blinked at me.

"I saw it in my father's memories. It's hard to explain, but I don't think that's the last of him."

"What do we do?" John asked.

All around, the world was coming apart at the seams and he wanted directions from me?

But if I hesitated now, people could die.

"Wake everyone up. Get the other trolls to help move everyone to the upper deck. It'll take longer for the water to reach them there. All we can do is buy time. Beth, find and heal Dr. Targyne, if you can, then find me over there." I rattled off orders like I knew what I was doing, but inside, my knees shook. Outside, everything shook because I was drenched in cold seawater.

Dripping–both blood and water–I searched through the wrecked cubicles for Kin. Around me, trolls bustled to follow John's barked orders. Felix lay in his human form, surrounded by feathers. His jacket had torn open, and a rib poked out through the skin, but he breathed. I knelt beside him, and smoothed back his hair. My tears splashed onto his face, and I collected his feathers. They seemed like golden treasures to me, lying amongst the wreckage. As I put them into a neat pile, the enormity of it all shook through me.

My father was dead.

I killed him.

I'd had these ideas about who my father was, dreams about him as a person. I had fantasies about him coming to pick me up from school, or one day he'd just drop in and say "I've retired, and I can live with you now." Never had I dreamt he was a kidnapping murderer.

And knowing–knowing beyond a doubt–that my father was personally responsible for the death and ruin of families, I still wanted to know him. How much of *him* was in me? Would I fall into his mistakes and traps like pitfalls, set there before I was even born just for being his daughter?

One day, would I be responsible for so much death and destruction?

Now he was gone, and I couldn't ask him.

My hopes and fantasies had been a physical part of me, and I ached where they'd been torn out. I had killed the father I had never known.

He was gone forever. I'd never even said hello.

He'd known me though. At the end, he recognized me.

I sobbed harder.

"That arm will need looking at, Miss Takata," Dr. Targyne said. He stood over me.

I'd missed his approach, and seeing him startled me. My hand brushed the hissing sword, and my finger caught on one of the many sharp places, slicing it open. Blood welled up.

"It is a moody blade, said to be a gift imparted from its donor." He raised an eyebrow at me.

"Yeah, well, it's effective."

Targyne nodded, his lips forming a thin line. He looked at Felix and scowled. "Well, your cure is quite effective, Miss Whitlocke, if you would be so kind," he said, indicating Felix. Beth sliced open the palm of her hand with a dagger John produced. Her blood fell into Felix's open wound, and color returned to his cheeks. He groaned. I almost cried with relief. He would live.

Felix's sky-blue eyes fluttered open, and his gaze met mine. "Did we win?"

What a question. I turned to find the body of my father, but green flames and a plume of greasy smoke rose over him. My father, who made the world's biggest mistake, lay in a smoking pyre fueled by his own heart fire–at least, I assumed that's why he was on fire.

Others would take this moment as a victory.

And if we could just get everyone off the boat, we could save a couple hundred lives.

Perspective, I guess. I forced a smile.

"Yeah, we won."

He smiled back, but I couldn't say anything else around the lump in my throat.

"Your turn, Miss Takata," Dr. Targyne said, putting a hand on my shoulder. He looked at Beth, and she took my shoulders.

"Sorry," she whispered, "but this part is going to hurt."

Dr. Targyne held up a syringe filled with Beth's blood and nodded. Beth's grip tightened to bone crushing and Dr. Targyne took my arm in his hands and gave me the shot. Then he yanked my arm into place, manipulating the broken bones. Pain swarmed me and threatened to black me out. Fire and razor blades ran up my arm. Lightning seared through me as the bones ground together. Then, like magic, the pain dissolved into a cold drink of water on a hot day, relief at last.

I must have screamed because everyone stared at me. I panted like I'd run a marathon and shivered. "What are you looking at?" I stood up, trying to hide how much I still hurt. "We have to move these people. Hurry up!"

Everyone sprang into action. We carried people up the stairs in an endless train of weak and damaged Kin. Some were so thin they looked like skeletons with skin. Others looked to be more recent additions. Once we had everyone on deck, it was obvious there was a problem with our boat. Smoke rose in a plume over the derelict ship, and it developed a pronounced list.

When we finished moving people to the deck, the first hints of dawn colored the sky an abysmal grey. I wandered around trying to figure out what to do next. I stopped pacing when my aunt grabbed my shoulder. Without a word she wrapped me in a hug. Days as a prisoner and she still smelled of piñon. I tried to speak, but my throat clogged with everything I couldn't quite bring myself to admit.

Steve stood on the deck, waiting for me. It was such a relief to see him in the flesh, walking around.

He gave me a sad half smile in return. "Beth told me," he said. "Thank you for what you did." He paused for a moment. "I'm sorry about your father."

Fresh tears sprang to my eyes and slid down my cheeks. I

looked away.

Dr. Targyne snapped his phone closed. "I've called Mr. June. He says he'll drop the accusations at the hearing."

Beth nodded like it was nothing more than she expected, but fire stirred in my belly, a welcome relief to the pain of grief.

"Wait, hearing? We just saved the day, solved the biggest missing person's problem in the last century, and she still has to go through with a hearing?" My voice rose higher in pitch with each word. Felix, Aunt Agnes, and John stood beside Beth and I.

Beth put a hand on my shoulder. "It's okay, they do everything with pomp and circumstance."

"They'll not censure her, Miss Takata," Dr. Targyne said.

"Damned right they won't."

"Could I borrow that?" Felix asked, pointing to the phone. Dr. Targyne handed it over, and Felix grabbed my hand and pulled me away. He led me to one of the rescued Kin, and I instantly recognized her as Hazel. Her hair had more grey than my father's memories of her, but there was no mistaking her.

"Mom," Felix said, "I'd like you to meet Allyson."

She looked up at me, shriveled and tiny compared to her previous self and smiled. "You look like your father."

Again, tears welled in my eyes, and I couldn't speak. I nodded. I wanted to say, he was trying to help hide you all. He didn't mean to hurt so many people. He wasn't the terrible person everyone thought. I opened my mouth, but no words came out.

She nodded. "Your father was very brave. Even after Kurt, he risked much."

Silence stretched between us, and Felix took my hand in a reassuring squeeze. "I need to call Dad," he said, breaking the silence. He punched the numbers. "Hi Dad, it's me, yeah, look, we're somewhere in the North Bay Area—"

"The Ghost Fleet, in Suisun Bay. That's 680." I pointed at the bridge over the waters.

Felix repeated the landmarks to his father. "Mom's here. She's okay." His voice went quiet. "We didn't find Lucia or Jessie." He paused again. "I'm okay, just–uh oh. I've gotta go, Dad. I'll call as soon as I can."

I turned to see what Felix was looking at: four motor boats on fast approach to our ship. Spotlights flared to life and drenched us in pools of light. I shaded my eyes with a hand.

"You are trespassing on federal property! You are under arrest! Put your hands in the air, and don't make any sudden moves!" The loudspeaker crackled.

A hand touched my shoulder from behind. "I've gotta go," my aunt said. "Don't worry about those guys, kid. Just keep your teeth together. They have no right to question you without legal representation."

"Where are you going?" I asked.

"To get legal representation. I'll take this." She held up the plastic bag with Kurt's severed hand. My aunt melted into the rusty deck, instantly camouflaged, and I lost sight of her. Her wings whispered on the breeze as she flew away.

Humorless men with guns swarmed the ship. A group with backpacks and reflective tape everywhere went through the door to the hold. By some unspoken pact, we stood with the unconscious Kin, leaving the other trolls to try to look innocent, but no matter what, we looked like something bad went down.

The men in camouflage and guns rounded us up. It wasn't like the movies, and not once did someone read us our rights. Beth rolled her eyes as they put a zip tie around her wrists, but they proceeded to tie everyone's hands that way. The man who pulled my zip-tie handcuffs on put them in front, but I stole a glance and saw that Dr. Targyne's were cuffed behind his back. They searched us for weapons and took our phones and the Kornus Blade. One by one, they pulled everyone down onto barges; first the unconscious Kin, then us trespassing fugitives. By the time I stood on the deck of the barge, my shaking was uncontrollable. Someone gave me a scratchy wool blanket, and I wrapped myself in it as best as I could. They sailed us under the bridge, past a peninsula and to a pier with long, factory style brick buildings along the shore.

A fleet of ambulances waited, and the infirm were taken from the boats in an efficient stream of EMTs and firefighters. The rest of us got to watch from under armed guard. Once the ambulances left, the men with guns marched us into one of the brick factory buildings. Inside, it was empty except for train tracks on the floor. Armed guards stood at all the entrances, stony faced and rigid.

The trolls stood off to one side, struggling to look as human as possible. They did everything right, stood up straight, kept their knuckles from scraping the ground as they walked, but their lopsided faces were impossible to disguise. The military people called us out one by one. No one called out returned.

Diffuse light spread into the building from high, grimy windows, but I couldn't tell what time it was. I didn't care anymore. I sat on the floor, back to back with Beth, John, Felix, and Steve. Dr. Targyne didn't sit, but whenever he walked, he hobbled. He hadn't had the benefit of someone setting his bones straight when Beth healed him.

After the last of the adults had been taken away for questioning, a short man in a military uniform walked into the room. He held a stack of papers in one hand and kept the other tucked at the small of his back. He stopped in front of Steve and passed a piece of paper to him. With both hands still in zip ties, Steve fumbled with the paper.

"Is that you?" the uniformed man asked.

I looked over his shoulder, and there was Steve smiling out from the paper. Beneath his picture, bold print read *Have You Seen This Child?*

Steve frowned at the paper. "It is."

The man in the uniform passed out similar papers to Beth, Felix, and me. My mom must have used a picture from when we lived in Vermont. In the picture, I had my guitar, and I was smiling. I scowled

216

at the paper. When I looked up, the uniformed man watched me.

He nodded towards the paper. "If that's not you, I need to know."

"It's me," I said.

He moved his lip so his mustache pointed more to the sides. Then he knelt in the dirt next to me. He pulled out a knife and cut my zip ties before moving on to Steve and the others. I rubbed my wrist, but that only made them ache more. When he was finished he stood in front of us.

"My name is Erik Matherson." He took us in individually, and we sat like mice waiting for the cat to pick which of us would be its dinner. He jabbed a finger at me. "I'd like to talk to you first, Miss Takata."

I pointed at my chest, and he gave a curt nod. When I stood up, I brushed at the sticky dust, but only succeeded at getting my hands dirty. My clothes were clammy but almost dry.

Matherson walked over to the wall of armed men, and they parted to let us pass. I should have felt near panic. I was being held under armed guards on military property, but I just couldn't muster the effort. Everything had already been drained from me. I might be able to feel things like panic later, but exhaustion and loss blotted out the world.

I followed the short man to a room in the next brick building. It was another warehouse, but a desk and two chairs sat in the center of the echoing room. The Kornus Blade sat on the desktop wrapped in a giant plastic bag.

He took a seat and gestured to the other chair. I sat with a thump, like a puppet with my strings cut.

Matherson folded his hands together and rested his chin on top. "Would you like to tell me what happened?"

The laugh that escaped my teeth rang with hysteria, bouncing off the walls. Explain how I chased kidnappers across the southwest, got shot at, hunted down my father only to kill him with the bloodthirsty sword on the table and still failed to actually stop the man responsible? "No," I said. The word squeaked out, escaping my throat before the sob close on its heels.

My father was dead.

The pit where my heart used to live wrenched open, and I tried not to fall into the reality of what I'd done. "I don't want to talk about it."

Matherson's eyes narrowed at me. "I was hoping you might help me out. There's a battleship in the bay, and from what I can piece together, one of the biggest human trafficking rings this decade was based there. What happened? Who attacked you? Why did *you* have *that?*" He pointed his pencil at the Kornus Blade. "Is it even yours?"

An excellent question.

He leaned forward. "Are there more places like this? Places where we might find other missing children?"

His eyes bored into me.

Like images through a fog, memories of other facilities drifted past my mind's eye. They weren't places I'd seen before. They were my father's memories. There were other places where Kin slept, their lifeblood fueling the youth and power of Kurt Stein. But what could I say? What could I tell this military man? 'There's a mad man with magic–stolen from *my* family!–and he is running this crazy trafficking ring.' It was too crazy.

And worse, Kurt could be a very powerful man in the human world, too. What if he'd bought off the Army, or whoever these guys were? Who could be trusted?

"I don't know." I stuttered, tripping over the truth, and his glower deepened until his eyebrows nearly touched the tops of his cheeks. I stumbled on. "I had nothing to do with that ship or the people there."

"Who were they? Any information you have could help us find people; other children are in danger." He folded his hands on the table as if patiently listening.

Reggie's words haunted me. *Like when my boy disappeared.*

"I–I don't know if you can help."

"Try me."

I looked down at the gleaming blade between us. Despite cutting off a hand and tasting the chest cavity of Kurt, there was no blood on it. Every nook and cranny gleamed a brilliant silver white. It pulsed as if it could sense me. It wanted more blood.

A guard held the door open, and a man in a business suit entered the room. "Stop!" His words echoed in the large room. Despite the suit and glasses, I knew he was Kin. There was no mistaking it now. The glasses were a fake to make him look more normal. He smelled like blackberries and mint, but that wasn't enough to tell what kind of mythical creature he was. "I am her legal representation," he said, turning to me. "Miss Takata, say nothing."

A memory of this man surfaced in my mind. He took the Kornus Blade in its protected form and placed the blade in a padded suitcase. I recognized it as my father's memory, but now I knew his name.

"Mr. Jordan," I said in way of greeting.

He blinked before carrying on. "I have documentation from her family that she is to be released into my care immediately." Mr. Jordan backed up his words with papers and slid a stack across the table. The piece on top was a pristine copy of my birth certificate complete with the embossed seal. I'd never even seen the copy my mother had.

Matherson took a deep breath, but his jaw didn't relax. He riffled through the stack of papers and turned back to me. "What's the story behind the sword?"

Jordan held up a hand towards me. "It is a family heirloom that recently went missing. The Takata family thanks you for recovering such an important artifact."

One side of Matherson's mustache twitched to the side, and he held my gaze. "I'm trying to save people. I can help. If you change your mind, give me a call." He pulled a business card from his breast pocket and handed it to me. As Mr. Jordan reached for it, Matherson produced a second just for the lawyer.

Jordan traded him, one card for another piece of paper. Clearly, lawyers fought a paper war.

"What's this?" Matherson asked.

"It's an injunction for the return of my client's property."

Matherson's eyes darted to the Kornus Blade and back again. He raised an eye in question, but Jordan's stone mask didn't crack.

"Is that all?" Matherson asked.

Jordan produced another stack of documents. "No, I am also here representing Mr. Smith, Mr. Giovanni, Mr. June, Dr. Targyne, and Miss Whitlocke. If you would be so kind as to bring them out, I would appreciate it." Mr. Jordan passed over a business card. "Also, if you wish to speak with Miss Takata in the future, you can arrange it through me."

"We'll be in contact," Matherson said.

Jordan ushered me through the door, holding it open. On the opposite side, an armed guard waited. He watched us, but made no move to intercept us. Matherson slipped through the door just behind us, and headed off towards a different brick building.

"What is this place?" I asked Mr. Jordan as we waited.

"Mare Island. They used to refurbish nuclear submarines here."

"Now what do they do with it? Keep it for interrogating kidnapping victims?"

A wan smile cracked his lips. "Mostly, they sell the rights to use some of the buildings to entrepreneurs."

I watched the clouds streak by in thin wisps. The scent of the sea permeated everything, and the hollow breeze hissed through the loose bricks as we waited.

The others rounded the corner. "Well?" Beth asked.

I looked up at Mr. Jordan, and he shook his head.

"Not here," I said.

Mr. Jordan pointed away from the sea, and we walked along the road with rail tracks sunk into the pavement. The others fell in behind me. The road went between two modern looking buildings, cinderblock instead of brick, before turning a corner around a cinderblock building.

When we rounded the corner, a hastily constructed fence marked the edge of the gun-toting men's reign. Four guards stood at the gate. They didn't move to stop us, but one talked into his radio as we approached and waved us through with a sharp gesture.

Beyond the gate, news vans waited. Cameramen hastily jumped to catch a better view of us. Great, I was soaked in mud, blood and seawater, and I was going to be on the news.

Nearly two-dozen motorcycles roared to life. In a pack, they swarmed us creating a barrier between the cameras and us. The burly gryphons riding the bikes looked every inch a motorcycle gang with their leathers and vests. Instead of skulls and flames, their embroidered gear had claws and wings. Some of their vests had bulges suspiciously shaped like guns.

They escorted us to a limousine parked across several spaces. My aunt stepped out of the limo. Her teal business suit gave her the air of a CEO, but I knew it was an act. The menacing corporate executive look was designed to intimidate people.

Joe waited next to the limo, smiling. He wrapped Felix in a bear hug. I turned my head so I wouldn't see. The scent of piñon engulfed me, and my aunt caught my gaze in her deep brown eyes.

Her hands on my shoulders, she looked into my eyes. "You did better than I could have."

I opened my mouth, but words failed me.

"Miss Takata, we need to get out of the open," Mr. Jordan said. "Your recent activities will have gained you numerous enemies." He held open the limo door, and I nodded.

"Wait," Felix said, running the few steps from his father to me. He brushed a lock of hair out of my eyes, pushing it back over my ear. Lightning shocks jumped through my body where he touched my ear. My heart pounded in my throat at his nearness, and he leaned in. I met him half way, and the second our lips touched, reality exploded. Nothing existed beyond the two of us. The world spun like I was flying. My skin burned, and something rushed in my chest.

He broke off, and leaned back. "Come visit over spring break?"

"Yeah," I said. It came out in a breathless sigh.

"Please, Miss Takata," Jordan said, looking pointedly in the direction of the news vans. My eyes rose, but I didn't see any cameras. Then again, Stein was a mage. Maybe the clouds reported to him. With one last look at Felix, I let myself be herded into the limo.

The inside was everything a limousine should be, and I was everything that should not be riding in one. I hadn't bathed or slept in more than twenty-four hours, and I was covered in dust and grime from the factory floor.

Beth, John, my aunt, Steve, and Dr. Targyne climbed in before Mr. Jordan. Seats lined the inside, and on one seat, my backpack and jacket waited. Mr. Jordan sat down facing backwards and knocked on the wall nearest the driver. The car pulled away, and motorcycles kept pace around us.

Felix rode behind his father, wearing a black helmet. They waved once, then the pack gunned past us, eating up the pavement.

Beth wagged her eyebrows at me. I threw a rolled up t-shirt at her.

Mr. Jordan pinched the bridge of his nose, pushing up his fake glasses. "Ladies," he said with the same long-suffering tone my mother used when she was tired or thinking about the bills. The glasses knocked his greased hair away from his ears, and a pointed ear popped up through the black hair.

"He's an elf!" Beth squealed

Jordan sighed. "And if I am not entirely mistaken, Miss Whitlocke, you are half-troll," he said calmly.

Beth's mouth snapped shut.

Mr. Jordan turned to me. "Your father set up a fund to help keep you safe upon his death. I have activated it."

"What does that mean?"

Aunt Agnes folded her arms. "It means you now have a pointy-eared shadow." Then she leaned forward. "So what's this I hear about my car?"

"I didn't shoot at it." I pointed at Dr. Targyne. "And where are the rest of your people?"

"Determined trolls are dangerous. The others were wounded. I continued on after I had seen to their safety."

"You shot my car?" Agnes asked.

"I was under the impression your niece was a kidnapper," Dr. Targyne said.

"It wasn't her," Steve said.

"I'm glad we've cleared that up," Mr. Jordan said, blandly. "I'm certain we can reacquire your car."

"So what happens next?" Beth asked. Everyone's eyes suddenly turned to me.

Memories from my father took hold, and I saw warehouses and caves, all filled with people, giving their life to Kurt Stein. Other dragons and other trolls were out there. Thousands of Kin waited.

I blinked back the foreign memories. "We get the sword back, and we do it again."

ACKNOWLEDGEMENTS

Turns out, a book is one part toil, five parts polish, and two parts luck, and this book was no exception.

Toil:

Thank you to my family. I never could have written any of this without your help and support. Thank you, Mom, for reading to me when I was young, and thank you again for reading everything I put under your nose later in life. Thank you, Dad, for never doubting, even if dragons, faeries, and spaceships weren't things you enjoyed. Thank you Tracy and Ben for being supportive of your crazy little sister. Most importantly, thank you Heidi and Marillion. I know writing takes me away from you, but know that even when I'm typing, I am always thinking of you. Both of you turn up in ever story I write. You have made everything in my life possible.

Polish:

Along the way, I've thrown my works at many people, and some have been kind enough to send me feedback—others know to just send chocolate. Without their camaraderie, I wouldn't be sane, and my writing wouldn't be what it is today, so thank you Mason, Liz with Aliens, Liz with Zombies, Tara, Sara, Michelle, Meribeth, the League of Extraordinary Renas, the critiquers at Marathon and of course my many beta readers, especially Kelley Lynn who read an early version of this book and made significant improvements by offering her heartfelt feedback.

Luck:

Even with all that support, this book might not have happened. Without the help of Stacy Nash and the Aussie Owned and Read team, Kathleen Kubasiak might not have ever seen the pitch and asked for more. Lucky for me, Kathleen acquired my book, and from there an amazing team formed. Jessa Russo whipped my flabby words into shape; Merethe made sure my ts were crossed; Amalia Chitulescu made my amazing cover, and the whole Curiosity Quills team worked so hard: Thank you Lisa, Andrew, Eugene, Clare and Nikki. This book is so much more amazing than I ever could have dreamed. Thank you.

ABOUT THE AUTHOR

Like most mad scientists, **Rena Rocford**'s early works were largely met with scorn and mockery, but she bided her time. After all, what did her fellow kindergarteners know about literature? From that day forward, Rena kept her writing on the mythical back burner as she pursued more logical goals. Today, crayons. Tomorrow, the world. She moved on to essays and egg drops, followed by experiments in shady laboratories. She tried her hand at everything, learning from anyone who would teach her. She even moonlighted as a horseback riding instructor.

Admittedly, living as a muggle brought Rena some levels of success such as completing her master's degree, but always the stories returned, calling her to the keyboard in the dark of night. Now, having built armies from words, Rena has set her sights on world domination, one book at a time.

From her secret base in the wine country, Rena has enlisted the help of her cats, her loyal dogs, and her family—who can be relied upon to hide the launch codes at a moment's notice. You can find Rena at her blog, follow her on Twitter, or find her on Facebook.

THANK YOU FOR READING

Dead Girl, by B.C. Johnson

Lucy Day, 15 years old, is murdered on her very first date. Not one to take that kind of thing lying down, she awakens a day later with a seemingly human body and more than a little confusion. Lucy must put her mangled life back together, escape re-death, and learn to control her burgeoning powers while staying one step ahead of Abraham, her personal grim reaper. But when she learns the devastating price of coming back from the dead, Lucy is forced to make the hardest decision of her re-life.

Catch Me When I Fall, by Vicki Leigh

Seventeen-year-old Daniel Graham has spent two-hundred years guarding humans from the Nightmares that feed off people's fears. Then he's given an assignment to watch over sixteen-year-old Kayla Bartlett, a patient in a psychiatric ward. When the Nightmares take an unprecedented interest in her, a vicious attack forces Daniel to whisk her away to Rome where others like him can keep her safe. But when the Protectors are betrayed and Kayla is kidnapped, Daniel will risk everything to save her—even his immortality.

CPSIA information can be obtained at www.ICGtesting.com
Printed in the USA
BVOW08s0711030116

431505BV00004BA/132/P

9 781620 070437